LOVE DEEP

COLORADO CLUB BILLIONAIRES
BOOK 2

LOUISE BAY

ISBN-13: 978-1-80456-046-4

ONE

Juniper

I can't remember the last time I was excited about seeing a guy. I pop the lid off my new eyeliner and try to perfect the eye flick I saw an influencer on the 'Gram doing. I rarely wear makeup. It feels like one more daily chore, and I have enough of those. Tonight, I'm making an exception. The last time I had a crush, I was in high school. That was over a decade ago, and it's been two years since my last date. But this evening, I'm pretty sure I'm going to be in the same general vicinity of the British friend of a guy I went to high school with.

Byron—who grew up in this town but moved to New York as soon as he could—has built a fancy resort on the edge of town. The grand opening for all the super wealthy VIPs is tonight. I'm not going there, even though *eighteen* of my paintings now hang in the Club after Byron purchased them. Fancy parties aren't my vibe. But Byron's throwing an after-party at Grizzly's, the local bar, and I'm pretty sure his friend Fisher is going to be there.

I feel like I'm sixteen, desperate to spot the quarterback in the school halls.

He might not even show.

It's not like we're heading out on a date.

We haven't even met.

Fisher was introduced to a group of us at Grizzly's when he and Byron were on their way out a few weeks ago, but it was a *Hey, everyone, this is Fisher, Fisher, this is everyone* kinda deal. I'm not sure he even saw me, but I definitely saw him. I had to try very hard not to pass out. It wouldn't surprise me if he turned out to be Henry Cavill's hotter younger brother.

The first things I noticed were his broad shoulders and muscular forearms. My gaze trailed up, and I took in his dirty-blond hair and wide smile, and I shuddered. I actually shook from looking at the guy. When he slid his hand along his strong, stubbled jaw, it sent a jolt of electricity between my legs. I've never had such a physical reaction to just being close to a man.

But tonight... Byron says he's going to introduce me to Fisher because Fisher might know someone who might want to buy my artwork. I think that's what he said. Or he might know someone who wants to help me do something with my art. I don't remember the details—just that Byron wanted to introduce me to the tall, blond British guy who made my body weak when I first saw him.

I'm good with that. Very good.

I'm not sure if it's because Fisher's new in town that had my body reacting the way it did. Maybe it's because he's British and the accent is like molten chocolate. It could be that he has the biggest, warmest smile I've ever seen. Tick here for all of the above. All I know is that when I first laid eyes on him, it was like I was hit with a thunderbolt and my vagina woke from a decade-long hibernation and told me she was ready for business.

It's not like I'm expecting to... I don't know... fall in love or have Fisher fall in love with me. He lives in New York and is only here to celebrate the opening of Byron's private members resort, the Colorado Club. Soon enough, he'll be back in New York, and I'll still be here in Star Falls. But it's nice to remember what it feels like to be attracted to someone again. It's been a long time.

I drop my eyeliner back in the pencil pot Riley made me for my birthday and comb my fingers through my long, wavy hair. I can't brush it. It will just frizz. It will have to do.

An agonizing groan comes from the other side of my bedroom door, and I go out to investigate.

"Riley?" I ask as I pop my head into her bedroom.

But she's not in there. The TV is blaring from the living room, but she's not in there, either.

"Riley?" I call out.

"Moooom!" A strangled cry comes from the bathroom.

I rush into the bathroom to find Riley, my normally full-of-beans eight-year-old daughter hunched over the toilet bowl.

"Mom," she cries. "I threw up."

My stomach hits the floor, and my heart sinks down beside it. I kneel down next to her, rubbing circles on her back with my palm. "I'm here, my sweet girl."

I place my free hand across her forehead. She's burning hot.

"I think I'm going to throw—"

After she throws up what's left of her lunch, I strip off her pajamas and put her in the shower.

"Mom, why am I sick?"

"I don't know, sweetheart. We all get sick."

I grab some shower gel and soap down her body. She barely moves. Normally, she'd be dancing about, singing a Vivian Cross song.

My mom calls out, "Where are you girls?"

"In here, Mom," I call back and open the bathroom door.

My mom is holding a foil-covered dish—because my mom never comes over without food. Not ever. I mean, I love it. She's a great cook, and it saves me a job, but I think she thinks we'd both starve without her.

"Fizzy, I'm sick," Riley calls from behind our cat-print shower curtain. Each cat has a name and its own unique identity.

"Oh, my darling girl," my mom says. "It's good Fizzy's here. You can have some slow-cooked chicken. It will make you feel much better."

Riley groans, and I maneuver Mom out of the doorway and back into our living space. The last thing I want is Riley vomiting again.

"Mom, can you make me a plate of that chicken? I can't wait to try it. I'll just go and get Riley out of the shower."

"Won't you eat at Grizzly's?" she calls, as I head back down the hall to the bathroom.

"I'm not going to leave Riley."

I'm equally sad for Riley being sick and sad for me that I'm no longer heading out to Grizzly's to meet Fisher. But life rarely works out how you planned. There's no way I'll leave my daughter when she's sick. It's not that I don't trust my mother—of course I do. But I'm Riley's mom, and she needs to know that she comes first for me. Her dad has shown her often enough that she doesn't come first for him, and she doesn't need that message from two parents.

I knew when I became a mom that I'd make sacrifices, and I've always embraced them. What I get from being a mother far outweighs anything I give up. Even if it's an encounter with a suave Englishman. Yeah, maybe I'm overprotective, but that's who I am. It's who I *have* to be. My mom and dad help out, but Riley's my responsibility and always has been, even when her father lived in Star Falls.

"Oh, Juney," she says, and that's the last thing I hear.

"How's my sweet girl doing in here?" I ask.

"I'm cold," she says as steam billows in the bathroom.

I turn off the faucet and pull back the curtain. "Let's get you dry." I cover her with a towel and help her out of the shower.

"Mommy, Fizzy's going to make me eat that chicken, and I just can't."

I press a kiss to her head and start to dry her off like I used to when she was too little to dry herself. I miss these little moments, now that she's bigger. The times when she used to need me, but she needs me less and less. She's growing so fast. Riley's eight going on eighteen.

"Fizzy's not going to make you eat that chicken. I won't let her."

"As soon as you leave, she will. Please don't go, Mom."

"I'm not going anywhere," I say, rubbing the towel over her brown curls, which always appear when her hair is wet. "How can I leave my sweet girl when she's sick?"

"Really, Mommy? You're going to stay?" She says it like I'm always out.

A couple of times a month, I make it a mile down the road to Grizzly's. It's not like I'm shaking my booty in... New York. Regret pulls at my stomach. I won't see Fisher now.

But it doesn't matter. It's not like anything could have

come of that anyway. He's some hotshot in New York, and I'm a single mom in Star Falls, Colorado. I laugh at myself. What was I thinking?

"What's so funny?" Riley asks.

"Oh, just life," I say, patting her head as we go into her bedroom. "Now, which PJs do you want? The blue ones with the cats?"

While she changes, I go back to my room, pull my hair into a ponytail, and swap my jeans for sweats. I'm more comfortable like this anyhow.

Riley's coming out of her bedroom with Miss Paws just as I come out of mine. "I'm sorry I ruined your night. I bet you and Eva were going to have a lot of fun, right?"

"Not as much fun as I'll have here with you."

She grins up at me and holds up her stuffie. "Don't forget Miss Paws. She's fun too."

"Super fun," I reply. "The funnest."

"Mommy," she says, "*funnest* isn't an actual word, you know."

"It isn't?" I ask, not wanting to doubt her. "Well, it's in my special Mom dictionary."

"Along with huggles?" she asks.

"Exactly. Because moms are the only people who can give a hug and a cuddle at the same time."

"So, who wants chicken?" Mom asks as we walk into the living room, and Riley groans.

"Just me, Mom. But we might wait an hour. Let Riley recover a while. You can get home to Dad if you want. Now that I'm not going out."

"Are you sure you won't go?" she asks. "I thought you were looking forward to tonight. Isn't there a party at Grizzly's? You never know who you might meet."

My mom is always trying to find me a husband. It's not

something I'm looking for, but I don't bother to tell her. Riley comes first, second, and third in my life. There isn't really room for anyone else. They'd have to be really special to get a seat at the table in my house.

"Mom, I would have seen *Eva* there. She's only working half a shift. We might have met people I've known for thirty years. No one new comes into Grizzly's."

The exception is Byron's friends, but I don't say that to Mom. She doesn't need more reasons to try to convince me to go out tonight. I want to stay in with Riley.

"You know they're having that big opening at the Colorado Club tonight. I heard Justin Timberlake is playing. You never know, he might swing by Grizzly's for the locals' after-party."

We both start to laugh, and then Riley asks, "Who's Justin Timberlake?" Our laughs deepen, and I officially feel as old as the sky.

"But seriously," Mom says, "isn't Byron throwing a party at Grizzly's? That's what Donna said when I saw her earlier."

"Yeah, but it's Grizzly's. That place will be here when the three of us are dead and buried. I can go to Grizzly's next week."

Next week, when the Colorado Club is open to the world and no doubt Fisher will have returned to New York.

Sometimes, life works out the way it's meant to. Just me at home with my sweet girl. Tonight, I can dream of handsome Englishmen with messy hair and broad smiles that make me shudder. Fisher can stay my fantasy. That's all he was ever going to be anyway.

TWO

Fisher

I spent the first eight years of my life in England, just outside London. Then I moved to Pennsylvania with my mom and dad and have been in the US ever since. I don't know if it's my British accent, but I've always felt like a bit of an outsider. Somehow, eating chicken wings in a bar in Colorado feels more like being at home than it should.

"They really are incredible. I've never had food so good," I say, taking another bite.

Byron chuckles. "You eat out every night in New York at some of the best restaurants in the world."

"Right," I say. "And this chicken is better than all that shit."

"If you say so."

"You completely underestimate it because you've had it

your entire life." I take a swig of my beer, and somehow the chicken makes the beer taste better, and vice versa.

"Wrong," Byron says. "I left Star Falls way before it was legal for me to eat wings at Grizzly's."

"Then your taste buds have shriveled up and died," I say.

"That must be it. You think we should bring Vivian here? You think your world-famous pop star of a client would enjoy the chicken wings?" he asks.

"It's a guy thing," Rosey, Byron's fiancée, says, sliding into the booth next to Byron.

"What's a guy thing?" I ask.

"Loving the wings. Loving chicken. It's like genetic. Or chromosomal or something. Is that the same thing? Anyway, Vivian might enjoy the wings, but she's not going to worship them in the same way you guys do. Her husband might. He's with her, right?"

"Yeah, and her baby," I say. "But, Rosey, you can't say a word to anyone about her being here."

"I know," she says, pressing a finger to her lips.

"I don't worship the wings," Byron says. Rosey shoots him a look that calls bullshit. "What?" he protests. "I don't. I'm not saying I don't enjoy them, but I don't love them like Fisher and Worth and... all of them."

"No one could love them like your best friends love them." Rosey glances around. "You think you'll get Vivian out of the gilded cage of the Club and down here to sample small-town life including the chicken wings? She's one of the biggest stars on the planet, but there's nowhere like Star Falls. She should experience some of its magic."

"So, I worship wings, but you think Star Falls is magic?" I ask Rosey.

She gives me a pitying look. "Maybe you haven't been here long enough."

"I've been here a lot. It's beautiful. I love it. You know that."

"Yes, but seeing it is one thing. Living it is another," she says with a sparkle in her eye.

She looks over my shoulder, and her eyes brighten as she sees someone or something. I turn, and a woman just arrived. She's scanning the patrons, no doubt trying to find whoever she's meeting. She's got wavy blonde hair and bright eyes that I can tell are blue from over here, five yards away.

Rosey catches her eye, and the woman breaks out into the biggest infectious smile that even has me grinning. She waves at Rosey, and I watch as she heads off to one of the booths on the other side of the bar.

She's bloody beautiful.

"That's Juniper," Rosey says before I get a chance to ask. "She's the artist we've been telling you about."

I frown and take another bite of the wing while I try to think back to whether I remember Rosey or Byron mentioning an artist from Star Falls. I'm used to people mentioning singers they've seen on YouTube or guitar players they're following on Instagram and telling me I need to check them out. Almost always, it's immediately clear why they're not signed to a record label. But Juniper has something about her. Star quality is such a bullshit concept. Except it's not. You either have it or you don't. And maybe Juniper has it.

"She a singer?"

Byron starts to make an up-and-down motion with his hands, like he's gently flapping.

"She's a painter," Rosey says, clarifying Byron's miming.

"You know, the one who painted some of the pieces in the Colorado Club. In fact, one of her paintings is opposite your bed in your lodge."

"Ohhh," I say, everything clicking into place. "And you wanted to know if I knew of anyone who might be able to help her in New York." I nod. I should have paid more attention. "I know a few people."

"Shall I go and get her?" Rosey asks, half out of her seat already.

I'm not complaining. I wouldn't mind being introduced to her.

"Sit down and let the man eat his chicken," Byron says.

"She used to go to school with Byron," Rosey says. "They've known each other since they were kids."

I can't decide whether I'm imagining it or whether Rosey is putting a little too much effort into our conversation. She's usually way more relaxed than this.

"So, how's it going with Vivian?" Byron asks, awkwardly changing the subject.

I nod, still fixated on the beauty across the bar. I can't take my eyes off her. She's laughing with a group of friends on the other side, by the door, and they all seem as equally transfixed as I am.

"Really good," I reply. "She seems exactly as she comes across to the public—focused on being a new mom and wife. She's low-key and... great."

Vivian Cross is probably the most successful singer on the planet right now. And I just signed her to my record label. She's recording her next album up at the Colorado Club, which is why I'm here in Star Falls.

"You sound surprised," Rosey says. "She *always* comes across as low-key and great when I see her interviewed."

"I've been in this industry a long time," I say. "The

image you see on TV is usually just a fabrication of how the artist's team wants them to come across. How they think they'll appeal to the widest audience possible."

I don't know how I ended up in an industry that revolves around pretense when authenticity is what I value most. Actually, I know how—the music. I've loved music since I can remember, and I've managed to make it my work. I'm lucky.

"So, you thought America's sweetheart, Vivian Cross, would be a total diva bitch?" Rosey asks.

I finally pull my gaze from Juniper and grin at Rosey. "I thought she might be more demanding than she seems to be. At the moment. Yes."

"Does she like the recording studio?" Byron asks, always focused on the Club and what people like and don't like about it.

"What's not to like?" I ask. "It's state of the art. You put in everything I'd asked."

I sneak another glance across the bar. Juniper's making faces as she's talking, completely unselfconscious and relaxed. I have to press my lips together to stop myself from smiling at her obvious joy.

"I just wrote the checks," Byron says. "I don't know if what you suggested is any good."

"It will pay for itself eventually," I say. "You're going to get loads of people coming out here to record. It's so fucking peaceful. Vivian loves that it's so private as well. She's excited that she's going to be able to take a hike without worrying she's going to get recognized."

I glance across to see Juniper again, but she's gone from where she was sitting. My gaze flits across the bar to try to find her. Did she leave?

"What does she think about her lodge?" Rosey asks.

"It's one of my favorites of the ones that aren't already taken."

"She loves it. Plenty of space but cozy, is what she said. Everything's good."

Rosey wrinkles up her nose. "Okay, so she's all settled, and her producer is staying at the Snowdrop Inn. So, why are you still here?"

I raise my eyebrows in mock horror.

"It's lovely having you here, but I just don't get it. You're the CEO of the label. Are all stars like this? They need babysitting?"

I laugh. "A lot of them. But their managers do that, mostly. But she doesn't want her manager on-site because she wants to focus on her family when she's not in the studio. He only agreed to stay away if I was around. I'm here just to make sure she's happy. If anything comes up, I'm not at the end of the phone. I'm here, ready to sprint into action."

"But you're the head of the record label. You can't do that for all your artists," Rosey says.

"Right, but Vivian Cross is the biggest recording star in the world. And the biggest signing Right Records has ever had. I don't want to fuck that up. Whether her manager wants me here or not, I'm here. But the fact that he does want me here means I'm not going anywhere."

I also can't be hovering around Vivian like some over-protective guard dog. I've just got to make sure she's happy. And leave her alone to create her next album. Signing someone like Vivian, when every label would have cut off their right arm to have her, is a big fucking deal. If I fuck up, everyone will be waiting to pounce. Vivian has only signed for this one album. I need to make sure it goes smoothly.

Right Records might be the biggest independent record

label in the business, but it's a small fry compared to the big players. If Vivian's signing goes well and she's happy, I expect others will want to come aboard. It could be completely transformational for my business.

"You're not going to fuck anything up. You're in Star Falls," Rosey says. "It's all going to be great." She's looking behind me, and then she starts to wave. "Oh, Juniper!" Rosey calls out and beckons her over.

I turn, and Juniper and a couple of friends are heading toward the pool table in the back. Juniper says something to them and then leaves them and heads to our table.

"Have you met Fisher?" she asks.

Juniper's gaze turns to me, and her eyelashes flutter, and her lips part. I swallow, like she's unexpected royalty or something. Her cheeks are dusted in pink, and her skin glows under the dim lights of the bar. Her eyes sparkle as she smiles.

"Hey, Fisher."

"He's the friend from New York Byron's been telling you about." Rosey turns to me. "I'm sure you can help Juniper out with her art career. You know so many artistic people in New York."

Juniper laughs, and the scent of orange blossom and jasmine fills my nose. "I don't have an art career. I'm a teaching assistant."

"You're so talented," Rosey says. "I'm sure if more people knew about you, you'd be a wild success."

Juniper smiles like she's half indulging Rosey and half pleased to receive her praise. But it's a real smile. A smile that I can tell she means to her core. It fills me with lightness and energy.

"Fisher's staying in one of the lodges that has one of your paintings in it."

"It's beautiful," I say, even though I can't even remember it. But everything about the lodge is beautiful, so I can't be lying.

She lays her palm flat on her chest. "Thank you. That means a lot."

"What is it you're looking for?" I ask. "An agent? A gallery to exhibit you?"

A whisper of panic crosses her face. "Oh, I... I'm not really—I paint for fun. I sell one now and again. Twilight Latte always has one up and a few other stores in nearby towns. I don't expect I'm going to make it or anything."

She lets out a nervous laugh at the end, like she's ridiculous for even thinking she might be successful. Part of me wants to scoop her up and tell her it's going to happen for her—just like I have done with countless artists over the years when they've doubted themselves. But I haven't seen her work, and so I won't say that to her. I made a promise to myself a long time ago that I wouldn't give people false hope. It's too painful in the long run. One thing I pride myself on is I don't say things just to inflate people's egos.

"I'd like to see your work," I say before I have a chance to think about it. "I don't know much about art, but..."

"Great. That sounds like fun. You just tell me when you're free."

I nod like I can't form a sentence, like speaking and looking at the woman in front of me takes up too much brain capacity or something.

She glances down at my plate. "Finished your wings?"

I grin like an idiot. "They were good."

"They were great," she corrects me with a smile. She glances over toward the back of the bar. "You all want to come and play pool?"

"Sure," Rosey says for all of us, and she's out of her seat before anyone can say anything otherwise.

Byron and I take our beers and follow Juniper and Rosey.

"Juney's nice," Byron says, and then he sighs. "That's it. That's all I'm doing. If she asks, tell Rosey I told you that Juney's the greatest woman on the planet."

Realization dawns. "Oh, I see. It's like that, is it?" I'm being set up. But I'm not mad about it.

Byron groans.

"Don't sweat it," I say. "She just wants everyone to be as happy as the two of you are. It's nice."

"I know. But people have to find their own path, and it's not like you're going to come live in Star Falls forever, is it?"

I chuckle. "Unlikely. But I'm here for the next six weeks."

"Well, Juney is... well, she grew up a lot since high school. As you know, until the Club, I hadn't come back to Star Falls since leaving, so she could have become a serial killer in the intervening years. We've been in touch a little since I came back to town, but we don't hang out a lot. But tell Rosey I told you she's amazing."

"Deal."

We knock together our beer bottles and arrive at the back of the bar, where the pool table is. There are a few women gathered around, but Rosey and Juniper seem to have already started a game.

Rosey breaks and then turns to me and Byron. "Doubles?"

Rosey hooks her arm around Byron's, leaving me and Juniper standing here and gazing at each other.

"You in?" I croon as I tilt my head toward Juniper.

She smiles and saunters past me, and I very happily follow.

I couldn't have picked a prettier partner.

THREE

Juniper

Playing pool with Fisher was not what I had on my bingo card for tonight. He was the last person I was expecting to run into. After missing Byron's party a couple of months back, I'd almost forgotten about him. Kinda. Not really.

"So, you here to catch up with Byron and Rosey?" I ask him.

He looks at me, and it's almost like I can tell he's imagining me naked. It's kind of a dirty look. Like he's thinking about sex. Or maybe I'm thinking about sex. *I'm* definitely thinking about sex. It's impossible not to, being so close to Fisher.

"Yeah, and I'm here for work too."

He's tall, and his shirtsleeves are rolled up, showing bronzed skin pulled tight across muscled forearms. I don't think I've ever noticed the forearms on a man, but Fisher's are mesmerizing. He laughs, and it feels like I'm standing next to a log fire. He's warm and comforting at the same time as being sexy as all holy hell.

"Work?" I ask. "What do you do?"

"I'm in the music business," he explains. "I have an artist recording up at the Club."

"Recording? Is there a studio up there?"

He nods.

"Oh, wow. I had no idea. How fun."

He grins at me like I've said exactly the right thing, and I return his smile. He's gorgeous. Perfect white teeth and blond hair that's slightly wavy.

"Your turn," Byron bellows across the room.

I jump in surprise. Fisher raises his eyebrows, still grinning.

"I guess it's our turn," he says.

"You go first," I say, and not just because I want to see what his ass looks like in those jeans he's wearing.

"You want to see what my ass looks like, don't you?" Fisher asks.

Embarrassment sweeps up my body, and my eyes widen. "I do not!"

Fisher dissolves into laughter and knocks me with his elbow. "I'm kidding. Relax." He takes my pool cue from me and heads over to the table.

I try and look everywhere apart from Fisher's ass, but it's difficult. I swear he chooses a shot that gives me a pretty good view of his backside. And it's nice. Tight. Round. I hate a guy with no ass. And Fisher has plenty. He sinks two balls and then misses on the third.

"How was it?" he asks, grabbing his ass cheek.

"Not as nice as mine," I deadpan.

He grins and nods. "I bet."

Rosey misses her shot, so it's me up next. When I pocket the green ball, my ass is facing away from Fisher. It's a silent victory. I miss the blue, and I head back to my pool partner.

"You did that on purpose, didn't you?" he asks. His accent makes him sound very formal.

"What?" I ask with a shrug. "Take a shot that had me leaning away from you? I don't know what you mean."

Fisher laughs, and I order another beer from Eva. Fisher mumbles something I've never heard of to Eva. He probably had some fancy beer shipped in especially or something.

"So, you live in New York even though you're British?" I ask.

"My family came over when I was eight. So, I don't feel British, even though I still have a trace of an accent."

"A trace?" I laugh. "You sound like Prince William to me."

"Oh, yeah?" he asks. "Well, I'm definitely not Prince William. What about you? You went to school with Byron?"

"High school, yeah. I was... different back then. I always had paint in my hair and all over my clothes. I was obsessed with art. It's all I ever thought about."

He looks at me, waiting for me to say more. When I don't, he asks, "What changed?"

I smile. "Real life."

I think back to all the emotions of the time. I had to make a choice, and I chose Star Falls. I don't think I realized back then what I was sacrificing.

"That's all you're giving me?"

"It's a long story," I say.

Fisher must see my expression because he doesn't press me.

"One for another time," I assure him.

"But you still paint?" he asks.

"When I get the chance," I say.

Truthfully, I do it more now than I have for a while. Riley's older and more independent. And she likes coming to the studio with me. Painting with Riley is... different, but I still like it. Sharing that time with my daughter is so important. It feels sacred or something.

"So, what did you say you do for work?"

"I work in a school. I'm a teaching assistant."

"Wow." He slides his palm over his jaw. "I don't know how you have the patience."

I laugh. "It's a question of lowering your expectations."

He narrows his eyes, like he's taking in something profound. "Yeah. I like that way of thinking about it. It's a good way of going through life, too," he says.

"What? Having low expectations?" I ask.

"Yeah, that way, you're not disappointed."

Something niggles in me at his observation. "I'm not so sure that's true," I say. "I mean, if you expect a six-year-old to behave like an adult, then you're going to spend your life frustrated and annoyed. But in life? You gotta have expectations or... I find people live up or down to your expectations, whatever they may be."

Fisher holds my gaze, and he's about to speak when Byron interrupts.

"Hold that thought," Fisher says.

He takes a shot, and I swear he misses on purpose. He barely looks at the table. I'm not complaining because that means he comes back to me quickly.

"Is that true in your experience?" he asks.

"What?" I ask.

"That if you expect people to be one way, they generally are."

I take in a breath. I've not really thought about it before. "Yeah. I think so."

"And if you expect nothing of someone, they'll give you nothing?"

I shrug. This conversation has taken a turn I wasn't expecting. I hadn't planned to give him philosophical insight, just an understanding that, in my experience, people tend to turn out to be what you expect.

"I think I assume people are going to be assholes," he says.

I tilt my head and look at him. He seems so carefree on first glance, but maybe that's not true if you dig a bit deeper.

"I'm not sure," I say.

"That people are assholes?" he asks.

"That you assume everyone's going to be an asshole."

His eyes widen in surprise, and then he regains his friendly expression and grins at me. "You're an interesting woman, Juniper."

"And it's my shot."

I manage to sink a couple of balls, and then when I miss, my pulse starts to race—because it means I get to hang out some more with Fisher.

"Do you go back to the UK a lot?" I ask.

"Not really. Home is New York, but I travel for work. What about you? You lived in Star Falls your entire life?"

"Sure have. Never even traveled out of state."

He nods. "Right. That's..."

"A little pathetic?" I suggest and laugh. "I agree. But, you know, life happens. And you have to pick. We get one life, and we can't be the person who sees the world and the person who knows everybody in Star Falls to their bones."

Fisher smiles, his eyes fixed on me, like he's trying to figure me out. "I don't think many people think about life like that. Like it's a series of choices that will lead them to have one kind of life or another."

"Really?" I ask. "I'm not saying you plan it out, but there are crossroads in anyone's life and moments where you know whatever decision you take, your life will end up in two different places."

"God, Juniper," he says and groans, and I'm not sure if I'm boring him or something.

"What?" I ask. "Am I talking too much?"

He shakes his head. "I think I could talk to you all night. You and your take on life is... bewitching."

I scrunch up my nose. "I'm not sure that's a compliment."

"It very definitely is."

His gaze is so intense, I can almost feel it pressing into me, surrounding me, daring me to say more.

I reach over to him, because I can't *not* touch him any longer, and I rest my hand on his muscular arm for a beat, then two, then I force myself to pull away. "Thank you," I say. "I'll take any compliments you're giving out."

FOUR

Breakfast at the Colorado Club is a banquet fit for a king. And certainly, the reigning queen of pop.

Vivian slides into the booth opposite me. "Never bring me here again."

My stomach churns. Did I make a mistake, bringing her to Colorado? It's certainly different from any place I've ever recorded, and I've been to a lot of different studios. New York, Tokyo, London, LA—even Sheffield, Alabama. And the tech is state of the art. But that's not always what it's about.

"You don't like it?" I ask.

My concentration has been shot since seeing Juniper the night before last. The way she talked about people living down or up to expectations. I can't stop thinking about it. Maybe I've been missing signs that Vivian wasn't happy over the last twenty-four hours. I need to refocus on Vivian. I'm not here to have a six-week fling with a beautiful blonde who got pulled away by her friends after pool and then left before I could get her number.

"It's phenomenal. And the food is too good. I might never want to leave."

I exhale. Thank god. I need Vivian to be happy.

"I'm leaving twenty pounds heavier at least. And I'm blaming it on you."

"I'm good with that."

"And your mate put in all the equipment because you told him to? It must have cost him a fortune."

I chuckle. "Hearing you say *mate* in an American accent is hilarious."

"I'm learning all your Britishisms from my husband. *Mate* is a favorite."

"It's a good one. And, yes, Byron wanted it to be a place where artists who didn't want to go out partying could come and work, but also immerse themselves in the surrounding space."

"It's wonderful. And the fact that Beau and baby Victoria can come and it can be family time when I'm not in the studio is such a bonus."

"Yeah, I have to say, I'm not used to seeing artists at breakfast while they're recording."

She laughs. "Well, I'm a mama now. I've been able to spend a couple of hours with Victoria this morning, and then we can do some time in the studio before I get her into bed. That's what's so great about having Beau and Victoria on-site. I can do it all."

She beams at me. It's such a relief to have her happy. I would never have believed that I could sign a star like Vivian when I was starting Right Records. I just wanted to start a record label that didn't treat everyone like shit and then pretend it was art.

"As long as you're okay."

"Couldn't be happier," Vivian says. "Oh god, speaking of the exact opposite of happy. Did you hear the news about Gerry Banks?"

My stomach hits the floor at the mention of my old nemesis, and I freeze. What's she going to say?

"Re Records tried so hard to sign me, and I'm so freaking glad I didn't. My manager was definitely pro Re. But something didn't feel right, despite them being the biggest label in North America. And now with Gerry taking over? Do you know the guy?"

"Wait, Gerry Banks is taking over Re Records?"

Vivian takes a spoonful of the yogurt thing that's in front of her and groans at the taste. Then she turns her attention back to me. "Yeah. Can you believe it? I thought he was all about management, but apparently not."

Gerry and I were both in A&R at EMG Records way back when. And when the place went under, Gerry started managing artists. He's been pretty successful.

"He's a strange guy," I say. "I used to work with him."

"Is he as cutthroat as people say he is?"

I don't like to speak badly of people, but Gerry Banks is loathsome. He's one of the few people I've ever met who I'd cross the street to avoid, and that's saying something. There are plenty of snakes in the world of entertainment.

"We were both quite young when we were at EMG, but he was... I could never prove it, but I'm pretty sure he targeted artists I was forming relationships with and would swoop in and..."

"Steal them?" she offers, nodding. "Doesn't surprise me. The guy is... he's not a good guy."

"I certainly didn't like working with him."

He's invited me to a few showcases since those days.

Even tried to set up a meeting with me about an artist one time. But I've tried to dodge all contact. I've never wanted anything to do with him.

"But it's hard to avoid the bad guys in this industry, right?" she asks.

"I think it's the same in any industry where there's money to be made, but resources are scarce. There aren't many real stars, and there are lots of people who want to find what there is."

There are plenty of untrustworthy people in the music industry, but Gerry is another level of bad. He's rotten. To his core. Not only did he steal artists from me. He started various rumors about me. And tried to get me fired. I have no idea how the guy has ended up as the head of Re. It doesn't make sense. He's been out of that game for so long now. There must have been plenty of more qualified people. I really want to ditch Vivian and go and investigate what's going on.

Luckily for me, Vivian wants to know what's going on almost as much as I do. She pulls out her phone and starts searching for information.

"I guess," Vivian says. "I think Gerry takes it to another level." She holds out her phone.

Gerry looks exactly the same as when I last saw him. Slick. Polished. Smiling. I fight the urge to shudder.

"Well, as long as he leaves me alone."

While I'm looking at Vivian's phone, a call comes through. Re Records flashes up on the screen. Does she have their number saved or did it come up automatically?

My mind starts to race, and I nod toward the phone. "Looks like someone's calling you."

Vivian sees who's calling and grimaces. "Why would

they be calling me? And how in the hell do they have my number?"

"You could answer," I suggest. Curiosity is probably going to be the death of *me*, as well as the cat.

She shrugs and accepts the call. "Hello? Who is this?"

She listens. The tinny chatter of someone talking on the other end of the line fills the silence between Vivian and me.

"No, sorry, I'm not interested, and anyway, any requests should be put through my assistant or my manager and—"

My jaw tenses. They're trying to poach her. Typical.

She's interrupted, and then goes silent, listening to whatever it is the other person has to say. She glances at me, rolls her eyes, and finally says, "Fine." Then she hangs up.

"Speak of the devil, and the devil shall appear." She groans. "Can you believe that was Gerry freaking Banks?"

My stomach roils, and my hands ball into fists. What a fucking snake.

"I don't know why he decided to call me, and I don't know how the hell he got my number."

"Did he say why he was calling?" As soon as the words leave my mouth, I feel like an idiot.

We both know why he was calling. He wants to lure Vivian over to Re. He's got balls—I gotta give him that. And I'd really like to chop them off if I get a chance.

"He said he's having a small dinner to mark his new job and wanted to know if I'd go."

She makes a face like she's tasting vinegar, and I appreciate it. Maybe she really hates him. Maybe she doesn't. Despite what Juniper said the other night, I have very clear expectations when it comes to talent—they won't necessarily tell you if they're thinking of jumping ship. They leave their managers to give bad news.

I pull in a breath, trying to stay calm. What I want to do is punch something. Go for a run. All of a sudden, I have all this pent-up energy inside me that needs a release.

"That's weird," I say.

I want to try and figure out exactly what Gerry's plan is. The fact that he's calling Vivian—Right Records' biggest-ever signing—straight out of the gate seems like an act of war. And wars are won and lost not on who has the biggest gun, but who has the best intelligence. I want to know everything about Gerry fucking Banks' plans. Because then I'll be in a better position to be able to defend myself.

"Maybe," she says. "I was between Re and Right Records when I was signing. He's probably wondering whether he can win me over."

I chuckle. "I'm absolutely certain that's what he's wondering."

Vivian holds up her croissant like it's a microphone and then takes a bite off the end. "Well, he can fuck off. He's a dick."

Could have ignored the call, I don't say.

Could have hung up as soon as you knew who it was, I don't say.

Could have said no to dinner, I don't say. I didn't hear her decline. The last thing she said was, "Fine." My jaw clenches. That could have been, *Fine, I'll think about it. Fine, I'll come for an hour. Fine, send the invitation over to my manager.*

And god knows what incentives Gerry dangled to try to get his own way. *I've got X, Y, and Z hot actor or actress coming, and they would love to meet you.* Or, *Afterwards, there's a private showing of an art exhibition or a movie.*

With his new position, Gerry is now one of the most powerful people in the entertainment industry. There are a lot of things he could offer Vivian that might be appealing to her.

"Can you believe we were just talking about him, and then he just called? How bizarre!"

"I'm sure he's calling all my clients." My stomach drops as I say the words, and I ball my hands into fists.

Of *course* that's what he'll be doing. If I was right, and he targeted me personally at EMG, he may well do the same now. Maybe I'm being paranoid, and the guy has forgotten I exist, but something tells me he's shooting his shot, and I'm his bull's-eye.

This couldn't have happened at a worse time. I need to be back in New York, at my desk, on the phone, my ear close to the ground. Or I should be putting in face time with my artists. With their managers. But I'm stuck here. In Star Falls, Colorado. And my gut says Gerry Banks is going to do his best to fuck with me.

FIVE

Juniper

Riley's chatting with Pat, behind the deli counter, about school. I swear, she never tells me anything about her day. Eva—my best friend since high school—is engrossed in her phone as she follows me up the aisles of the grocery store. On my way into town from school, Eva called and said she wanted to catch up. I told her it would have to be while shopping for groceries because our cupboards were bare.

"I'm going to get vegetables," I call out to Riley.

"Okay, Mom."

Eva shuffles behind me like an elderly dog, still looking on her phone. I'm not quite sure what she wanted to catch up about. Maybe her cell battery.

"The guy is rich," Eva says out of nowhere.

"What guy?" I ask.

"Your guy," she says.

I frown. "I don't have a guy," I say. "What are you looking at on your phone?"

"I saw the chemistry between you and Fisher the other night. There's no way things can end there. We just need to find a way for you two to run into each other again."

I roll my eyes and head to the vegetables section of the market. Eva is out of her mind. No change there.

The sale of eighteen pieces of art to the Colorado Club has been pretty life-changing. I put most of the money aside into a college fund for Riley, but I kept some to help with the day-to-day. Now, instead of having to worry about whether I can afford rice *and* cannellini beans this week, I can pick healthy, nutritious ingredients and know that my card won't be declined when I get to the cashier.

It also means I can treat Riley to a packet of Snoballs and not feel bad about it. I see a packet of the less-than-nutritious snack on the shelf and toss it into my cart and grin at what I know will be her expression when she sees what I bought. Then I continue to find something green and leafy to counteract the sugar and chemicals in the Snoballs when I almost run into Rosey.

"Hey, Juniper!" she calls.

Rosey's lovely. She's one of those women who's always smiling and happy. I wonder what that must be like.

"Hey, Rosey. How ya doing?" I glance behind me. "This is my friend Eva."

"We know each other," Eva says, and they exchange smiles. "Excuse me for a second. I just need to try outside for a better signal."

"It's so good to see you!" Rosey says. There's a little bounce to her step, which is just adorable. "It was great hanging out at Grizzly's the other night. All of us out together was so fun, especially with Fisher."

So much Fisher talk this afternoon. Fisher wasn't

exactly what I had expected him to be. Yes, he was hot as all holy hell. He was charming and flirtatious. But there was something more to him that came as a bit of a surprise. He was a little deeper than I'd thought he would be. Not at first, but as we talked, he really seemed to want to hear what I had to say, and he... thought about what I'd said. It's been a while since I've even talked to someone I haven't known at least twenty years—and usually since one of us was born. Fisher was not only new, but he was genuinely interested in what I had to say. And I was interested in him.

It was nice. More than nice.

"It was really fun," I say.

"You and Fisher seemed to get along."

I nod, trying to think of what I should say that doesn't include how hot I think he is. "Yeah, he seems great."

"He really is. Such a good man. And so kind."

Her eyebrows pull together a little, like there's more to it than she's telling me. No doubt there is plenty about Fisher I don't know.

"Even Byron had a good time," she adds with a laugh. "Fisher always enjoys himself," she says. I wonder if that's true. "He's single, you know."

I smile. "I gathered that. He was quite flirtatious. But I get the impression that's part of what makes him, *him*."

"Yeah. I think he's flirtatious by nature. But he was *particularly* flirtatious with you."

I can't tell if she's just trying to make me feel better or if she's telling me Fisher liked me. Although I'm not sure it matters either way.

"Well, I appreciated it," I say.

It's true. He's built like a Greek god, and he had a way of looking at me like the rest of the world just disappeared—

like the world could go up in flames and he wouldn't care as long as he could keep talking to me. Keep smiling at me. Keep making flirtatious little jokes.

Truthfully, I haven't enjoyed myself so much at a night out at Grizzly's for—well, ever.

Rosey grins at me, and all I can do is shrug. It's not like we're going to date or anything. He lives in New York. That might as well be the moon. I've never been outside of Colorado before, let alone a city as big as New York.

"He just needs a woman to be his partner in crime," she says.

"Well, I'm sure he'll find someone." I imagine there's more than one who's interested in fulfilling that particular role.

"I think so," she says. "Hey, would you like to come up to the Club for dinner? Tonight even?"

"The Club?" I ask, trying to buy myself some time. I'm ninety-nine percent certain my mom would come and sit Riley, but I have no idea what I'd even wear to a place like the Colorado Club, and I'm one hundred percent certain I don't own it, whatever it is.

I don't know if my expression gives me away, but Rosey follows it up with, "It will be super relaxed. In our lodge. So, just jeans and sweaters. No need to dress up."

I want to ask her whether Fisher will be there, but it seems rude. Would it be? I'm not sure of the etiquette when it comes to dinner invitations. And if she says yes, would that make me more or less likely to want to go? Maybe it's better that I don't know.

"We'd love to have you," she says.

I've spent the last eight years trying to make sure Riley's life is as stable and consistent as possible. Especially since her dad left town, I've worked hard to keep all her other routines in place. To make sure she always knows what comes next. Riley feeling safe, secure, and loved has been and *is* my absolute priority. A last-minute change of plans shouldn't be a big deal. Riley's routine wouldn't change. It would just be my mom in my place.

I wouldn't normally go out during the week, but talking to Fisher the other evening shifted something. Swapping stories with someone who didn't already know everything about my life and I didn't know anything about theirs—well, it was kinda refreshing. And I don't think it was just because he was hot. It was as if something long dormant inside of me woke up. Like maybe I could have something for me.

"I'd have to check whether I can because—"

"I don't think I have your number." She pulls out her phone. "No pressure. Just let me know by six. Does that work?"

We swap numbers.

"Oh, and don't worry. I'm not cooking. Owner's perk is getting delicious food delivered right from the Colorado Club kitchens."

"But will you have Grizzly's chicken wings?" I ask with a smile. "I don't know if I can come if you say no, Rosey. It's a deal-breaker."

She laughs. "If it means you'll be at our place at seven, I can make that happen."

It's so nice of her to invite me. She seems so insistent.

"Okay, well, I'll let you know. Thank you for the invitation."

Eva appears from wherever she was, and she and Rosey say hi and bye to each other again.

Then Eva turns back to me, her mouth hanging open. "I think I made that happen," she says.

"Made what happen?"

"Rosey appear and invite you up to the Colorado Club. With Fisher."

"She didn't mention Fisher."

"You're going on a double date!" She looks like she just found out she won the lottery.

"First, I haven't said I'm going yet, and second, I have no clue if Fisher will even be there."

She rolls her eyes. "I can watch Riley if your mom can't. And where's your phone? You need to text her right away and say you'll be there."

"Eva!" I say. "You can't go around just making decisions for me. I need to think about it. And ask my mom."

"There's nothing to think about. You're going. Riley will be looked after by either me or your mom, and you're going to go and enjoy yourself. I swear to god, Juniper, you never do anything for yourself." I go to speak, but Eva cuts me off before I can get any words out. "And a night out at Grizzly's twice a month doesn't count. You're going to have a great time. Time to blow some cobwebs out of your vagina." She pulls her eyebrows together. "Out of your vagina? From your vagina? Whichever way, the cobwebs in the vicinity of your vagina shall be gone."

I groan. "Stop saying vagina."

"Vagina," she says. "I'll only stop saying it if you promise me you'll go tonight."

"I'm definitely not leaving my kid with you."

"So, you'll go? Your mom will definitely sit for you."

I start trying to think about whether I *want* to go. Do I want to see Fisher? Do I want to miss the opportunity to see him again?

"Vagina," Eva repeats.

"Okay, I'll go. And you know what? I'll bank an opportunity to terrorize you about something one day."

She shrugs. "So be it. As long as you go tonight, you will not hear another V-word from my lips."

I grab a head of cauliflower and dump it in my cart. My mom makes great cauliflower cheese. She and Riley can make it tonight. While I'm out.

SIX

Fisher

I'm scanning my emails to see if anything else has come in about Gerry. If he's sniffing around Vivian, there must be other artists of mine he's approached. I just don't know if any of them would tell me. I don't even know if Vivian would have told me about his call if I hadn't been there when it came through.

My assistant, Frankie, messages me. It's late in New York. She's sent through a link. I click, and it's a gossip site's coverage of a celebrity party.

Why did she send me this?

I scan the text, then scroll down to see the pictures. It's loads of people from the music industry in attendance. Then I scroll back up to see what I'm looking at.

The stars were out in force for music industry power-house player Gerry Banks' welcome to Re Records party. He's taken the position of CEO of the third-largest record label...

I don't need to read any more. But I want to see who's

there. I scroll down again, this time making sure I clock people in the background as well as the talent who the camera is focused on.

I scroll farther and farther down. He got a lot of big names to attend. It looks like no expense was spared. He certainly spent PR money on the party. Why else would a private party get so much media coverage—even if it did have some of the biggest music industry stars of the moment attending?

As I get closer to the bottom, I notice country artist Alison Banks is there. I screenshot it. She's in the middle of a three-album deal with me. What the hell is she doing at a Re Records event?

And just before I hit the bottom of the page, another Right Records artist is pictured—Jax Cinq. He's a pain in my ass. I'd happily hand him over to Gerry. It would take a load off my plate.

I'm pissed about Alison, though. I examine her picture more closely. Maybe she accompanied someone who has ties to Re Records. I can't remember who she's dating.

I type out a quick text to Frankie. She responds right away to say she's already gone through possible scenarios, but Alison is secretly dating her manager, so it's not because she was someone's plus-one. I ask her to set up a call with Alison and shove my phone into my pocket.

I'm due over at Byron and Rosey's cabin, and I don't want to be late. I've been eating there most nights, so it's not like it's a big deal, but still. I expected to be having dinner with Vivian more often. I thought I'd even have taken her down to Grizzly's by now. But she's very low-key and incredibly low-maintenance. When she's not in the studio, she just wants to hang out with her husband and kid. It's great. But I feel a bit like a spare part. Especially with all this stuff with

Gerry going on. I've got more time to ruminate on it, and I wish I could be back in New York, where I'd be able to do more. In my experience, meeting in person is the only way to understand properly if someone's telling the whole truth.

But I promised her manager I wouldn't leave. Plus, keeping Vivian happy is more important than ever if Gerry is going to steal Alison from me—and presumably, he has other artists of mine in his crosshairs.

I head over to the cabin right next to mine. The security here is great. I don't even lock my door. It's like being transported back to the 1950s. Vivian has said a few times how safe she feels here. That's what I wanted for her. As a mom, I'm sure safety for her family is at the forefront of her mind. I got that right. I just wish I hadn't committed to Vivian's manager that I'd be here all the time. She really doesn't need me. But I only have myself to blame. I was the one who agreed to be here. I'm not going to go back on my word.

Rosey throws open the door with her typical enthusiasm. "Hey!" she says. "Juniper's joined us for dinner."

I look over Rosey's shoulder to see Juniper talking to Byron. She turns, and it's like the world shifts into slow motion. I swear I can hear rivers gurgling and birds tweeting as our eyes meet, almost like she's putting some kind of calming spell on me. I raise my hand and give her a half wave, and she lets out a small smile that's completely beguiling.

"Can I get you a beer?" Rosey asks.

"Sure, thanks."

When I reach Byron and Juniper, I bend and drop a kiss on her cheek. She smells sweet and floral—that jasmine scent again. I breathe her in, and my heart rate drops, and my shoulders lower.

"So good to see you again."

"And you. I didn't realize it would be the four of us." She glances over at Rosey.

I grin. Rosey's playing matchmaker.

"I'm glad it is," I say. Juniper's good company, and she's made me feel better already tonight.

A slight blush crosses her face, and she presses her lips together, her smile stretching to her eyes.

"We have some gorgeous chateaubriand tonight," Rosey says, handing me a bottle of beer. "Byron's favorite. Oh, Juniper, do you like beef? I can get something else—"

"Beef works for me," Juniper says. "Fancy beef works too."

I chuckle and clink my beer bottle against hers. I like that she calls it as she sees it.

"Did you know that the painting in your bedroom is one of Juniper's?" Rosey asks.

"I did," I reply.

The fact is, since I found that out, I think of her every time I see it. The pale colors and abstract shapes pull me in and are incredibly calming.

"I like it a lot. I've actually put in a few calls to contacts I have in the art world back in New York. Do you have anything I can send to them?"

Juniper looks surprised. "You did? That's really kind. You really didn't have to. I'm not sure I fit into the New York art scene."

"You should give him your QR code thing that you have," Rosey says.

"Oh, sure," Juniper says and pulls out her phone. "I can do that." She brings up a screen with a QR code, and I scan it. "That's my number and my website. A lot of the stuff on there is sold, thanks to Byron. But it gives them an indication of what I do."

"Is it all landscapes?" I ask. "They're beautiful. Peaceful."

"Mainly. There's plenty of inspiration around here. But I dabble in other things too. Portraits. Some abstract stuff. In fact, my landscapes become more and more abstract."

"I meant to tell you that we've had members take your details," Byron says. "Have you had anyone reach out?"

Juniper shakes her head. "You've done so much for me, Byron. I don't have any expectations that—"

"Good things are happening for you, Juniper," Rosey says. "Let's eat."

I pull out Juniper's chair for her, and she blushes again as she sits. Is it bad that I think the fact that I can elicit blushes from her is kinda hot? It gives me a feeling of power that I enjoy more than I should. As I let go of her chair, I run my fingers over her back. She shivers, and my dick twitches.

Fuck.

Juniper's sexy.

She clears her throat like she's trying to refocus. "So, how long are you in Colorado for, Fisher?"

"Around six weeks."

"That's how long it takes to record an album?" she asks.

"Every artist's different, but that's how long my artist has allocated in their schedule."

She narrows her eyes. "So, are they writing the songs here, or do they have them written, and then they just record them here?"

"I think she has a few ideas about the direction of this album, and from what I understand, she has one song that's pretty much written and a hook for another one, but the rest she'll write while she's here."

"Wow. So, she writes on a schedule? I've never given much thought to it, but I assumed songwriters wrote when the muse struck them."

"Is that how you paint?"

She glances up at the ceiling, like she's really thinking about my question. "No. Not at all. I get really limited time in my studio, and when I'm in there, I just let the canvas take me where I'm going. Occasionally, I'll have an idea of a technique or a feeling I want to evoke in the painting, but usually I just do whatever I feel at the time."

"I think songwriting is the same," I say.

"Have you ever written any songs?"

I pull in a breath. "I have. I've cowritten quite a bit as well. It's fun, writing with other people. Collaborating. You know, I haven't done it in a while. I used to produce as well." It's been a while since I've done any writing. The business side of having a record label is more and more demanding.

"I didn't know that," Rosey chimes in, and it's like she's broken through some kind of private bubble Juniper and I had been in. It feels sharper and less welcome than it should.

I don't take my eyes from Juniper. I'm not sure what I'm hoping to see.

"I'd love to hear your songs sometime," she says, and then as if she suggested something entirely intimate, she jolts slightly and shakes her head. "I mean, if you were comfortable sharing them, and obviously, I don't expect you to—"

I place my hand on her arm. "It's fine. I'd love to share with you. But it's not like how I imagine painting would be.

The songwriting I've done was very collaborative. So, it's hard to necessarily tell what I did and what a particular artist did or another producer or cowriter."

"Yeah, painting is quite solitary, but then again, it's really not. At least it never feels lonely. Quite the opposite, actually. I can lose myself in my studio because I'm so completely in the work, if that makes sense?" She talks passionately, and she comes to life when she's describing the process.

"Yeah, it makes complete sense," I say.

"Do you wish it could be full-time?" Byron asks. "I remember you at school, and art seemed to be who you were."

Juniper takes a big breath. "Honestly, I'm not sure. I'm not a kid anymore. Life can't be one thing. And I might fall out of love with it if I had to make a living from painting. Would I feel pressure to create, you know? Maybe if I were some trust-fund kid who didn't have to worry about the water bill, it would be different."

"I get that," I say. "I love parts of my industry. The creativity. The passion. The life that it creates in people. It's the show-business side that I hate. The pretense. The image. The packaging. Sometimes, it takes the shine off of things."

Juniper laughs, and I can't help but smile. "You're a music industry executive. Surely, the image and the packaging are what sells records. Isn't that what you're trying to do?"

"I'd probably be more financially successful if that's what I loved. It's not about the money for me. Not anymore."

Juniper doesn't say anything. She just nods.

"Maybe that's why music works for you, Fisher, and

why art works for you, Juniper," Byron says. "Money isn't the primary consideration for either of you."

Is it me, or is Byron trying to matchmake now by pointing out things we have in common?

"Still going to introduce you to some people if I can," I say.

Juniper smiles awkwardly, like she doesn't want to expect anything of me. She's so humble. I'm used to seeing the *humble act*. The public likes nothing more than a successful, super talented artist to act like they're working a day job at Duane Reade. Often, it's the ones who come across as humble on the chat-show circuit who are the biggest monsters.

But with Juniper, there's nothing fake about her modesty. None of it is for show. Maybe it's because she's never made it big. It makes me want to know more. I want to know everything about her.

The four of us fall into easy conversation. I'm used to the dynamic when it's Byron, Rosey, and me, but with Juniper, it doesn't feel off-balance. It's the opposite. Somehow, she fits in like it's always been the four of us. She teases Byron, just like any of us would. She laughs at Rosey's take on the world. There's no pretense. No guards up.

And when I have her attention, everything falls away, and it's like nothing else matters.

SEVEN

Juniper

I'm pretty sure tonight will go down as one of my favorite evenings of my life that doesn't involve my daughter. Great food, great wine, and some of the very best company. And I'm getting a ride home after I snagged a ride on the employee bus on the way up here.

"I had a really good time tonight," Fisher says from where he's sitting next to me in the driver's seat.

I can't remember the last time a man drove me home after a... not that we've been on a date.

"I was just thinking the exact same thing. And thank you for bringing me home. You really didn't have to. It's just on the left, in the gap between the trees."

He clicks on the turn signal of Byron's truck, which he's borrowing, although there's no one else on this road, and then he turns into my driveway.

"It's my pleasure. And anyway, Rosey would have never forgiven me if I hadn't."

I laugh. "Yeah, I think tonight was a setup. I didn't know you were going to be at dinner."

He chuckles and glances at me, a crackle of electricity sparking between us. "Me neither. But I'm really pleased you were."

His expression makes me think that he's been waiting his entire life to spend an evening in my company. There's something intoxicating about being with a person so interested in me. I can't remember any of the guys I've dated—not even Riley's dad—being so focused on me.

"Me too."

"It's good to hear the stories of Byron when he was younger. It's strange to think of him growing up here, in Star Falls. He's so rooted in New York for me. I guess because that's the only place I've ever known him."

"How did you two meet?" I ask.

"We met over a decade ago at business school. There were six of us who were tight. We're still tight."

"Like a *pack* of business school grads."

He laughs. "Kinda."

"Well, now you know your friend a little better. You know the Star Falls part of him."

"Yeah. Still the same Byron though."

We pull up outside my small one-story home. Fisher kills the engine. I don't reach for the door handle. It's nice, just the two of us.

"Yeah. He always was a good guy." I shift in my seat so I can see him better, my back against the door. "I like talking to you about music. You're obviously really passionate about it. It's... cool."

"I like talking to you too. About music. And other stuff too..." His mouth parts, and he inhales.

His eyes grow dark in the moonlight, and I find I'm

desperate to know what he's about to say. He turns so he's facing me, and heat runs through me as our eyes meet.

"I *really* like talking to you," he says, his voice deeper now. His hand reaches up and cups my face.

I know he's only in town for a short while, but all I want to think about is how his skin feels against mine and how his tongue darts out to wet his lips, like he's just about to—

The front door to my house crashes open, and Fisher's hand falls from my face. Riley stands in the doorway, her hands to her eyes like they're make-believe binoculars.

I laugh because unless they're make-believe infrared binoculars, she's not going to see anything. It's dark out here where the truck is parked.

Fisher turns to me, and my smile fades as I take in his shocked expression.

"That's my daughter, Riley."

He raises his eyebrows. "You never mentioned you had a daughter."

What does he mean? Of course I mentioned I have a daughter. There isn't anyone in a fifty-mile radius who hasn't heard me brag about the amazing eight-year-old who rules my life. I pull my eyebrows together, trying to remember when I would have said something. "I'm sure I did."

When we met at Grizzly's, we were having snatched pockets of flirtations... and it felt good to be talking to a handsome man. I got swept up in the moment, and I can't say for certain that I did tell him. But I didn't hide it. I couldn't if I tried. Everyone in this town knows I'm a mother. *Everyone*, including Byron and Rosey. Surely, they would have told their friend.

"I'm sorry if I didn't," I say. "I wasn't hiding her. I never would."

He turns back to the windshield and puts both hands on the steering wheel. "No," he says.

And I'm not quite sure what he's saying no to.

No, I didn't know you had a daughter?

No, I don't want you now that I know?

No, I don't want to know you?

We watch straight ahead out of the windshield as my mom pulls Riley back inside.

Fisher's expression has hardened; the air has shifted between us.

I could try and justify my omission, but I don't owe Fisher anything. He doesn't deserve to know anything about me. We're not dating. We haven't even kissed. There are no expectations on my side, and there shouldn't be on his.

"I'm sorry," I say, because I mean it. I'm sorry he feels like I kept something from him.

His entire demeanor shifts, and his expression is pained. "You have nothing to be sorry about. We don't know each other." He clears his throat like he's done with this conversation.

I sigh. I should get out of the car and go home and get Riley snuggles. But I'm not ready to. Not yet. I don't want to get out of the car when whatever it is that Fisher and I have shared is still broken.

We sit in silence for a few beats.

It feels hopeless.

"I'm going to go inside now and get myself some eight-year-old snuggles. But I really did have an incredible evening tonight. And I'm really pleased you were there."

I pause. Then I turn and press a kiss onto his shoulder. For some reason, it feels like the right thing to do. It's almost a promise of what might have happened between us. He smells of expensive shower gel and newly mowed grass, and

I try and commit it to memory because it's probably the last time I'll ever see Fisher again.

Although no doubt he'll live on when my mom teases me for sniffing strangers and kissing New Yorkers on the shoulder.

"Good night, Fisher."

"Good night, Juniper."

I offer him a small smile, but he stays facing ahead. I get out of the truck, and when I get to the porch, I turn back, but he's busy turning the truck around.

If nothing else, Fisher proved my vagina hasn't curled up and died. Maybe one day, a guy will ride into town who won't only be here for six weeks, who won't mind that I'm a mother, and who I'll like as much as I started to like Fisher.

And maybe hell will freeze over and people of Star Falls will stop talking about the Colorado Club.

But there's always hope. That's what life's taught me these last thirty-two years—there's always hope.

EIGHT

Juniper

Riley and I probably look like children's entertainers as we walk down Main Street in our matching outfits. We're both wearing paint-splattered overalls and blue t-shirts, and our hair is in scarves. Except Riley's outfit is a little smaller than mine.

"Mom, can you take my picture? None of my friends believe that I'm an artist."

"You want a picture in front of Marv?" I ask, nodding toward the life-sized moose that sits outside Snail Trail—the outdoors store on Main Street.

She rolls her eyes like she's barely tolerating me. "No, Mom. I grew out of photographs with Marv two years ago."

"Oh, sorry. But it's cute, having pictures of the two of you together over the years."

"Mom!" she yells, like I'm insisting Marv be in all our family photographs. "I just want the mountains in the background."

"Okay," I reply. "So, go stand with the mountains in the background."

My studio is in the old candy store. Everyone told Mrs. Peters that a candy store in the middle of Star Falls wasn't ever going to be a moneymaker, but she didn't care. She wanted a candy store. She was convinced Star Falls was going to be the next Vail, and she wouldn't listen to anyone. Mrs. Peters has more money than all the residents of Star Falls combined, so when she finally closed the doors of Candy Cane, no one called it a failure. Mrs. Peters had wanted a candy store, and she'd gotten one.

It was Mrs. Peters who'd offered it up to give me a place to paint. Just until she found someone to rent the premises. I don't know if commercial real estate is going through a downturn in Colorado, but I can't remember Mrs. Peters even having anyone looking at the place. Anyway, I give her a painting of the bluebells in the woods behind her house every springtime, and I get a place to paint.

Riley strikes a pose, hands on hips, one leg out in front of the other. I have no idea how my child decided she was going to pose like a Hollywood movie star, but here we are. Eight, going on eighteen.

"You look gorgeous," I say, and swipe to show her the shots I took before she can ask.

She fiddles with her headscarf and smiles. "We match, Mommy. I love it when we wear the same thing."

I laugh and scoop up her hand, wondering how long it will be until wearing outfits that match with mine will be the last thing she wants to do. The time is passing by so quickly. Just a second ago, she was the long-awaited, desperately wanted baby in my arms.

She groans. "Don't get mushy on me, Mom. I know

when your eyes go like that, you're about to say something mushy."

I nudge her with my elbow. "I'm allowed to be mushy. Mom's prerogative."

"Hey, you two!" a woman's voice calls from behind us.

I spin around, and Rosey's coming toward us. I haven't seen her since I went to dinner the other night. The night when I kissed Fisher's shoulder.

I've replayed the evening over and over in my head. I don't understand how the subject of Riley didn't come up. I can't help but wonder what his reaction would have been. It's not like it makes a difference. Would he have proposed marriage to me if I hadn't had a kid? No way. So, why am I still thinking about it?

"You two are dressed like twins!" Rosey's eyes are wide.

"It's how we like to hang out, isn't it?" I ask Riley. I hand her my keys. "Why don't you go and get set up?"

"Thanks, Mom."

It kind of breaks my heart and fills me with joy at how she takes the keys with such enthusiasm. Even a year ago, she wouldn't have wanted to go without me. Now, she can't wait.

"She's growing so tall," Rosey says as we watch her sprint toward the back of the old candy store.

"So tall. But better than the opposite."

Rosey laughs. "Well, I suppose that's true."

"Thanks again for dinner the other night. It was such great food. The people up there at the Club are super lucky, eating like that every night."

"Right?" Rosey asks. "Although sometimes, I just wanna eat Cheetos and M&M's. But maybe that's just me."

"I get it. Sometimes, cheese and crackers is the best meal."

"Totally."

I can tell she's itching to ask me something. Probably about Fisher. It's not like Rosey to hold back.

"So, it was nice of Fisher to drive you home, right?"

I try and hold back my chuckle. "Super nice. He seems like a really good guy."

"A *really* good guy," she says. "And you two have a bit of chemistry."

I smile. "Maybe." I sigh. "But, you know, he lives in New York."

"But so did Byron when I met him," Rosey says. "You can't rule him out just because of that. If I'd done that with Byron, we would have never gotten together, and now I'm with the love of my life, and we're making it work in Star Falls *and* New York."

A rush of shame pushes through my chest. "It's not just that. I'm a single mom, Rosey."

"So? Riley's the best, and Fisher is so kind."

"Except I didn't tell him about Riley." I explain how Riley came out when we were sitting in Byron's truck, and how Fisher went cold. "And then when he found out... I think he thought I'd deliberately not told him, but that wasn't the case at all. I don't know how—because she's my whole world—but she just didn't come up."

"I get it. You don't have to explain yourself. And no one could doubt your love for your daughter. Fisher has broad shoulders. Literally and figuratively. He won't hold it against you."

"But he also doesn't want to get involved with a single mom in her early thirties who lives in Star Falls, Colorado. I'm sure he gets his pick of women back in New York."

Rosey puts her hands on her hips. "One thing I've learned in this life is you have to back yourself. Because no one else is going to. If Fisher is put off by you being a mom, then screw him."

I let out a small laugh at Rosey's unexpected turn. She's fierce, and I love her for it.

"And even if I opened up and told him things I haven't spoken about in years, even though I just met him, then screw him again. Or maybe don't screw him." Rosey laughs, and I feel lighter about the whole goddamn situation.

"It's fine. I doubt I'll lay eyes on him again. Honestly, just talking to someone new was fun."

Rosey sighs. "I'm not sure that's true. He'll be around for a while yet. I think you're such a good match for each other."

I want to roll my eyes, but I don't. Rosey's so sweet to be so invested.

"I'm going to go and find out what my daughter is doing in the studio."

We say our goodbyes, and I head to the back of Candy Cane.

"Mom!" Riley says excitedly as I step inside the store. "I found some painter's tape. Can I put this on my canvas and then paint? I figure it will look cool when I pull it off."

My heart lifts in my chest. There's nothing better than seeing Riley getting creative. "I think that sounds like a great idea. I might even do the same."

"Really?" Riley says, beaming at me as I set down my bag.

"Really," I reassure her. "I think you could make some really creative effects with that."

She nods. "That's what I thought."

She pulls out one of her blank "canvases" and gets to work. She's organized, getting her water and paints together, just like I showed her. I try not to smile as I watch her out of the corner of my eye.

About a year ago, she said she wanted to work on canvases, just like me. Riley is a prolific producer of art, so keeping her in a supply of canvases was going to be expensive. But we came up with a solution. I use some old frames I have, and instead of having canvas stretched over them, I got some large sheets of paper and stapled them to the frames. It looks almost as good. When she's finished, I cut around the frame and release the picture. I've got hundreds. And I'm never getting rid of any of them. She's so talented, and as we paint side by side, we create so many incredible memories that I never want to forget.

"What are you going to paint, Mommy?" she asks.

"I'm going to start something new today," I reply.

"Mountains?" she asks.

I shake my head. I've been through a real mountain phase recently, and today, I want something different. "Maybe trees," I say. "But not firs."

"Oak trees?" she asks.

"Maybe." I pull out my phone and start searching what kind of trees they have on the East Coast.

Life seems so opposite there compared to life in Star Falls. I bet their trees are different too. I come across an image of some silver birch trees. Their narrow, bright white trunks are like spindly fingers poking out of the ground, and their leaves are a delicate green. Yeah, I think I might be onto something. I pull up more images of silver birch trees. They are so delicate and graceful compared to the solidity of the firs and other trees we have in Star Falls. But gorgeous. I imagine myself in the forest, the small leaves all around me, fluttering in the breeze as if they were talking to me.

I set a fresh canvas on my easel. I take another roll of painter's tape and get to work, tearing long strips of tape, cutting them, pressing them to the canvas. At the moment, my tree trunks are blue, sticking up from the ground. But when I fill in the background and then peel away the tape, hopefully, I'll achieve the bright white I want.

"You love my idea about the painter's tape, don't you, Mommy?"

"I really do. You're an inspiration, Riley. Now and always. Don't ever forget it."

NINE

Fisher

There isn't a world where I thought I'd be driving around rural Colorado in a truck. But as Vivian is fully occupied in the studio or with her baby and husband, I have a lot of free time on my hands, and Byron's truck means I can get off the grounds of the Colorado Club. I guess I should rent something. I just didn't expect to need to leave the Club. Apart from to get some wings at Grizzly's

But I'm not heading to Grizzly's today. I'm headed back to Juniper's place. I'm still a little pissed she didn't tell me about her daughter. But I'm also pissed that I'm pissed. I know it's slightly irrational. She didn't owe me anything. It's just I thought I knew her. It felt like I could see into her soul at times. I'm not often wrong about people. Not anymore. But now? Now it feels like I got Juniper wrong, and it fucking bites.

Since my parents divorced, I don't let people in often, not really. I don't want to give more than I get. I don't trust you unless I know you. Properly know you. Until I've seen you weak and vulnerable. I might have been a kid, but my parents spent years pretending they were happy and then turned around and upended my world by telling me it had all been a lie. So, now I assume everyone's a liar until they prove me otherwise.

Everyone sees the affable, happy Fisher, but they don't get any deeper than that. But Juniper did. She scratched the surface, and getting her wrong stings.

I pull up outside her house. The light's on inside, and I figure at eight thirty, her daughter is in bed.

I get out of the truck and look up, and Juniper is on the porch. She offers me a small smile, and it hurts in my gut. Her normal wide, warm smile is tamped down, and I don't like it.

"Hey," I say, arriving at the top of the steps to the porch.

"Hey, Fisher. I wasn't expecting to see you."

She's sitting on a bench, and she has a glass of wine in her hand. There's a book on the table beside her, the cover facing down, a bookmark poking out of the top. Her hair is down, and she doesn't have a scrap of makeup on. She seems so completely herself, and it pulls me in like I've never experienced before. But why when I don't know her?

"I said I'd put you in contact with someone in the art world in New York. I'm a man of my word. I didn't have your number, because my phone ate it or something, I'm not sure what happened. Anyway, I wanted to drop off Grace's details to you."

She narrows her eyes slightly, like she wasn't expecting me to say what I just said. "That's very nice of you."

"I said I'd do it. And so here we are."

"Here we are," she says in a mock British accent. She smiles. "But seriously, I know you're..." She takes in a breath. "Pissed off. Angry. I'm sorry..." Juniper doesn't meet my eye. "I didn't lie to you," she says. "But I'm heartbroken about the fact that Riley wasn't the first thing you knew about me. She's the most important thing in my life. I feel like a horrible mother. I obviously got caught up in a silly fantasy for a second there. But this is my real life." She laughs. "*She's* my whole life. And she's great."

All my anger and resentment are swept away, and I believe her completely. It's like something unknots in my stomach, and I can breathe again. I truly believe she wasn't lying.

"There was no reason to tell me. We've met each other twice, and... I get it."

She laughs, and it's a deep belly laugh, and it warms something in me.

"Well, I'm not sure you get it, Fisher. But I appreciate it."

She pats the bench next to her, and I gladly take a seat. Being mad at Juniper felt like swallowing sand when I was expecting caviar. Now, here with her, everything is back to how it should be. I don't know how to explain it, but I feel better when I'm with her than I have for years.

"You want some wine? Beer?"

I shake my head. "I'm driving. I'm not saying no because I'm mad. I'm not. It's just... I'm... particularly sensitive when I'm caught by surprise by someone."

"That's an interesting way to describe yourself. Tell me more, Fisher from New York."

I pull in a breath. I expected to drive down here, hand her Grace's contact details, and then head out. I wasn't expecting to get into this conversation. But I don't want to leave.

"I suppose I pride myself on reading people. I don't often get people wrong. And..."

"And you got me wrong," she says.

It's not a question, and I get a dull prod in my heart at the timbre of her voice.

I think about it. When I met her, I saw Juniper as a big-hearted country girl who never got out of the small town she had been born in, but if she had, she could have done anything she wanted. She's talented and likeable, and listening to her talk about art is captivating.

The fact is, I don't know if I got her wrong. But I didn't expect her to have a kid.

"I don't know anything anymore." I sigh and sit back on the bench, pushing my hands through my hair.

"I'm not a monster," she says.

"I know. And you're no pool hustler, either."

She laughs. It's light and breezy, and I can't help but smile at her.

"Can we start again?" she asks.

That's an easy question to answer. I'd give her the same answer whether I believed she was a liar or not. The thing is, I don't think she is. I think she's been living in a small town a long time, and she's not used to speaking to people who don't know her story. Or at least the part of her story where she has a kid.

"We can definitely do that."

"My name's Juniper, and I'm a thirty-two-year-old single mom of an eight-year-old girl named Riley, who has the biggest heart of anyone I've ever met."

Her love for her daughter shines from her like the sun. And it warms me.

"Good to meet you, Juniper, mom of Riley with the big heart."

She grins at me like I just hung the moon, and it tugs at my heart.

I pull out my phone from my pocket. "Let me give you Grace's details. What's your number? And I'll send them over."

"Are you coming to me with excuses about why you need my number?"

I chuckle. "Maybe I am."

We exchange numbers, the old fashioned way, without a QR code, and I send Grace's details to her.

"She owns Grace Astor Fine Art in New York, LA, and Miami. She's very well known in art circles, and she's got a big network of clients. I sent her the link to your website, and she seemed enthusiastic. She said she'd welcome a conversation."

"Fisher!" Juniper says. "That's so incredibly sweet of you, but you can't be forcing ladies like this to take my calls."

"Juniper, I'm not forcing anyone. Grace is part of the New York establishment. She doesn't do things she doesn't want to."

"But you called in a favor," she says. "And you didn't need to."

"No, I called a friend and said that I knew of an artist and asked if I could send her the website. She was excited. Grace isn't about to pretend she's excited about an artist when she isn't. She's not made that way."

"I'm sorry. I wasn't being ungrateful. I just... people like that usually like art from twenty-two-year-olds who went to some fancy college, not some hick from nowhere Colorado, who paints in an empty candy store, for goodness' sake."

"Juniper, your paintings are good. I don't know much about art, but they're fresh and atmospheric, and there's something... big about them. I feel something when I look at them."

I turn to her to see if I've offended her. Her cheeks are pink and her lips pouted. She's fucking beautiful.

"That's the nicest thing anyone has ever said about my art."

"Really?" I ask. "You're so talented. Grace isn't doing me a favor. I'm doing *her* a favor. She's lucky I introduced her."

"Staap, I can't take all these compliments. It's too much."

I'm not lavishing her with praise. I'm telling her the truth. She's clearly not used to people appreciating her art.

"You need to call her," I say. "You promise?"

She winces slightly. "Maybe."

"I think you could be a big deal, Juniper."

She sighs. "But really, I'm a mom. I can't go chasing off to New York City to meet some fancy gallery owner. And anyway, say she likes my work, she's going to want more of it. Byron bought a lot of the stuff I had. And it's not like I have loads of time to make more. I have a job. I get to paint once a week, if I'm lucky. And I've usually got an eight-year-old tagging along who wants regular snack breaks, so those Saturdays are not particularly productive."

"You're counting yourself out," I say to her.

"I'm being realistic, is what I'm doing."

"Or maybe you just don't believe in yourself."

She laughs. "Oh, well, that's probably true. I can't deny it. Why would I possibly do that? I'm a teaching assistant who likes to paint. I'm not the next Van Gogh."

Now it's my turn to laugh. "Maybe not, but all I'm saying is, make the call. Maybe Grace says that unless you get on a flight to New York, she's not going to speak to you. But maybe she doesn't. Maybe Grace comes to the Colorado Club. For all I know, she and her husband are already members. And maybe she does want more art from you. Isn't school vacation coming up? But maybe you're inspired and you paint more. I don't know. I just think it's a bloody shame if you give up when you don't even know what's possible."

"But there are so many reasons why it wouldn't work. Why would I waste my time?"

"You don't need to imagine the obstacles. There will be enough real ones—that's just life. But you owe it to yourself. You owe it to Riley to do your best to fulfill your potential."

"Fisher, are you using mom guilt to get me to call Grace Astor?"

I nudge her. "Whatever it takes."

"You're sweet, Fisher."

I chuckle. "I'm not always, trust me."

"Do you have a secret dark side?" she asks me, like she wants to know.

I smile. I don't know about a dark side, but there's part of my past I'd rather forget. "Doesn't everyone?"

She raises an eyebrow, like she thinks I'm talking bollocks.

"I have my moments." I shift, and our legs brush together. She's beautiful, and I need to get out of here before I get myself in the kind of trouble I don't want to get out of. "Call Grace," I say, before standing and head the hell off Juniper's porch.

TEN

Fisher

Despite the incredible breakfasts at the Colorado Club, my favorite place to get my first meal of the day is the Galaxy Grill. The cherry-red seats are like something out of the fifties. The uniforms that the waitresses wear are fifties appropriate, and the black-and-white tiles on the floor are a vibe. It doesn't hurt that the waffles here are sent directly from heaven. I wonder how much of Star Falls has changed in the last seventy-five years. Probably less than most of America.

"You want a table by the window?" The waitress nods to the row of booths that can fit six people, and I bite back a smile.

"Sure," I say. "Thanks."

I love the view down Main Street with the mountains climbing up and out from behind. It feels like the town was plonked here in the middle of nowhere and doesn't really belong, with the mountains so domineering of the landscape. It's so different from New York.

I follow the redheaded waitress over to the booths. When we pass the first one, something catches out of the corner of my eye, and I do a double take. There, in the first booth, is Juniper. My gaze slides to the person opposite her. It's a kid. Her kid, presumably.

"Hi," I stutter like I'm a fucking awkward teenager.

She smiles a wide, warm smile. "Hi, Fisher. This is Riley. My daughter."

"Hi," I say, nodding at Riley.

Riley's hair is slightly darker than her mom's, but she has the exact same smile. She lifts her palm up, and it takes me a second to realize she's offering me a high five.

I slap my palm against hers and raise my eyebrows. "It's good to meet you."

"Fisher's one of Byron's friends, Riley."

"Byron who you went to high school with? The dude who lives in the Colorado Club?"

"Dude?" Juniper asks on a laugh. "When did *dude* appear in your vocabulary?"

Riley just rolls her eyes, like her mom is the worst.

"So, it's nice to meet you, Riley." I nod to the next table, where the waitress has left me a menu. "I'll see you—"

"You're welcome to join us, if you want." She gives me another smile, and I feel it in my gut. "But I completely understand if you don't want to endure the attitude of a hungry eight-year-old." She winks at her daughter.

"I won't be hungry as soon as my pancakes get here."

"Well, that's true." She glances back up at me. "But it's completely fine if you want to eat on your own."

"Ahhh, pancakes," Riley says, leaning forward so she can see around me to where the waitress is heading toward their table with a plate of pancakes. The plate is stacked high, and I wonder if it's possible for an eight-year-old to even make a dent in that many pancakes.

Now I'm making it awkward. I need to fucking sit down. I'm hovering like I'm an indecisive bee.

"Sure, I'd love to join you, if you don't mind sharing your space?"

Juniper and Riley both shuffle up, leaving room for me to sit next to either of them.

More decisions. I really should have skipped breakfast. Although there's a part of me that's glad I didn't.

"Come sit, Fisher. You're making me nervous." Juniper pats the bench next to her, and I slide in.

"Pancakes, huh?" I say, nodding toward Riley's plate.

Riley shoots me a look like I'm a loser. And she wouldn't be wrong. I just don't know what to say to an eight-year-old.

"Oh, and here's mine," Juniper says as the waitress sets down another plate.

"You're a table of three now!" the waitress says. "How perfect."

Something passes between her and Juniper.

"Don't start, Donna," Juniper says. "Or I'll send my mom after you."

"What are you talking about? Your mom would be on my side." The waitress laughs and turns to me. "What can I get you? You had the waffles and strawberries last time you were in, right? You want the same again? With a black coffee?"

"You memorized my order?" I ask. Am I being stalked?

Juniper laughs beside me. "Donna has a photographic memory. Don't worry; she's not your personal stalker." She stops herself. "Although, she has the skills."

"I absolutely do; you're right," Donna says. "So, what's it going to be? Same as last time?"

"Sure," I say. What else *can* I say? I'm slightly concerned that if I order something different, it will be entered into a database somewhere, and Donna will be able to tell me what I'm going to be doing five years from now.

"You want the whipped cream?" Donna asks. "You said no yesterday."

"Now you're just freaking me out," I say. "But no, no cream, thanks."

Donna writes it down and disappears, and I watch her go, wondering if she's going to note down my order somewhere so she can pull it out next time I'm in. Or maybe she really does remember everyone's order.

"Does she really have a photographic memory?" I ask, watching Donna.

"I'm not lying, Fisher," Juniper says sharply.

Before I have a chance to respond, Riley says, "Donna remembers everything. My birthday. Everyone's birthday actually. Even Albert's birthday."

"Right," Juniper says. "Let's not bring Albert into this."

Albert is clearly a topic of controversy.

"But, Mom, please can I have another Albert? I promise I'll do all my chores for a month without complaining?"

Juniper shakes her head. "I am not buying you another fish. They die, Riley. That's what fish do. And you wouldn't leave your room for three entire days when Albert died. I'm not doing it again."

I try to bite back a smile, because I thought Albert might be the ex-husband or something. But Albert's a fish. And Donna remembers his birthday. This town sure has its quirks.

"What are you up to today?" Juniper asks, clearly and desperately trying to turn the conversation away from Albert.

"Well, breakfast for a start. Then I'm going to text you to see if you called Grace Astor."

She laughs. "You don't give up, do you?"

I shrug. "Tenacity is my superpower."

"What's tenacity?" Riley asks, her mouth half full with pancakes.

"Don't talk and eat," Juniper says. "Tenacity means persistence. Like when you ask me to visit the diner after a studio session. You don't quit until I say yes. That's tenacity."

"So, tenacity is my superpower too." Riley raises her hand for another high five, and I slap mine against hers.

"So?" I ask.

"So, calling Grace is on my list of things to do."

"And what's the time frame for getting through your to-do list?" I ask.

She winces. "Average life expectancy is what? Eighty-two or something, right?"

I shake my head, wondering what I can do to convince her to pick up the phone.

"I really appreciate you giving me her number."

"You need to use it," I say as my phone buzzes.

I realize I haven't checked my emails yet today. Back in New York, it wouldn't matter what day of the week it was, the first thing I do in the morning is check my emails. Here in Colorado, all the days are merging together, and I'm out of routine. After I wondered when Juniper painted the picture opposite my bed, the first thing I thought of today was what the view would look like and whether it would be the same as yesterday. In New York, I don't contemplate the view. I'm down to business right away.

"Sorry, I just need a second."

I scroll through my phone and see something from the

manager of the biggest group that's signed to Right Records at the moment—The Homecoming Kings. He's a decent guy. A straight shooter.

I open the email, which is headed as *Contract*. I scan the email. He wants to discuss the marketing around the last album... blah, blah—and then I hit the crux of the message.

The band has been talking about whether Right Records is the right place for them.

I groan and sit back. There's no way this isn't connected to Gerry Banks. He's got to have been sniffing around them. The Kings are building some serious momentum in their career. They write all their own music. They're not idiots. Or more accurately, only the drummer is an idiot. They have real long-term potential. Of course Gerry wants them.

Fuck.

"They won't be long with the waffles," Riley says encouragingly.

"You okay?" Juniper asks.

"Yeah, fine. Sorry, I haven't checked my emails today, and they're building up."

"Relax. You're in Star Falls. You don't need to get all *The Scream*." She puts her hands up to her face, and Riley does the same thing. They both open their mouths, imitating Edvard Munch's famous painting.

Even though I don't feel very happy, I can't help but laugh at the two of them.

"It's not that. I just got some bad news at work. That's all."

"What kind of bad news?" Riley asks. "Did you lose your job? That happened to Anna's dad. That's why they had to move. They've gone to Denver now."

"No, I didn't lose my job. Although it feels like someone's trying to bury me professionally."

"Is it that cutthroat?" Juniper asks as Donna delivers my waffles.

"Not usually. Well, yes, it is, but I can handle it. I know when to expect the blows. And usually, I'm in New York, so I've got my gloves on. But someone from my past has come back to haunt me, and it feels like... I don't know. It's strange. It feels weirdly personal. And now I'm starting to sound paranoid."

She gives me a reassuring smile. "You seem to me like a man who has good instincts. Maybe it *is* personal."

But why would it be? It wasn't like I got a promotion at EMG and he didn't or something. We were both the same level. Maybe I had more of a knack for sniffing out talent than he did. I certainly got more artists signed than he did during our time as co-workers. But he stole artists right from under my nose. If anything, I should have a personal vendetta against him.

"I can't see how." I shrug.

"I think the waffles will make you feel better," Riley says. "I'm feeling better after some of my pancakes. Mom says it's the sugar."

I grin at her. "Good advice, Riley." I dig into my waffles.

"Pancakes and mom snuggles. That's the secret sauce that always cheers me up."

I glance sideways at Juniper, and she's trying not to laugh.

"I'm not sure I qualify for mom snuggles," I reply. "But these waffles are delicious."

"Best in the tristate area," Riley says wisely.

Juniper laughs. "The tristate area? Who made you, kid?"

"You did! And Dad." Riley's expression turns sullen. "My dad moved to Orlando with his new family."

A pang of sadness hits me in my chest. I know that feeling. Everything changing and you not being able to do anything about it. Not knowing if you're going to see your dad again. It's all... a lot.

Juniper chews on her bottom lip. "It's an adjustment," she says.

"Yeah, I get that," I say. "My mom and dad got divorced when I was a kid."

"Really?" Riley asks.

"Really," I say, trying to keep my voice even. "It takes time, but new becomes old pretty quick."

"What does that mean?" she asks.

"It means it hurts. And it's difficult to imagine, but it will hurt less someday."

Riley shrugs and takes another mouthful of pancakes.

Juniper slides her hand onto my thigh and pats it under the table before going back to her eggs. I'm not sure if it's a thank-you for trying to make Riley feel better or an *I'm sorry you went through that*. Maybe it's both. It's nice. *She's* nice. So's Riley. Juniper's not someone trying to make me think she's one person when she's actually another. She's still the beautiful, insightful woman I met. But she's also a mother.

"Riley, what do you think about me taking your mom to dinner sometime this week?" I ask.

Out of the corner of my eye, I see Juniper's eyebrows rise up into her hairline.

"What, like at Pizza Meet Ya?"

"Pizza Meet Ya?" I ask. "Wow, that's a mouthful."

Juniper laughs. "The pizza place on the corner," she clarifies.

"Maybe," I say. "Does she like Pizza Meet Ya?"

"She does," Riley says. "We don't go very often though."

I glance at Juniper. Her expression is open and happy. It's comforting and warm.

"If you'd like to go to dinner, that is?" I ask her.

She nods. "That would be nice."

"Do you want to be her boyfriend?" Riley asks.

Juniper splutters on her drink and goes to speak.

I chuckle. "I just wanna get dinner," I say. "I get really, really hungry."

"Okay," Riley says.

"Okay?" I look at Juniper.

"Okay," she says with a wide smile.

ELEVEN

Juniper

I don't know what I was thinking, saying yes to dinner with Fisher. Not that I don't melt every time he's near. I don't find him any less attractive than I ever did. But I know it's heading nowhere, so why dinner? He was just so cute with Riley at the diner. I couldn't help myself. And the way he fielded the question about him wanting to be my boyfriend was expert. Being able to cope with awkward questions from an eight-year-old is an aphrodisiac I never knew existed.

"Are you ready?" Mom calls from the living room.

"Nearly!" I call back. It's a lie. I can't decide what to wear.

This is just a casual one-off date. I'm not about to date a guy who lives nearly two thousand miles away. Or eighteen hundred forty-seven miles away—I looked it up on Google. But I want to look nice. I want to feel attractive. I want *him* to find me attractive. Most of my semi-nice clothes I wear to work. And the ones I don't wear to work are mainly covered in paint.

Lights flash across my bedroom window. Lights of a car. Of Byron's truck.

Shit.

I pull on some jeans and a white camisole. It's casual. But maybe it's too casual if we're going up to the Colorado Club. I pull off my jeans and top and grab the green dress I bought to wear to school, but haven't worn yet. It's still casual enough for Pizza Meet Ya, but it could pass at the Club. I think. I bend over, ruffle my hair and then flip back to standing. That will have to do.

I stumble out of my bedroom just as Fisher knocks on the front door.

"I'll get it," I yell.

But it's too late. Riley and my mom are already opening the door. The last thing I need is for Fisher to be interrogated by my mom. She's fiercely protective of me, and she has been the exact same way since I got pregnant. The first time.

"Come in," Mom says. "Can I get you a drink?"

I practically sprint into the living room. "We can't stop, Mom. We have reservations."

As I'm talking, I lock eyes with Fisher. He looks... incredible. His hair looks like it's still damp from the shower. He's grinning from ear to ear at me, and it fills me with liquid joy.

I scan his body to make sure I'm not too off with what I'm wearing. His jeans skim his legs like they were tailored for him. And he's wearing a white shirt, which lights up his face like he's a movie star or something. He might be the best-looking man I've ever laid eyes on.

"I'm not inviting him to spend the entire evening with

us, watching *Jeopardy*," Mom says. "I asked the man if he wanted a drink."

"That's very kind of you," Fisher replies.

"My, I love your accent. Say something else," my mom says.

I roll my eyes. Is my mom flirting with my date?

I press a kiss to the top of Riley's head and scoot under Fisher's arm. "Gotta go. Love you, sweet girl."

I take the stairs down to the driveway like the house is on fire as Fisher says goodbye to Riley and my mom.

"Wow, you really didn't want me to quench my thirst. That's kinda mean," Fisher says. My eyes widen, and he bursts into laughter. "I'm kidding. But really, you couldn't get out of there quick enough."

He opens the truck door for me.

"Believe me," I say as I get in. "I saved you from a fate worse than death. I've not been on a date in nearly three years. My mom would have wanted to know your inseam measurement before we were allowed to leave if she'd convinced you to take a beverage."

Fisher brings up his hand. "Hold that thought." He shuts my car door, rounds the hood, and climbs into the driver's seat. "You haven't been on a date in three years? What the fuck is the matter with the men of Star Falls? You're beautiful. And fun and—"

"I'm not interested in the men of Star Falls."

"Surely, there's got to be some good ones."

"I grew up with all these guys. It kinda takes the edge off. Anyway, I've been focusing on Riley. With her dad moving away, it's been tough on her. I didn't want her to think I was going anywhere. I wanted to make things the same for her for a while."

Fisher nods as we head along the road back toward the town.

"So, where are we headed?" I ask, trying not to ogle him as he drives. It's just difficult.

His oh-so-hot forearms are on full display, and I can't seem to look away. And the cut of his jaw? I swear, I should have brought a change of panties.

"We have a choice," he says.

"A choice?" I repeat. "You know you're in Star Falls, not New York City. We don't have restaurants on every block." I grin at him, and he turns his head.

"You're so pretty," he says.

The man makes me melt.

"*You're* so pretty," I reply.

He chuckles. "But seriously, we actually do have a choice. I didn't book Pizza Meet Ya. I think that needs to go in a top ten somewhere for weird names for a pizza restaurant."

"I'm pretty sure it already is."

"But we can go there if the pizza's good."

"The pizza's okay," I say tentatively. "And we won't need a reservation." Honestly, I'd really prefer not to go to Pizza Meet Ya, but I might go just about anywhere with Fisher.

"We could head up to the Club. The owner owes me a few favors. We can go to any of the restaurants up there."

"There's more than one restaurant?" I ask.

Fisher just laughs, but I'm genuinely interested in the number of restaurants up there. How many restaurants does the place need?

"Or you could show me your favorite spot in Star Falls, and we could have a nighttime picnic. I've packed some food in the back."

"You do?"

"I figured you might not want to go to Pizza Meet Ya because you've probably been a thousand times before. And the Club... well, Rosey will have her spies out, and I'm not sure how relaxing it would be if we had a full-on cheer squad in the corner."

I laugh. "That's true. She's very enthusiastic about the two of us... being friends."

Fisher nods. "Right. So, is there anywhere you think would be good for a picnic?"

"Absolutely," I say. "The falls this town is named after. Take the next left."

When we pull up to the parking spot for the falls, Fisher cuts the engine. "Is it weird that I didn't expect there to be waterfalls here?"

"Why else would we be called Star Falls?"

"I think I thought it was about the stars. And that maybe there was a shooting star spotted."

"Oh, we have a lot of shooting stars, too," I say. "But the best place to see them is by the falls."

Fisher unloads the fancy picnic basket from the back of the truck. There's a separate bag that Fisher also carries. He won't accept any help as we head toward the path.

"How long is the trek to see them?"

"You're going to be severely disappointed if you were expecting a trek," I say. "It's about twenty yards behind the car."

Fisher laughs. "Good. This basket is heavy."

"Sure you can manage it?" I ask in an overly concerned voice. "Those weedy little arms are going to get so tired."

Fisher tries not to laugh. "Thanks for the concern."

I laugh. "Come on. It's almost a full moon tonight, so it's a perfect evening to visit the falls."

They come into view, and even I can't help but be struck by how beautiful they are. The water cascades over rocks into a pool below. It's more than the trickle it can be sometimes. The moon reflects in the pool, making the black water glow.

"I haven't been up here for ages."

"I guess when it's on your doorstep, you can take it for granted. But it's beautiful."

We find a place to sit. The ground is still warm from the sun, and we could sit right on the mossy grass, but Fisher has come prepared and brought a blanket.

"This is cute. Do you normally take women on picnics? In Central Park, maybe?"

"Hmm," Fisher responds, straightening out the blanket. "Never been on a picnic date before."

"Me neither," I say. "Although I have kissed a couple of boys up here."

"Oh, right? So, I have the ghosts of boyfriends past to contend with as well as the backdrop."

"Right," I reply. "I was sixteen, and a game of Truth or Dare meant my first kiss was with Johnny Radlett up here."

"Lucky Johnny," Fisher replies, and his eyebrows pulse up.

I can't help but grin. Fisher opens the picnic basket.

"Holy shit. Who else did you invite?" I ask.

There is a ton of food in the basket. He brings everything out and sets it on the blanket like he's arranging it for a photo shoot or something.

"It's a feast," I say.

There are three different types of salads, cold meats, pasta, smoked salmon. It's like he went to a store and said, *I'll take one of everything.*

He hands me a glass and pours out some white wine.

"A feast," he repeats.

"You're not telling me you got this all from the store in town?"

"No, I'm not. I can't even take credit for picking it or packing it. I just told someone at the Club I was taking a beautiful woman on a picnic date and I wanted to impress her."

Butterflies dance in my stomach at his compliment. Fisher impresses me just by standing there, but he does a nice line in compliments, too. I'm glad it's dark, and he can't see the heat in my cheeks.

"Well, color me impressed. But I'm not sure it's the picnic that's done that."

Being with Fisher feels so different. I'm not used to guys who like talking to me about art or have experience living outside of Colorado.

"Tell me about life in New York," I say. Then I immediately regret it. Maybe I don't want to hear about how great his life is outside of Star Falls. Maybe I want to believe that he might stay a little longer than he's planning to. "Do you hate it?" I ask. "Because they say, once you come to Star Falls, nowhere will ever be as nice."

He sees right through me and my one-woman marketing of Star Falls and laughs. "I don't hate it. New York is... you can't compare it to here. Star Falls is totally different."

"We don't have skyscrapers."

"Right."

"Or pollution."

"Or the ability to get takeout twenty-four hours a day."

"I'll take clean air over twenty-four-hour takeout."

Fisher chuckles. "You're right. I guess what I mean is that New York isn't just like any city. There's a place for everyone there. You don't have to pretend to be anyone because everyone is welcome."

"Huh," I reply. "That's a really nice way of describing a place."

"It's true. New York is a cornucopia of the world. And that's what makes it so fascinating. You never know who you're going to meet."

"That's definitely not the case with Star Falls." I can't help but laugh at myself. "I definitely know who I'm going to meet on any given day. Or at least I have a good idea."

"Have you known everyone in this town your whole life?" he asks.

"Pretty much. Some move away for college and come back. The odd ones leave completely."

"You never moved away for college?"

I pause. Am I going to get into this with Fisher? I stare at him. He's got the prettiest blue eyes I've ever seen. They're warm and inviting. They make me want to share all my stories.

"I thought about going to art school. No, I didn't just think about it. I really wanted to go to art school." I take a breath. "I got accepted into a great program in New York. One of the best in the country. Even got a full scholarship." I try and keep my voice steady. "But I got pregnant just as my acceptance form was due."

Fisher frowns. "With Riley?"

I shake my head. "No, not with Riley. I lost the baby at six months."

It's been a long time, and I'm past the devastation the miscarriage created. But I don't think I'll ever be truly over it. Every year on my due date, I want to shut myself away and cry. And paint. And cry some more.

"I'm so sorry," he says, his eyes full of concern.

"It was tricky. And then all I was focused on was getting pregnant again. I wanted so desperately to fill the gap the miscarriage had left. I think I put too much pressure on myself, and I couldn't get pregnant, but I couldn't think about anything else. Art school wasn't a possibility then, even though I could have probably applied again and gotten in for the following year. It wasn't what I wanted at that point. I wanted a baby. A baby to make up for the baby I'd lost. A baby to take away the pain."

Fisher sighs. "That's tough."

"Yeah, it was difficult. And I was young. Really young. It's weird. When you're that young, you don't realize how the decisions you make then can affect the rest of your life. I didn't really comprehend the impact of the decisions I was making back then. Not that I regret any of them. Riley's the best thing in my life, but having her meant I gave up the idea of having an art career."

Fisher just nods.

I smile up at him. "Our lives couldn't be more different, right? Where did you go to college? Yale?"

"I'm not some trust-fund guy," he says. "I've worked hard for what I've got." He smiles at me. "Different lives—you're right. But we have a lot of things that... overlap."

Our gazes lock.

I can't help it. Suddenly, I burst into laughter. "What are we doing?"

Fisher's smiling at me like he seems to whenever I laugh. I've noticed that when I smile, he wears this expression, like watching me is making *him* smile, and it makes me feel warm and good, and I want more of it.

"Having a picnic by the falls," he suggests. "Enjoying each other's company. I like you, Juniper."

I press my lips together, trying not to grin like I'm fourteen and my pop-star crush just told me he liked me. "I like you too, Fisher."

"But you're right, I'm not living here in Star Falls. It's not like we can..."

"Turn into anything?"

"Right."

I hold his gaze so he focuses on what I'm about to say. "But we can have fun and enjoy each other's company while you're here."

His tongue darts out to lick his lips, and my cheeks heat.

"I'm sorry. I just don't want to... I don't want to pretend."

I smile. "I like that about you, Fisher. No pretending."

He nods.

I glance over to the falls. "You know what I've never done?"

"Tell me," he says.

"I've never skinny-dipped at the bottom of the falls."

Fisher's eyes flare in the darkness. "Well, that seems to be a huge error of judgment. On your part and mine." Without skipping a beat, he starts to unbutton his shirt, and then he stands. "Come on. What are you waiting for?"

"I think I need another glass of wine."

"Chicken," he goads, toeing off his boots.

"Well, I can't have a fancy New Yorker tell me I'm chicken now, can I? Turn around so I can get naked."

"Do I have to?"

"You absolutely do have to."

He groans but does as I asked.

Turns out, there are some firsts left in my life. First time I've ever been on a picnic date, first time I've ever been on a date with a guy from New York, and the first time I've ever skinny-dipped at the bottom of the falls in Star Falls.

TWELVE

Fisher

The air is still warm even though it's nearly ten. Which is just as well because I'm stark bollock naked.

The splash of water tells me Juniper has reached the pool.

"You okay? Careful you don't slip."

"You worry about your New York ass slipping. I've known these rocks my entire life. I can map each dip and edge with my eyes closed. Which is a good freaking thing because it's dark as hell down here."

I laugh. "Can I turn my New York ass around?"

"Hang on... yeah, you're good."

I have no idea how much she can see in this light, but for a second, I think about cupping my manhood as I head over to the water, but what's the point? It's all going to be out as I climb in.

She lets out a yelp and then calls, "I've turned around."

I chuckle. "Did you get a fright, seeing my New York ass naked?"

"Just get in here already and quit teasing me."

I slip into the water. "Fuck! It's freezing."

Juniper is in front of me, her blonde hair twisted up behind her, and the water hits her just below her shoulders. I can't see any part of her below the water. But I know she's naked, and I feel myself thicken at being so close to this beautiful woman when neither of us is wearing clothes.

Juniper laughs. "It's not the Caribbean. That what you're used to?"

I shake my head. "You need to stop your teasing."

She wets her lips. "Or what?"

"Or I might kiss you."

Her eyes widen like I've shocked her. But she's not shocked. Not really. She didn't think we were getting into this water for a play fight.

"Oh, yeah? So, all I gotta do to get you to kiss me is tease you a little more?"

I step toward her and take her face in my hands. "You don't even have to do that."

I press my lips against hers, and she tastes of sweet honey. Something inside me clicks—together or apart, I can't tell—and somehow, I get a sense that I'm right where I need to be. All the stuff about Gerry Banks and Vivian and The Homecoming Kings melts away, and all I can think about is how this kiss feels inevitable.

Fated.

She moans and moves closer. Her hands find my waist, and I gasp into her mouth at the contact. I don't know if it's because we're both naked or if it's the darkness or the water, but I've never felt a kiss all over my body in the way I do now. It sweeps over and through my skin and into the darkest parts of me. Her hands stroke up my sides, the water lapping at our skin, and out of primal instinct, I wrap a hand around her waist and pull her closer.

I'm hard as fucking steel, and I press against her soft belly. Her sharp nipples graze my torso.

Fuck. I want more of this woman. I want all of her.

Our mouths explore each other. Ravenous. Desperate. Is it because it's the first kiss and it's been a long time coming? Is it her? I'm lost in her. Dizzy with need for her.

She pulls back a little. Her eyes trail over the parts of my body not submerged in the water. She sweeps her hands over my lips, along my jaw—all the while, our gazes locked. Her hands skirt my body. My shoulders, my arms, my chest, my hips, my ass. Everywhere, except there. It feels almost ceremonial. She's mapping me in some Star Falls tradition.

I mirror her, sliding my hands down her neck, over her arms. The water laps at her chest, her breasts hidden below the surface. My hands dip to feel their shape. I trail lower, over her stomach, her hips, and around her ass.

We both exhale, and she lets out a small smile. The ceremony is over, and it's time to move on to the next stage.

I circle my arms around her and pull her closer. Our mouths fit together, and she sinks into me. Our kiss is more this time. Deeper. More connected. But it's still not enough. She must feel the same way because her arms come around my neck, and then she lifts her legs around my waist.

I have to break our kiss because the sensations, the feel of the water and her being wrapped around me—it's all too much.

"Too much?" she asks, reading my thoughts, and goes to shift back down.

I grab her ass with both hands, keeping her in place. "Not enough, Juniper. Not enough."

She smiles, fiddles with something behind her head, and her hair falls down behind her.

Fuck. If I die now, I'm not sure I've ever been so fucking happy.

"I'm really fucking hard," I grunt out.

She parts her lips and shifts in my arms, teasing the crown of my cock. "I can tell."

"Don't do that," I say. "I'm going to come, and I'm going to be really embarrassed. I'll have to go back to New York early."

"Not before you've fucked me, you won't," she says on a smile.

I groan, and she squirms in my arms, and I tip my head back. She's half heaven, half hell. An angel and the devil himself.

"I want you," she whispers, then presses a kiss to my neck. "I want to have as much fun as possible with you before you leave."

Our mouths meet again, and with the tip of my cock enveloped in the folds of her pussy, our tongues clash together. I'm so close to thrusting up inside her. I'm not sure how I find the strength to hold back. I'm so hard. So desperate for her, and she's like a siren, urging me closer.

"Fuck, Juniper." I pull away from her and set her down on her feet as far as my arms will reach. "You're... too sexy. I want you too much."

"Do you have condoms?" she asks.

"Yeah." I try to think if I've ever had sex in water before. I don't think I have. I don't know how condoms work in water. Is it safe?

"Let's get out," she says. An easy solution that I couldn't think of; my brain is so frazzled from being so close to Juniper.

Back on solid ground, I pick up the blanket, letting what's left of our picnic fall onto the grass, and then I set it back down again.

She sits, and I can't look away. I'm mesmerized by her every movement. The way she looks at me. Her body. She's incredible.

"Condoms," she says, pulling me back to the moment.

"Right," I say.

I get my wallet and join her on the blanket. We're lying on our sides, our heads propped up on our hands. I try and keep my eyes focused on her face, but her body in the moonlight is lit up like she's carved out of marble. She's timeless. Perfect.

"If you haven't dated in three years, does that mean..."

"I haven't had sex in a long time." She trails her finger over my shoulder. The same shoulder she kissed in the truck after I drove her home. Despite the heat, it sends a shiver down my spine. "So, no need to get performance anxiety on my behalf."

I grin. "Oh, I'm not worried I won't perform. I'm slightly worried I might break you though."

She takes my hand and places it over her breast. "You won't break me, Fisher."

Her breasts are full and firm and so soft. I pull her against me and then flip her to her back, my entire body over hers, pinning her to the ground.

"You're so beautiful, Juniper."

She opens her legs, and my cock connects with her pussy. Except the wetness this time isn't water. It's all her. Jesus. I want to slide into her bare and feel her all around me, drenching my cock. But I need to think straight.

I drop my face to her neck and hold her arms out wide to give me access to all of her. I press kisses over her collarbones, over her arms, down between her breasts. I take her nipple in my mouth, sucking, licking, grazing my teeth over the puckered flesh until she's squirming underneath me.

But squirming won't do it.

I want her to beg.

Releasing her arms, I skirt down her body, my hand going between us. I want to feel her wetness on my fingers. I slide a finger over her clit, and her juices cover me. Looking her in the eye, I lift my finger and put it in my mouth.

"Pure honey," I say. "I want more."

I work my way down her body, kissing, pressing, touching. When I get to her pussy, I press her legs wide open. The moonlight isn't enough. I want a goddamn surgical light to examine her in all her perfection.

"Fisher," she calls.

"What was that?" I ask.

"Fisher," she says louder.

"Yes, baby? What is it?"

Her breaths are heavy, and she arches her back. "Please, Fisher. I want you."

I groan. That's what I want to hear—pure desperation.

I dive between her legs. She's so sweet. So wet. So perfectly mine.

Her hands fly to my hair as I work my tongue over her clit, down her folds, around her entrance. She cries out, bucking up against me, and I have to pin her hips to the floor.

All too soon, she's shuddering on my tongue, rocking against my face like she can't get enough, and then she explodes, her body limp and lifeless as she falls back down to earth.

I crawl back up her body and cage her in on either side of her face. "Now, you can have that one for free. You were so wet. You needed it so badly. But next time, you won't come without asking. Do you hear?"

Her chest heaves between us, and our gazes are locked.

"Really?" she asks eventually.

I nod. "Really. You can't come without my permission."

Is my need to control her orgasm a kink? Maybe. But it *is* a need. It's a requirement I have of her.

I kneel, take the condom, and roll it on. I have to get inside her. I need to feel her around me the next time she comes.

"You ready?" I ask.

She nods. She looks like she's not entirely sure.

"It's going to be good," I assure her. "So good."

She nods again, and I hold her gaze as I slowly slide into her.

She's so. Fucking. Tight. When I'm as deep as I can get, I exhale, trying to gather myself. I don't know how long I've got.

"You feel so perfect, Juniper."

She threads her hands into the back of my hair, and it feels so intimate; it provokes such a feeling of familiarity, of closeness, that for a moment it feels like I've known her an entire lifetime, and I will know her for another.

"You too," she whispers.

I start to move. Slowly pulling out of her. Her mouth falls open in a silent cry. I try and create a rhythm, but it's stuttering. She's so beautiful it almost hurts. So delicate and warm and familiar and entirely new. She feels so soft and tight at the same time. It's hard to focus.

She shifts underneath me and moans, and I still, my jaw tight. It's too much. It hits me right in the center of myself. I'm on the edge, and there's no room to move before I fall. I'm so acutely aware of her pleasure, and it's so necessary to my own. It's never felt like this before. I'm so completely in tune with her. It's like I can see what's inside her head.

I pull out to give myself a little room to breathe. I need to gather myself.

"I'm close again," she says.

"Me too," I say on an exhale. "What are you doing to me?"

A small smile lifts the corners of her mouth. "Fisher," she says, like she doesn't quite believe what I'm saying.

"I mean it." I shake my head, incredulous. "You're... wonderful."

I push inside her again, and this time, I know I can't stop until we're both there. I won't be able to. I won't have the self-control.

Something animalistic inside me takes over, and I slam into her over and over. I feel her body tense.

Through gritted teeth, I hiss, "Ask me."

My breaths come short and ragged and our eyes meet. A line appears between her eyebrows, like she's really trying to focus, like she's doing everything she can not to climax.

"Ask me," I growl, louder this time.

"Please," she says.

"Please what?" I reply, slamming into her again, making her scream.

"Please, can I come? Please, can I come?" Her expression is desperate.

Her pleas are what tip me over the edge. I slam into her, up, deep, fast.

"Come," I command.

She dissolves under me, tightening around me, milking me.

I explode into her, and I can't catch my breath. It's like she's stolen a vital part of me.

Seconds, minutes, hours later, I can no longer hear the waterfall because of the pounding in my ears and the gasps of her breath. All sense of time and space is lost, and all I can do is feel. Her. Me. Together.

I collapse beside her, get rid of the condom, and pull her into my arms. Eventually, sounds of falling water finally trickle back, and the scent of honey follows.

It's as if all my senses shut down because all I could do was feel. Her.

Be.

With her.

Like she was the center of the universe and all that mattered.

She trails her fingers over my torso, and it starts to bring my cock to life. I capture her wrist.

"Be careful," I warn her. "Don't start something you can't finish."

She laughs beside me. "Oh, I don't have a problem finishing. Not with you."

I growl and flip us around so I'm over her again. I begin to kiss her. All over her skin. I want to know her. Know everything there is to know. Every freckle, every dip and curve.

"What happened here?" I ask, when I reach a small silver scar just above her elbow.

"I fell off a climbing frame when I was seven years old. Landed badly. Compound fracture."

I wince before pressing a kiss over it. I have an urge to take care of her, to protect her, and I can't remember having it before.

She plays with my hair as I press kisses everywhere and all over her. When I get to her breasts, I pull a nipple into my mouth. I suck and pull at it, and she squirms beneath me. I snake my hand down and reach between her thighs. She's wet, and I claim a silent victory. I push a finger through her folds, and she gasps.

"So ready, so quickly." I pinch her nipple between my finger and thumb.

She nods, like she wants more.

I push my finger deeper, my thumb working her clit. But I know that's not what she wants. "That feel good?"

She groans again. "I want you, Fisher," she cries.

"You have me," I say. I flick her nipple with my tongue.

She frowns, like I'm not cooperating, and it's so adorable that I let out a laugh.

"Tell me what you want."

She pauses for a second before she says, "I want you inside me."

"You do?" I ask, and teasingly, I work my finger deeper.

"Your cock, Fisher. I want your cock inside me."

I nod, like she got the answer right.

I grab another condom and put it over my straining erection.

"It makes you feel so good, doesn't it, Juniper?"

She nods as I position myself at her entrance.

"You like me filling you up, stretching you wide."

She pulls at me, urging me closer. I don't know how I'm holding myself back. I have the most beautiful, sexy woman underneath me. How am I managing not to slam into her and make her scream so the entire town of Star Falls can hear us fuck? But reveling in her need is almost better.

Almost.

"Shall I take it slow, baby?" I ask. "Because you're so tight. I'll just push in a little. Open you up a bit."

Her chest is heaving as she pants. She seems to be close even though I'm only just getting started.

"Oh, Juniper. You're so close. Remember to be a good girl and ask permission before you come."

I slam into her, and she dissolves around me, tight like a fist, her back arched, her hands grabbing at me.

"Oh dear," I say as I keep fucking her through her climax. "That wasn't polite, was it?"

Sweat sheens my body as I do my best not to follow her. My need to make her come again overrules my body, and I manage to push my orgasm back. I thrust into her over and over. Her expression when she realizes what's happening, when she knows another climax is building, nearly sends me off the edge. I have to shut my eyes for a second so I can get through. I shift and lift her legs up, place them over my shoulders. It gets me deeper, farther into her. And I can see her better like this. Watch as her breasts move with my thrusts, see how she shudders as I talk to her.

She reaches for me, but I'm too far back, so her hand falls to her pussy. To where we connect.

The visual is too much. I'm too far gone to bring myself back from the brink this time. I thrust harder, trying to feel everything. Trying to commit it all to memory in case life never gets this good again. And I need to get her there.

I didn't need to worry that she might not.

I grab her wrist and take her fingers in my mouth. "That's mine," I say.

"Fisher!" she cries. "Fisher, please, can I come?"

I circle my hips and thrust. "Come now."

I push into her, our eyes lock, and we both fall together.

THIRTEEN

Fisher

Vivian and I have fallen into a routine. The two of us meet every other day for breakfast and to catch up. I don't want to impose myself, but I want her to know that I'm here to support her.

"It sounds like it's all going perfectly," I say, in response to her talking about the album.

"How can it not when the pastries are this good?" she says.

I laugh. "So, that's the key to your creativity?" I ask. "Food?"

"More specifically, pastries," she says. "Or any high-fat, high-sugar, low-nutrition food."

"Got it."

"But seriously, you're welcome to come down. You can hear what we've done so far, if you'd like. In fact, I've got a little niggle with the current track. I wouldn't hate it if you put your producer hat on and gave me your thoughts on what you think it needs."

"It's been a while since I've been hands-on in the studio. I've been stuck behind a desk for years now."

"Oh, we'll blow off your cobwebs. Creativity is like riding a bike. You never forget it."

"Well, okay then. What are your plans for the day?"

"Same as all my days. I put Victoria down for a nap before I came to breakfast. Then I head down to the studio straight from here. I break at lunch for an hour and a half and go to see Victoria. Then back to work until dinner."

I nod, impressed. She's clearly committed to this album.

"I run a tight ship. Have to since Victoria was born. Otherwise, I'm not going to work again. And I like my job. Or I'm not going to see my kid, and I like my kid."

"Okay then. Finish your pastries, and then we'll get to work."

She lifts her hand, and I give her a high five. Her phone buzzes.

"It's Beau. Give me a second, will you?"

I go to slide out of the booth, but she puts out her hand to stop me, and she gets up.

Vivian Cross has been a star since she was a kid, but there's not an ounce of spoiled diva in her. I like her.

I pull out my phone and message Juniper. Last night was... pretty unbelievable, and as much as I'm excited to get back to work today, I didn't get much sleep last night, and my thoughts are still full of her. The arch of her back, the curve of her neck. Images of her are burned into my brain, and I'm not sure if I'm going to be good at just existing, let alone actually giving some helpful input on Vivian's album.

I ask Juniper how she's feeling. Tell her I had the best time and ask her when she's next free. She's a mom, and I understand that comes first, but I hope I don't have to wait too long until I can see her again.

I stuff my phone back in my pocket and see Byron coming down the stairs. He heads over when he sees me.

"You okay?" he says. "Eating alone? You can always eat with Rosey and me."

I grin at my friend. It's nice to see him so much a part of a couple when this time last year, I couldn't picture him ever settling down.

"Thanks. I'm eating with Vivian. She's just taking a call. But I don't mind eating alone."

Before he can respond, Vivian appears. "Hey, Byron," she says.

"How's the studio?" he asks. He spent a lot of money fitting it out, so it's no wonder he wants feedback.

"Err, absolutely *perfect*," she says, sliding back into the booth. "Everything about this place is incredible. And you know I'm practically British now. I can't give false compliments."

I laugh at her interpretation of the Brits. I may have only lived there for a few years of my life, but I had British parents. It runs through my veins. She's right; there's no praise when it's not due from a Brit.

"Good to hear it," Byron says. "If there's anything I can do, let me know."

She shakes her head. "Your very efficient manager, Hart, has you covered." She pats the table. "Come join us."

Byron sits, and immediately, there's a waitress asking him what he wants to eat and drink. Not just because he's the owner, but because that's how it is here. Everything's perfect.

Out of nowhere, Rosey appears, holding a cup of coffee. "Room for another?" She doesn't wait for a response before sitting down next to me. "Where's Beau?" she asks Vivian.

"With the baby," she says. "He's such a good dad. I

swear, I never thought I'd be able to become a mother in this business, but he makes me feel like anything is possible."

Rosey and Byron grin at each other. I'm sure they feel the same about each other.

"What about you, Fisher?" Vivian asks. "True love on the horizon for you?"

I chuckle, trying to ignore the images of Juniper from last night that fill my mind. "They tell me anything's possible in Star Falls."

"I believe it," Vivian says. "Look at the goddamn view!" She nods over to the huge windows that look out onto the valley and the town.

"How did it go last night with Juniper?" Rosey asks, her eyes bright and expectant.

Of *course* she has to ask in front of Vivian. Just what I need—two women who've found the loves of their lives, thinking it works out for everyone.

"It was good. We had dinner."

"Good? Dinner?" Rosey asks. "We want more details than that! Did you kiss? We know there's chemistry between you, but was there *chemistry* between you?"

I glance at Byron, but he just shrugs as if to say, *There's nothing I can do, mate.*

"It was good. And, yes, I'd say there was chemistry."

Rosey's eyes open wider. "So, the kiss was good. When are you seeing her again?"

"You need to manage your wife's expectations," I say to Byron.

He shakes his head. "Sounds more like *you* need to manage my wife's expectations."

"Seriously, Rosey," I say. "I'm here for a few more weeks. And then I'm back in New York. Juniper is lovely, but she has a life here in Star Falls."

"So what?" Rosey asks. "You're just going to write it off before you've even begun? Byron and I live between Star Falls and New York."

I laugh at her thinking that people living between New York and Star Falls is an everyday occurrence. "I'm saying, we both know this isn't going to turn into a long-term thing. But I like her. I think she likes me. I'd like to hang out some more."

"For the record," Vivian says. "Pardon the pun." She lets out a small laugh at her own joke. "I don't want to rain on your parade, Rosey, but Fisher, you don't need to be babysitting me in Colorado. If you need to be back in New York City, then you should go."

"Vivian!" Rosey exclaims. "That doesn't help."

Vivian shrugs. "Just saying."

"Seriously, Rosey, you're hoping for something that isn't going to happen," I say, ignoring the fact that Vivian just gave me permission to leave. I made a promise to her manager, not her.

It's just a fact of life that I'm not moving to Star Falls permanently, and Juniper has a kid and a job and an entire life here. She's not moving, either. No matter how much she makes me laugh. How good she feels naked. How incredible I think she is.

Rosey shrugs. "Five more weeks."

I shake my head, but I don't say anything. There's no point. I'm going to have to keep doing this to and fro with Rosey until I leave. Juniper is wonderful. I meant what I told her last night. And I hope she and I are going to enjoy each other's company while I'm here. But as much as my thoughts today might be all about her, I need to be realistic. We're a short-term fling. That's as far as it goes.

FOURTEEN

My head is a jumble of thoughts this morning.

"Do you have to bring that pirate costume in today?" I call out to Riley.

She pops up from right behind me. "No need to shout, Mom."

"I thought you were cleaning your teeth. Pirate costume is today, right?"

"No, next Friday," she says, looking at me like I've lost my mind. "It's for the assembly, which is next Friday."

"Oh, that's right."

"Did you not sleep good, Mommy?" she says. "And why did Fizzy have a sleepover?" she asks.

"No, I didn't get enough sleep. It's made my brain fuzzy. That's why I always tell you it's important to get enough sleep."

It isn't just the lack of sleep that's made my brain fuzzy, although it doesn't help. Every time I try and focus on something, my thoughts drift to Fisher. How he seemed to worship my body. How incredible he felt over me, under me, inside me.

Maybe it's just because I haven't had sex for a long time, but last night was like something that I'll never forget for as long as I live. He was so in control and commanding, but at the same time so incredibly attentive to what I needed and wanted from him. He was an equal mix of masculinity and fragility. He was just completely perfect.

I'd thought he was hot and fun before last night, and now? He's... special. A special man.

"Mom," Riley calls, pulling me out of more thoughts of Fisher.

"Yes, honey?"

"My lunch?" she says. "It's not in my bag."

"It's not?" I scan the countertops, but it's not out. "It's gotta be. I know I made it."

She opens her backpack wide, showing me that it's not in there. Where else could it be?

I pace up and down in front of the cabinets, like it's going to jump out at me.

"What about the refrigerator?" she asks.

I open the door, and there it is, like I prepared it for tomorrow or something.

I pull it out and hold it up.

"Mommy!" She collapses into giggles. "You need to wind up your brain today."

"You're right. I do. I hope yours is wound up too."

I place the lunchbox into her bag, and she zips it up.

"My brain is always wound."

I laugh. "Okay. You have your water?"

She nods.

"Sweater?"

"Mom, I'm wearing my sweater!"

I grin and wink at her. "You want another one?"

She rolls her eyes, and we head out. As we get to the car, a delivery guy pulls up.

"Mom," she says. "Who's that?"

The driver slides out of the cab. "Hey there. Got something for ya here."

I'm not expecting anything. He goes around the back of his truck and pulls out the biggest bouquet of flowers I've ever seen, already arranged in a vase.

Instantly, I know they're from Fisher. But how? I only left him about five hours ago. How on earth did he manage to get flowers delivered to me this early?

"Thanks," I say, signing for them.

They are the most beautiful shades of pink and yellow and green. They look almost wild. I look more closely and realize that the green foliage is juniper. My heart climbs in my chest at his thoughtful, romantic gesture.

"Can I take them?" Riley says.

"I think they might be a bit big for you," he says.

I laugh as she tries to take them. They're practically as big as her. I grab them, and we shuffle back into the house.

"Did you order these, Mommy?" she asks.

I shake my head.

"Then who sent them?"

I shrug, pull the card from where it's nestled in among the leaves, and slide it into the back pocket of my jeans. Riley doesn't notice. Why would she? I don't think I've ever had flowers delivered before.

"Let's get you to school," I say. "We're going to be late."

"But, Mommy, who sent us flowers?" she asks.

"I don't know. I guess we'll find out."

We get into my beat-up Honda and head out.

"I think it was Fisher," she says from the back, and my

heart splutters. How would she know that? "The guy from the diner. I think he likes you, Mommy. And when boys like girls, they give them flowers."

"Is that right?" I say.

"Yes, it's true. I saw it in a movie."

"Okay then."

"Is he going to be my new dad?"

I grip the steering wheel harder. I try and keep my voice as neutral as I can when I reply, "You have a dad, Riley. Why would you think Fisher is going to be your dad?"

She shrugs. "I never see my dad. If Fisher was my dad, I'd see him more."

"Oh, honey. Fisher isn't going to be your dad. Your *dad* is your dad. I know you wish you could see him more. Maybe I'll try and set up a FaceTime with him this weekend?"

"Okay," she says, sounding unenthusiastic.

Bill isn't great at keeping in touch with Riley between visits. It's not because he doesn't love her. I know he does. But he's busy and occupied. I just don't think she's at the front of his mind. Or at least, he doesn't put her at the front of his mind.

Before he left, I warned him that he'd need to put structures in place. Routines. If he wanted to stay a priority for her, she'd need to be a priority for him. He assured me that he would, and in the beginning, it was fine. He called every Sunday morning. And he'd send her postcards. But as his new family grew, he started rearranging calls or missing them completely.

Seeing the disappointment in her eyes was heartbreaking. It's still heartbreaking. All the hope that she's going to speak to someone who loves her, and then he cancels. Sometimes, I think it would be easier if he cut all contact. At least she could heal. But this way, she keeps being let down. She keeps getting hurt.

Whenever I raise the issue with Bill, he has an excuse. I can't force him to be more reliable for Riley. I can't see it ever changing. I get that she'd want to trade him in for another dad.

We pull up at school and I park. As we get out of the car, someone calls Riley's name, but she doesn't look up like she normally does.

"But if you married Fisher, then would he be my daddy?" she asks, as she turns to look at me.

It's like an arrow to my chest. I wish I could give her that. Hope for a new daddy. A better, attentive, more present father. But I can't. Certainly not with Fisher. But realistically, I can't see myself ever being married to anyone. I've managed this long.

"I'm not going to marry Fisher, sweet girl." I pull her in for a hug. "I'm sorry you're sad."

She pulls away and nods solemnly at me. "I am sad. I want a dad. Everyone has a dad except me."

"I get that," I say to her, and I pull her in for another hug. "It's so hard," I whisper against her pretty, soft hair.

Someone calls her name again.

"I'd better go, Mom. You need to get to work."

I smile. She's such an empathetic kid.

"I love you bunches," she says.

"Love you double," I reply, as I hook her backpack onto her arms.

She heads off over to the playground. Soon, she's smiling and playing her favorite clapping games with her three best friends, and it makes me feel slightly better that she's bounced back. For now.

I pull out the envelope that came with the flowers from my pocket and take out the card.

My heart soars in my chest at the message.

I'm still thinking of you.

You're wonderful.

—Fisher

It's been a while since a man thought I was wonderful. In fact, I'm not sure any man has ever thought I was wonderful. And it's the only time I've ever been sent flowers.

I tap the card against my chest. If Riley spends any time with Fisher, there's a danger her expectations will skyrocket. And I don't have much time when I'm not with her. Fisher might think I'm wonderful, and I think he's pretty wonderful, too. It's just, I'm not sure how much of him I'm going to be able to see before he goes back to New York and is gone forever.

FIFTEEN

Fisher

I'm in the next lodge over from Byron and Rosey, but of course, I can't tell if they're in there or not. I know for a fact that Byron has an office over at the main building, but he always works from his lodge. As does Rosey. So, I'm taking my chances and popping by for a cup of sugar. And their input on an idea I have.

I knock on the door and wait, glance back at the incredible views behind us. The mountains on the other side of the valley aren't as tall as the one we're on, but they're still imposing. This place is like a different planet to New York. I'm not sure how it's possible we all speak the same language.

Byron throws the door open and stares at me like he's been waiting for me. "Come in," he says.

I follow him to the back of their place. Their lodge is three times the size of mine. I have no idea why they're building a place outside of the Club when this place is an almost-palace.

I head to the fridge to grab a can of seltzer for me and one for Byron. "Where's Rosey?"

"Down at the new house," Byron says. "Keeping the contractors on their toes."

"Good for her. I still don't understand why you don't want to stay here. It's beautiful, and you have gourmet food yards away and—"

"But whenever I step out of my door, everyone knows I'm the boss. I don't want to be the boss all the time."

I hand him a seltzer and collapse onto the sofa.

Byron sits opposite me. "I have a call in twenty minutes, so what's up?" he asks.

I chuckle and take a swig of my drink. "I had a call with Grace Astor."

"Sam Shaw's wife?"

"Yeah, you know, she's got galleries throughout the US. But she also has an advisory service."

"Advisory?" he asks. "Advising on what? Art?"

"Exactly. She doesn't make a big thing about it. It's something she does herself for a few exclusive clients who want her help finding art for a new home or a refurb, that kind of thing. The clients that she works with are the kinds of people who are members of the Club."

"Okay," Byron says, trying to figure out what I'm going to say next. Or more likely, he knows exactly what I'm going to say, but he's wondering why I'm here in the middle of the day to talk to him about it.

"I thought it might be a service you want to offer your guests or members or whatever you call them while they're here."

"You want me to hand out a flyer or what?"

I chuckle. "Yeah. Or maybe wear a sandwich board and stand in the gym. But seriously, you could invite her to come to the Club and inform members they have an opportunity to have an initial meeting with her, while they're in the relaxed environment of the Club. Some of them might decide they want to work with her. Grace is a big name in the art world."

Byron's silent for a beat. "Won't they have people for stuff like this? My designer takes care of art at my place and here." He nods toward a painting that I can tell Juniper painted. Realization dawns on his face. "Oh, you want her out here so she can meet Juniper, and Juniper can't go to New York because of Riley."

"Partly," I say. "Juniper is why I called Grace, and we got to talking, and she told me of this consultancy service she offers. And she likes Juniper's work. She loves connecting with new artists. Even if she can't give Juniper a show at one of her galleries, she might be a fit for one of her clients she consults for. But Juniper and Grace need to meet. I'm sure if they do, Grace will be impressed with Juniper's work. But for some reason, Juniper won't call Grace. Or can't call her. I can see she wants it. But she won't... I don't know if she's scared or if she doesn't think she's good enough."

"Both probably," Byron says.

"Right. Makes sense. But Grace isn't coming to Star Falls just for Juniper."

"So, you want her to come and meet with Club members," he says out loud. "That way, she'll connect with potential clients for the work in her galleries and for her consultancy services. *And* she'll have an opportunity to meet Juniper and see her work. It'll give her an opportunity to kill two birds with one stone."

He pulls in a breath. "Club members don't like the hard sell, but we're talking about Grace Astor, so I don't have that to worry about. I think it's a good idea. But speak to marketing. The Club manager, Hart, can put you in touch with the right person."

He pauses, but I can tell he hasn't finished speaking.

"You're a good guy, Fisher, don't get me wrong. And honestly, I'd be a very happy man if you and Juniper ended up together. But she's never left Star Falls. I don't see you moving here—"

"We're just having fun. We both know this isn't a long-term thing," I say.

I like Juniper. I really like her, and the sex… it was more than phenomenal. But we don't work from a logistical perspective.

"And she definitely knows that?" he asks.

"Absolutely," I say. "I'm not about to make promises I can't keep."

"I know that's not what you would ever intend, but I would hate it if things got misconstrued. Juniper is a lovely woman."

"I know," I say. I get that Byron feels protective over his friend. Over this entire town. I'm not going to break Juniper's heart. "Juniper made it clear that we could only be casual."

Byron nods, satisfied. "It's good of you to help."

"She's talented," I reply. "And you know how I like to network."

"It's your greatest strength. Is there anyone in New York you don't know?"

"No one worth knowing," I say on a grin. I slide the seltzer onto the coffee table in front of me.

"Everything okay with Vivian?"

I nod. "I got to go back into the studio the other day. I helped her out on a couple of things."

"Like as a producer?"

I nod, skimming my palm over my jaw. "Yeah. I hadn't done it in a long while, but it felt good."

"Getting your hands dirty?"

"Getting back to basics. I love the music industry because I love music. All this other stuff sometimes takes away from that. Don't get me wrong, I don't hate the business side of what I do, but sometimes the music can get lost, you know?"

Byron stays silent for a beat, like he knows I've got more I need to get off my chest.

"Did I ever tell you about Gerry Banks?" I ask.

"The guy who used to steal all your artists before you could sign them when you were in A&R at EMG records. Haven't heard that name in a while."

"He went into artist management, but now he's running a rival record label. He's been reaching out to my clients."

"I guess he's trying to make a splash."

"It feels personal," I say.

"It's always felt personal to you. It's probably jealousy. It can drive people mad."

"Maybe it's that."

I just don't know why he would single me out. Especially now. As head of Re Records, he has more power than me. Yes, he answers to shareholders, and I don't, but Gerry could have done what I did and created his own label. I don't understand why he would be jealous of me. It doesn't make sense.

"You're not convinced?"

I shrug. There's something in my gut that tells me it's more than that, but I don't know what it could be. But my gut was wrong about Juniper. Or maybe it wasn't.

"Maybe you slept with his sister. Or mother. Or wife or something."

"It's something. I just don't know what. Being here makes me feel vulnerable, like he'll be picking over my business while I'm gone."

"Did you hear that we have the internet now? You can stay in touch with anyone wherever they are. It's a goddamn miracle."

"I have no idea why your career in stand-up never took off."

"Me neither," he deadpans. "Most of your artists aren't based in New York anyway, are they?"

"Some of them are, and a lot of them fly in and out all the time. So I catch up with people a lot in New York. And I fly to LA most months. I like doing things face-to-face. It builds trust. And looking someone in the eye it... I think you see more."

"Well, you certainly see their irises," Byron says.

"I mean about their intentions and character. And also, people tell you things face-to-face that they wouldn't tell you over a call. They'll gossip or mention something that wouldn't otherwise have come up. I never think you get the full picture over a call—even if it's video."

"So, go back. I'm sure Vivian wouldn't mind."

"It's not Vivian I'm worried about. I'm sure she'd be fine with it. Her manager and I made a deal that I'd be here because he can't be. I know *he* will mind if I take off. And I can't afford to piss him off. I could ask him—Vivian is so incredibly low-maintenance. I just don't want to rock the boat. Maybe I could suggest to him that I go back for a few days over a weekend. Vivian seems to treat recording like a nine-to-five job. Gotta admire her for it. She wants to carve out time with her family, but I've never seen anything like it. I'm used to rock stars who don't open their eyes before dinnertime and then work all through the night."

"She probably doesn't have the required drug habit."

I chuckle. "Right."

"Sounds like a good compromise. Go back to New York over a weekend. Check things out. But there's plenty you can do from here to figure out what Gerry's up to."

"Yeah, maybe I need to be more proactive instead of waiting to see what his next move is."

I need to take action instead of sitting here, waiting for Gerry to strike. I'm going to start by calling all the managers of my signed artists and catching up. Even if Vivian wants me in the studio, I can fit those calls in around that. And then I'll figure out the best time to fly back to New York.

SIXTEEN

I make sure I close the screen door as quietly as possible. Riley should be asleep by now, but I don't want to tempt fate. This is my golden hour. Today's chores are done. I have sixty minutes to myself before I need to head to bed.

I take a seat on the bench and open my book. I chose it from the library because it had a picture of the Empire State Building on the cover. Reading about it is the closest thing I'll ever get to visiting New York City.

Just as I finish the first paragraph, the headlights of a truck light up the porch.

Is it my dad? He didn't say he'd be coming by. As the truck swings to the side, my stomach flips. That's Byron's truck.

It's Fisher.

He offers me a grin through his window. I didn't realize how much I wanted to see him until right now.

We've been trading texts all day, trying to get another night on the calendar. It hasn't been easy. Mom has clubs most days—knitting, reading, pottery. And anyway, if I ask her to sit more than once in a week, she's going to pin me down and make me spill my guts. I can't face the idea of saying I'm having really great casual sex with an out-of-towner and I want to make the most of it. It's not that she's a prude; my mom would probably encourage it. I just don't want her—and everyone else, including Riley—thinking that Fisher and I are riding off into the sunset together. We're both clear this isn't anything it's not.

"Hey," I say as he takes the steps up to the porch. "I wasn't expecting you."

He grins, and my stomach flips like it's a goddamn dolphin's tail. It's just that he's so pretty and so, so good with his tongue.

"I thought I'd drop by and ask you out the old-fashioned way—face-to-face." He holds up a bottle of wine. "I brought a beverage this time."

I laugh and stand to get glasses. But I don't get a chance. Fisher puts the bottle on the table and wraps his hands around my waist.

He sweeps his lips against mine and lets out a groan. "God, you smell good."

He kisses my smile, and I sink into him, relaxing my body against his, threading my hands into his hair.

It shouldn't be this easy with him. But it is. It's like we've skipped three months of dating, and he knows exactly what I want from him. A long, slow kiss.

"I've been wanting to do that all day," he says. "In fact, all week, since the last time I saw you."

I wince. "Sorry. My schedule is—"

"You don't need to apologize. I know you have a lot going on. Doesn't mean I don't miss kissing you."

I tilt my head and push his hair from his face. "Well, I'm

available for kisses on my porch every evening from eight thirty till midnight."

I grin, but he doesn't laugh like I expected him to do.

"Don't make promises you can't keep."

"Fisher, if you wanna drive down here every night, then I'm more than happy to kiss you."

This time, he smiles and presses his lips against mine, pulling my body against his, sliding his tongue between my lips, finding mine eager and willing.

I feel him harden between us, and eventually, he pulls away.

"Tell me your mom isn't inside."

I laugh. "No. And Riley's in bed. But let me get some glasses, and we can... take a break."

I head into the house. Quickly, I check on Riley, but she's fast asleep. I grab two of my three wineglasses and a corkscrew and head out.

"How was your day?" Fisher asks from where he's sitting on the bench, his arm stretched out on the back. He takes the wine and expertly opens the bottle and pours out two glasses.

"Oh, you know, a lot like yesterday." I take a seat beside him, and he scoots me closer and puts his arm around me. I lean my head against him. "Except today, Riley and I had a difficult conversation about her trying out for cheer squad."

"You're worried she won't get in?" he asks, like he's genuinely interested. He's so sweet. He hands me a glass of the wine he poured.

"No, I'm worried she *will* get in. I hate the whole idea of cheer. I used to do it at school, and I know there are plenty of positives, but I don't like my daughter participating in something that's basically cheering on the boys doing a sport. It's gross."

"But it's a sport in its own right, right? I mean, they do gymnastics and stuff, don't they?"

I straighten my head and shrug. "Yeah, but ultimately, the idea of cheer is to hype up the crowd so they go wild for the boys. I don't like the message it sends. I want her to do gymnastics. To swim. Do any sport. But cheer?" I groan.

If Riley really wants to do it, I'll support her, but I don't like the message it sends to impressionable young brains.

"I imagine most parents are thrilled if their kid gets on the cheer squad."

"True," I say. "But I'm not most parents. I want more for Riley than cheering on the boys. I want people cheering *her* on."

He smiles at me like he's mesmerized.

"Sorry. I'll get down off my high horse now."

"Don't. You look hot up there, standing up for what you want. Cheers to that." He raises his glass, takes a sip, and sets it back down.

I shake my head, grinning at his cheesy joke. "Tell me about your day."

He pulls in a breath. "Well, I spent this morning in the studio. My artist wants my input on a couple of tracks, so I've been helping a little."

"Like giving it marks out of ten? What does input look like?"

"Can you imagine?" he asks, pulling me closer and pressing a kiss on the top of my head. "Me holding up numbers one to ten, depending on whether I like a track."

I laugh.

"I don't think that would go down well. Not because what she's doing isn't good, but..."

"Your artist is a woman?" I ask. "I don't know why, but I expected it to be a man."

"Yeah. She's here with her husband and child." He says it quickly and reassuringly, like he doesn't want me to think there's potentially another woman in the picture. It's kind and thoughtful, but that's not what I was thinking.

"You can't tell me who it is? Would I have heard of her?"

He sighs, and my hand, which is resting on his chest, rises and falls. "I'm sorry. I'm not trying to be an asshole, but I've promised her complete privacy."

"That's okay. I mean, I'd like to know, but I'm not getting my panties in a wedge because I don't. It's business. I get it." I pull away from him a little because I want to see him when he talks. "So, tell me. You go into the studio, and you don't pull out a paddle with a number out of ten on it. You're not scoring it. But what do you do? You say, *I liked that trombone, but I think your lyrics stink?*"

Fisher chuckles. "Not exactly that, but kinda. I used to dabble in record production and writing. And so I help with the mix, the arrangement, maybe even some of the lyrics and music."

"Wow. That's not what I thought you'd say. I expected you to be the money guy. I mean, you're friends with Byron, and he seems like the money guy."

"Byron's definitely the money guy," he says. "But I started off in A&R, scouting talent. Then I moved into production, building artists' careers, and matchmaking musicians together."

"I bet every day is different for you, huh?"

"Less so now. Because, like you say, I'm the money guy..."

"What?" I ask as his thoughts trail off.

"I was just thinking that you're right; my career has changed a lot from how I started before Right Records grew into what it is now. Before that, I was working with different people all the time. And even when I was working in A&R, I'd go to gigs all the time, scour YouTube for the latest thing. Now, I'm the guy that says yes or no across a desk."

"You miss being on the ground."

He pulls his eyebrows together in that way he does when he's really thinking about something. "I'm not sure. In some ways. I haven't questioned it in a long time. Right Records exploded after a couple of artists I was working with went viral and became overnight sensations. It happened one right after another. For a long time, I was just trying to keep up. I don't know if it's being here with one artist, or that I've been back in the studio, or maybe because Gerry Banks has resurfaced, but now I'm thinking about it."

"Huh, you know the other thing that's changed?" I point at myself, and then shake my head. "Don't go falling in love with me, blowing up your whole life."

A shy smile curls around his lips, and I can't help but lean forward and press my mouth to his. He's just so freaking adorable. As I go to pull back, he clasps my face and pushes his tongue through to meet mine. It's like he can't let me go without getting more first. The thought circles my heart and squeezes.

He grins. "I'll do my best."

I turn so I can't see him. Maybe if I can't see his expression, I'll be able to resist him easier.

"Now, tell me more about whoever the hell Gerry Banks is."

He chuckles and tells me the story of this guy who seems straight-up jealous of Fisher. And frankly, I'm not surprised.

"And you think it's only you who he targets? Does he have a reputation for being an asshole?"

"No more than anyone else in my industry—me excluded, of course."

"Of course," I say, feigning shock that he'd even suggest that he might be an asshole in business.

I pull out my phone. "Where did he go to school? Harvard, I bet. I heard everyone who goes to Harvard is an asshole."

"I have no idea."

"What do you mean, you have no idea? You must know everything about Gerry Banks. He's your nemesis."

"He's my nemesis, so I should know where he went to college?"

"You should know what he eats for breakfast and what his favorite tie is."

"We don't wear ties. No one in the industry wears ties."

"Okay then, not his favorite tie, but you need to know everything else about him. Have you never read *The Art of War?*"

He turns to me, a questioning expression on his face. "*The Art of War?* Why on everything that is Star Falls does teaching assistant-slash-very talented artist Juniper French need to have read *The Art of War?*"

I place my hand on his leg. "Oh, Fisher, do you only read books you *need* to read? I don't think I've ever heard anything so heartbreaking. I read sometimes just because I want to, or because someone told me it would make me laugh. And sometimes, I read because the cover is the perfect shade of azure blue, or because when I pull it off the library shelf, it seems to fit perfectly between my thumb and index finger. There are many reasons to read a book, Fisher. Need is only one of them."

He holds my gaze, a small smile on his lips. "You are quite something, Juniper French."

I want him. Really want him. In my bed. In my arms. Over me, looking down, as he fucks me. I want to wake up tomorrow morning and eat croissants and orange juice on the deck with him while Riley insists we play only Vivian Cross songs from the kitchen and then inhales two croissants.

I want him. But I can't have him. Not like that anyway.

"So, tell me what I've been missing from *The Art of War*."

"*If you know the enemy and know yourself, you need not fear the result of a hundred battles. If you know yourself but not the enemy, for every victory gained you will also suffer a defeat. If you know neither the enemy nor yourself, you will succumb in every battle.*"

"Thank you, Sun Tzu," he says.

"Honestly, the good thing about Star Falls is also the bad thing about Star Falls. Everyone knows everyone. Some more than others. You only have to meet Donna, who works at Galaxy Grill, once, and you'll know who she is instantly through and through. It's the same with her sister-in-law, Marge, who owns Snail Trail, the outdoor-wear store. And then there's Mrs. Gale, my next-door neighbor. Riley and I have lived here since Riley was born, and I know Mrs. Gale doesn't like cats, but does like daffodils. And she keeps to herself. Generally, you spend enough time with someone over enough years, and they're going to show you who they are."

"Planning to go into battle with Mrs. Gale?"

"Not on my list for this year. Who knows what next year might bring? My point is, you've been in Gerry Banks' orbit for a while now, and you know he's your enemy. And you think he's your intentional enemy. But you don't know where he went to college?"

"You think maybe he hates me because of the college he went to?"

"Now, if you keep teasing me, I'm going to throw your ass off this porch. And that would be a shame because I'd like a few more of those perfect kisses you're giving out." I give him a stern *don't fuck with me* look that only people who've actually wrestled with a two-year-old and a leaky diaper can know. "You need to know him. Figure out what makes him tick. Don't fixate on him fixating on *you*. Fixate on *him*."

He pulls in a breath, and I can't help but glance at his stomach as it moves under his shirt. I've seen those abs. I know how dangerous they are. I focus back on his face, and he smiles. He caught me checking him out.

"We need another date—soon," he says.

I nod. "Don't try and change the subject." I pull out my phone. "What did you say his name was? Gerry Banks? And he's at Re Records, you say?"

I start an internet search. His LinkedIn profile pops up first. His photograph is perfectly curated. It's clearly a professional photograph, but he looks relaxed and friendly. His bio is very pared down, with only job titles and time spent in each role. I scroll down to *Education*.

"Where did you go to college?"

"Penn State. Why?" he asks. "Did he go there?"

I shake my head. "He doesn't have a college listed, but his school... hang on. Let me check something." I copy and paste the name of his high school and do a search. "Yeah, he went to school in Pennsylvania."

Fisher chuckles. "You think he's been stalking me since kindergarten?"

"No, but it's worth filing away in your brain. Where did you grow up?"

"Pennsylvania."

"So, you both grew up in the same state. That's worth knowing."

"Is it?" he asks.

He clearly thinks I'm losing my mind.

"I'm just saying, you should do a bit of research. If nothing else, it might give you some insight into what he's doing so you know how to protect yourself."

"You're right," he says. "Oh, and while we're on the subject of our professional lives, I think Grace Astor is going to be coming to the Colorado Club."

My entire body turns to jelly, and if I wasn't sitting down, I'm sure I'd fall down.

"Why?" I snap.

She can't be coming to see me. I can't have some lady who knows about art coming all the way across the country to see my work.

Fisher frowns. "She wants to see your work, but actually, it's a great business opportunity for her as well. The marketing team is going to introduce her to some members of the Club they think would benefit from her expertise."

My body slowly regains its strength as he talks.

"So, she's not coming all this way just for me?"

"I'm getting the feeling you want me to say no when, if the answer was yes, that would be a huge compliment, so I'm completely confused."

I swallow. "Yeah. It's... I don't mean to sound ungrateful, but it's just little ole me in my studio, painting weirdo abstract landscapes, as my dad likes to describe my art. And I love that you like my painting, but I don't expect some lady from New York who owns galleries and stuff to like my work."

"Well, news flash: some lady from New York does like

your work. Don't think I had anything to do with her interest in you other than sending her the link to your website. She called me. I haven't pursued her. And anyway, this is Grace Astor. She doesn't owe me anything. And even if she did, she wouldn't gamble her reputation on anything. If she likes you, she likes you."

"I looked her up," I say. "She's a pretty big deal in New York. Well, all over the US."

"You're right. She is. All the more reason she's not going to fly out to Colorado and waste her time just as a favor to me."

"Are you sure you sent her the right website?"

"Juniper…" His tone is a warning, like I'm being ridiculous. But it's not me who's being ridiculous. It's this entire situation.

"I've been painting a long time," I say. "I love it. But I don't expect other people to. It was a shock when Byron's designer bought almost every piece I had."

"And you know Byron didn't do that as a favor, don't you?"

I don't know that. "There's no question that he did me a favor."

"Then you don't know Byron very well. If you asked him to buy a piece of your art, he definitely would. I'm not saying he's not generous. But he just wouldn't have been proactive about it. I can almost guarantee you that he gave your details to his designer and then forgot about it. He's not micromanaging the artwork at the Club."

I pull in a breath, trying to process what he's telling me. It makes sense that Byron wouldn't have wanted to micromanage the art buying.

"But I bet he told his designer to buy something."

"How many paintings did they buy?"

"Eighteen. She didn't like five that I have. Said they were a little bit dark. And one was too small."

"Right. So, he wouldn't have said, *Go buy eighteen paintings.*"

"He might have. He might have given her a budget."

He shakes his head and pulls out his phone. "We'll settle this."

He's going to call Byron. I'm mortified.

"What are you going to say?" I ask.

He doesn't respond. He sets the phone on speaker. "Hey," he says when Byron answers. "I wanted to ask you something. You know the paintings you bought from Juniper? Did you give your designer a steer on how much to spend?"

"There was an art budget, if that's what you mean," he replies.

My stomach dips a little. It's not that I didn't know he did me a favor. Of course he did. But hearing it? It hurts more than I expected.

"A budget for *Juniper's* art?"

"For art generally."

"So, not specifically for Juniper's work?"

"No. We didn't know we were going to buy Juniper's work until Rosalind, my designer, saw it."

"I guess I'm just asking if you bought Juniper's work as a favor to her."

I wish I could transport myself off this porch. I don't want to hear about Byron's pity purchase. I close my eyes and brace myself.

"Her stuff is all over the Club. There's no way Rosalind would let me compromise the work we put into the Club just to make Juniper happy. I'd rather have written Juniper a check. Rosalind liked the work, and it fit into her vision or aesthetic or something. Why are you asking me all this?"

My body relaxes, and I'm not sure I can quite believe what I just heard. Tentatively, I open my eyes, and Fisher gives me an *I told you so* look.

"Just getting clarity," Fisher says.

"Clarity for who? Grace?"

"No, just peace of mind. That's all. Gotta go." He hangs up before Byron can question him further. "Believe me now?" he asks.

I take in a deep breath. "Kinda."

"It would have been easier to write you a check if he wanted to do you a favor. Juniper, until you believe in yourself, I'm going to believe in you twice as hard to make up for it."

I don't think anyone has ever said anything so nice to me. I press my palm to his cheek and lean over and kiss him.

It's a *thank you.*

It's an *I like you.*

It's a *how did you appear in my life outta nowhere, giving me everything I need right now.*

He groans as our tongues meet and each hair on my body stands to attention. Every molecule of my body wants him. Wants all of him. I push my hands into his hair and he pulls me onto his lap, my knees on either side so I'm sitting astride him. His hands roam over my back and ass and tuck me against him. His hardness presses against my clit. His denim against the cotton of my leggings.

We're so close, but there's too much distance between us. I want him hard and bare and heavy against me. I want to feel his heat, trailing up and down my folds. I want to strip naked and feel him naked against me. I want more of him. I want all of him.

Instinctively, our bodies rub together and Fisher's kiss becomes more demanding, deeper, rougher, less controlled. My breaths come quicker, and I can feel the coil inside of me winding tighter and tighter. We're fully clothed and just kissing, but I'm vibrating. I'm needy. I'm dizzy with wanting.

"Juniper," he hisses, "Juniper." He says it like a warning, like we're about to cross a threshold or open a door to something, and he's trying to resist. Or trying to stop me. I can't decide.

I push against him, grinding on his thick cock, beneath the layers of fabric between us. But it's not enough.

I want more.

I reach a hand between us, my fingers fumbling for his zipper.

His hand clasps around my wrist. "Juniper. Riley is inside."

His sharp tone snaps me back to reality.

"It's fine," I say, my words come out like I'm panting. "She never wakes up so long as she's not sick." I'm not making excuses, it's true. The kid sleeps like a rock. But I get it. He doesn't want to risk it, and I don't want to make him feel uncomfortable.

I lift my hands to his shoulders and grind against him, my hips swaying and circling.

He gasps and his head falls back. "Juniper, you're going to make me come in my pants."

I grin and press a kiss against his neck, rough with the stubble of his beard. "I want you to," I whisper against his skin. "I want you to want me so bad, your dick doesn't need to be inside me."

He groans and grips my waist tightly, pulling my body against his. My clit is throbbing through the now soaked cotton of my leggings. My sharp nipples scrape against the cups of my bra and I moan, desperate for him to touch me. I just want to feel his fingers against my wetness, his shaft against my folds, his skin against mine. It would only take a second to push me off the edge.

"You're so beautiful, Juniper," he says.

I pull back slightly and gaze at him, lit up in the moonlight. I give him a small smile and press a kiss to the corner of his lips. He slips his hands to my hips and starts to rock me against him, over and over, small movements that feel tortuous. Why are we doing this to each other?

I whimper as the seam of his jeans connects to my clit, and I arch my back.

"Remember the rules, Juniper."

I groan at the growl in his voice, at his serious, demanding tone. "Tell me," I gasp out.

"You don't come unless you have permission."

Wetness renews between my legs at his words. I'm so close. My legs are trembling. My breaths are short and sharp. I'm almost there and he knows it.

He stills his hands, and I frown and try to move, but he's holding me tightly.

"Please," I whisper.

He lifts his chin in a request for more.

"Please," I say again. I lean forward, my mouth against his ear. "Please let me come for you."

He groans, and his hands rock me against him, over and over, hard and relentless, and panic starts to rise. I don't know if I'm going to be able to stop it. I can feel it like the rumble of clouds thundering through the sky. I don't know if I can—

I look at him in horror, but he sees my expression and takes pity on me.

"Come for me," he says on a growl.

That's all it takes for my orgasm to engulf me. I cry his name and he holds me tight against him and he groans out too, and I realize he's right there with me. Coming together, both fully clothed, so desperate for each other we'll take anything and everything we can get.

"Juniper French, I haven't come in my pants since I was a teenager. What are you doing to me?"

I wrap my arms around his neck, pressing our chests together, wanting to hold him tight, hold him so close he won't ever be able to leave.

SEVENTEEN

Juniper

It's difficult to dress up in Star Falls. Partly because everyone you run into will ask you why you're dressed up. Partly because there's no place to go when you *are* dressed up. So I'm wearing jeans and a white shirt and sandals. Because... no one can tell me I'm making too much effort when I'm wearing jeans.

I'm on the porch waiting for Fisher. Riley's in bed. Mom's in front of the TV with her knitting, which I'm pretty sure is going to be Riley's birthday present. I need to figure out how to break it to my mom that Riley doesn't want a home-knitted sweater. She's growing up so fast and my mom hasn't kept up. Riley wants to wear what all the other kids have. And no one wears a sweater knitted by their grandma. I don't know whose feelings to hurt. My mom's by telling her Riley isn't going to like her sweater, or Riley's by telling her Grandma is knitting for her.

When Fisher pulls up, my heart lifts so high in my chest I'm concerned my feet might leave the ground.

I dash down the stairs to the truck before my mom can come out and start chatting to Fisher like he's about to become her son-in-law. That's all I need. No one gets it except us. We like each other, but we're not ever going to turn into anything. He gets it. I get it. But no one else gets it. I don't want to listen to how it might work out or how long distance can work. Because that propels us into a future where both Fisher and I know we don't work. And I don't want to think about that. I just want to enjoy him while I have him.

"Hey, beautiful," he says.

"Hi," I snap, and I duck under his arm, avoiding his embrace and sliding into the truck.

He rounds the hood of the car, a frown on his face. He slides in next to me. "Is everything okay?" His tone is tentative.

"Yeah, sorry, just trying to dodge my mom. Can we get out of here?"

He chuckles and starts the engine. "Are we seventeen, sneaking out of our parents' place to meet up for a secret, passionate affair?"

"Well, neither of us is seventeen." I reach across and tuck a curl of his hair around his ear. "But you're not so far off with the rest."

He turns his head and places a kiss on my palm.

"You definitely want to go to Grizzly's?" I ask.

"Have you had their wings?" He casts a glance over to me, like he thinks I might be insane.

I laugh. Looks like we're going to Grizzly's. "You know the entire town will be there."

"We don't have to go if you don't want to."

"Have you had their wings?" I say, and he laughs. "I'm just saying, this town is pretty protective, so brace yourself if you think you're not going to be given the side eye by a couple of people."

"Will anyone challenge me to a duel?" he asks. "Ex-boyfriends?"

"My only ex is in Florida, so no need to worry about him."

"He's your only ex? You've been split up for how long?"

"Seven years."

"Phew," he says, turning what could be an awkward conversation into something that's no big deal. "I'm really not in the mood for a duel."

"Glad I could help out."

We pull up in front of Grizzly's. "Let's go get us some wings. Then I vote we go find a place we can make out. Or if you wanted to come back to my place or..."

I try not to grin at the idea of going up to the Colorado Club with this beautiful man. What will I learn about him? I know it's not his place, but I'm sure there will be signs of who he is around his room or lodge or whatever it's called.

"Sounds good," I say, reaching for the door handle.

Grizzly's is busier than usual. When we walk in at least half the place cops a look at the two of us arriving together, but they do their best not to gawp. Some more successfully than others.

We grab the same booth I was sitting in when I first laid eyes on Fisher. He was with two friends and they'd rolled into town in an RV. "What happened to your friends who you came to visit with last time? You know, when you came in the RVs."

"Oh, word gets around, doesn't it?"

"Kinda. I mean, those RVs were the talk of the town, and I was in Grizzly's the night you turned up to see Byron."

He narrows his eyes at me across the table. "You were in here? How the fuck did I miss you?"

My heart flips, and I can't wipe the smile from my face. I slide my leg against his under the table, and he reaches for my hand.

"Now what can I get you two lovebirds?" Eva asks. "You want a beer?" She looks at me.

"What are you having?" I ask Fisher.

"Wings," he replies, and I laugh.

"You don't want a drink?"

He shrugs. "Sure. As long as it comes with wings, I don't mind."

Eva nods at Fisher. "You got a hungry one there. Two portions of wings?" she asks.

"At least," Fisher says.

Eva pats him on the arm. "Let's start you off with two. You can always order more. And I'm going to grab you two beers, too."

"Are you sure you don't want to be alone with your wings?" I ask.

"Happy to not have any if it means I get you tonight?"

My blush starts at my feet and sweeps up my entire body.

"Let's get you some wings. And then I can help you work all those calories off."

He groans and traps my legs between his. "It's a good thing there's a table between us, or we might get arrested for public indecency."

My nipples pinch against the lace of my bra and I squeeze my thighs together.

"Those wings better come quickly, or I might decide they're not worth the wait."

"We have all evening," I reassure him.

"It won't be long enough," he volleys.

His words hit me in the chest because I know it's true. However long we have won't be enough.

Eva comes back with two beers and two orders of wings and we dig in. I'm hungry. I've not eaten all day. I'm always so busy preparing food for Riley and making sure she has lunch, sometimes I run out of time to make sure I'm fed. And I'm going to need my strength tonight if the look in Fisher's eye is anything to go by.

My phone buzzes and I flip it over on the table. "Sorry, I'm just going to check this," I say, when Mom flashes up on the screen.

Mom: Riley has a temperature.

Me: What is it?

Mom: 102.

"Shit," I mumble under my breath.

"Everything okay?" Fisher takes a swig of his beer.

"It's Riley. She has a temperature." I never leave Riley if she's sick. Ever. I know how quickly things can change when it comes to medical conditions. One minute you're fine and then you're not.

One minute you're pregnant. And then you're not.

Riley was fine when I tucked her into bed. She was chattering on about school and how she'd done on her math test. There wasn't any sign that she was sick. Things change quickly.

"Do you need to go?" he asks. "I'm happy to drive you back." It's so sweet of him to offer. I know he has different plans for where we go after Grizzly's. And so do I. I don't know what to do. What would I do if I were at home?

"Let me just text with my mom quickly."

"No problem. We can leave right away if that's better."

Me: Is she awake?

Mom: Yes. She says she has a headache.

Me: Does she have a rash?

There's a delay before she answers. I'm guessing Mom is checking for a rash.

Mom: No rash.

I'm torn. I want to be here with Fisher and Riley is probably fine, but I wish I were with my daughter, too.

Me: Please give her Tylenol in the cupboard and then let me know what her temperature is in thirty minutes.

"We're going to give it thirty minutes," I say. "See if the Tylenol kicks in."

We go back to our wings, but Fisher has released my legs and there's a shift between us. It's not as fun and flirty. Because, this is real life. And in real life I have a daughter who gets sick.

"So how's your mystery artist getting along?" I ask, trying to get us back on track. "You still don't like the trombone?"

"Man, the trombone sucks." Fisher chuckles. "She's getting along great. She loves the Club. Finds everything really easy. She's ahead of schedule and already has four tracks that could be... I mean, if we put the right marketing efforts behind them, they're going to be big."

"That's exciting."

"It is. Everything's working out great."

"You think you'll end up bringing more artists out here to record?" As soon as the question is out of my mouth, I wish I could stuff the words back in. What was I thinking? It looks like I'm asking him to come back before he's even left. I don't want him to think I think that what we have is anything but temporary.

"I'll definitely encourage artists to come out here. It's

only going to suit certain people. If they're wanting to party, then this isn't the best place for them."

I pull back and glare at him like I'm offended. "What could you mean? Are you saying the people of Star Falls don't know how to party? Have you ever seen Grizzly's after a storm? The entire town goes wild. Everyone's so happy to be alive. There's no atmosphere in one of your fancy-schmancy New York nightclubs that could compete."

Fisher chuckles. "Somehow I completely and utterly believe you. And on top of that, you have these wings."

I laugh. "Yeah, you need to take some back to New York and lure your artists out here with the wings."

"They'll be goners," he says. "There'll be a waiting list for the recording studio."

"True story."

I grin, but I can't help but glance at my phone to see if thirty minutes is up. I just want to know Riley is okay and then I can relax properly. I want to enjoy my evening with Fisher, but I can't do that if my daughter isn't well.

"Any news?" Fisher asks, as he sees me looking at the phone.

I shake my head. "Just checking the time. If her temperature is coming down with the Tylenol after thirty minutes, then I'm sure she'll be fine. Problem is, my mom is fully committed to her current knitting project, and I just want to make sure she checks Riley again when she's supposed to."

Fisher finishes his wings and calls over Eva. He gets the bill. "I'm going to take you back." He pulls out cash from his wallet as relief and disappointment mixes in my stomach.

"I'm sorry," I say.

"Please don't be. I just had the best meal of my life with the best company. If it's okay with you, I'll hang around and maybe we can have a drink on the porch when Riley is settled."

I narrow my eyes, trying to discover a trace of resentment or hostility in his face, but there's nothing.

"Come on," he says, shifting out of the booth. "Let's get you back with your daughter."

I stand, just as my phone buzzes.

Temperature is 103 now.

"Let's go," I say.

EIGHTEEN

Fisher

We pull into the driveway. "Shall I stay in the car?" I ask. I don't want to make anything more stressful for Juniper than it already is. I can't imagine what it would be like to have a daughter who isn't well. She must be worried sick.

"No, come in. Mom will be preoccupied with Riley. You're safe."

"I'm not worried about chatting to your mom," I say. I don't want to abandon her but at the same time I don't want to be in the way.

"Don't go," she says, and she squeezes my arm.

I kill the engine and she's out of the car and through the door to her house so quickly, I barely have time to blink.

I follow her, wondering if I should just go back to the Club.

I take a seat on the porch and wait. It's all I can do. Keep out of the way but be here. I can't pretend to know the best thing to do for a child. I've never even considered having children before. Back in New York, the only person I have to take care of is myself. I can't imagine the pressure Juniper must feel being responsible for Riley. I remember my mother being worried one time when I was sick. She and Dad both took me to the emergency room when I had stomach pain.

Huh. Maybe the signs that they weren't happy had been there, but I hadn't noticed because I was a kid and they weren't yelling at each other.

"We need to get Dr. Picuri to come out," I can hear Juniper say.

"You think we should bother him?" Juniper's mom asks. "It's a lot of money."

If money's an issue, I can cover a doctor's visit. But is it inappropriate of me to offer?

I hear nothing for a few moments.

"He's not answering. It just goes right to voicemail."

"Maybe he's at the hospital," Mom says. "The signal always goes dead if he's at the hospital."

"Shit," Juniper says.

I feel useless. As much as I want to stay out of the way, I want to be able to help.

I stand and open the screen door, poking my head in. "How's Riley?" I ask.

Juniper's face is ashen and they both look concerned. Juniper shakes her head. "Her temperature isn't coming down and she has a headache. She never has headaches. I just want someone to check her over."

"And the doctor?"

She shakes her head. "Not answering. And the drive to the hospital is over an hour."

I pull out my phone. "Hang on," I say, as I dial Byron's cell. "I'm going to check with Byron. I'm sure he has medical people up at the Club."

He answers on the second ring. "I thought you were out?"

"Riley's sick. The town doctor isn't available. Do you have anyone at the Club?" I ask.

"No. If she's really sick, we have a helicopter on site if she needs to go to the hospital."

I try to think. A medical evacuation seems like a big deal, but if Juniper's worried, then we should consider it. She may push back because of the cost but if we don't have any other options—

Then it hits me. Vivian's husband, Beau, is a doctor. I'm just not sure what kind.

"Okay, I'll let you know." I hang up. I don't think twice before I'm bringing up Vivian's name and pressing the call button.

"What's up, Fisher?" she answers, as if I call her at ten every night.

"I have a favor to ask you. The town doctor isn't contactable and the daughter of a friend of mine is sick—"

I don't even finish before she says, "Beau will be on his way. Tell me where he should go?"

I give her directions and then hang up the phone.

"My artist's husband is a doctor. He's on his way."

Juniper bursts into tears. "Oh my god, thank you, Fisher!" I step forward to comfort her, but she steps back, out of reach. Then she straightens and dries her eyes. "Sorry, just relief. That's all."

"You don't need to be sorry," I say.

"I'm going to make us all coffee," Juniper's mom says. She takes my hand and squeezes. "I'm very pleased you're here."

"I'm sorry," Juniper says, stepping toward me. "I knew if

you touched me, I'd completely collapse, and I need to be strong."

"I get it." I want to say Riley will be fine. That she doesn't have anything to worry about. Something that will make her feel better. But I don't have a clue what's going on. "The doctor will be here soon. You'll be able to speak to him and then..."

She nods vigorously. "Yeah. It's probably nothing. I'm just... her temperature normally goes down with Tylenol."

"It's okay." I want to reach out and touch her. Do anything that will comfort her, but she doesn't need that. She just needs a doctor.

"Go in and sit with her. You'll feel better."

"Thank you," she says, and turns and heads down the hallway.

"That's very kind of you to call your friend like that," her mother says from where she's making coffee.

"I just made a phone call."

"Well, I appreciate it. How do you like your coffee?"

I head over to the counter. "Black works."

She hands me a mug that says New York University on it. I must look confused, because Juniper's mom says, "That's where she was supposed to go to art school. They all wanted her. Everywhere from Yale to the School of Art in Chicago. She had scholarships coming out of her ass, that kid." Shit. I had no idea Juniper gave up so much. "But she wanted New York," her mom continues. "It was always New York." She nods. "It was her dream. And then Riley became her dream. You'll sacrifice anything for your kid." She looks at me pointedly, as if she's trying to convey more than she's saying.

I offer her a smile. Juniper mentioned she had a place at art school in New York. I guess that's the heart of the art scene in the US. It makes sense. I can't think what else her mom is wanting me to know.

"I'm going to give this to Juniper," she says, lifting the mug and heading out. "Make yourself at home."

I take my mug of coffee out onto the deck to wait for Beau. My thoughts are swirling, trying to piece together the scraps of information I just got from Juniper's mom. I can't shake the feeling that she was trying to tell me something beyond the words. Was she saying that Juniper would never come to New York because of Riley? I already know that. And I'm two dates in with Juniper. There are no expectations.

Two dates in and head over heels for her.

Minutes later, a car pulls into the drive and I stand.

Beau opens the back passenger door. Byron has drivers on standby twenty-four hours a day. Thankfully.

"Thanks for coming," I say as he comes up the steps. "I wouldn't have asked, but the family is really upset."

"It's not a problem. I've worked in a lab for a long time, but I think I still remember the basics. If nothing else, I'll know if we need someone else to look at her."

"Great." I lead Beau inside and call out. "Juniper. The doctor is here."

Juniper's mom appears in the corridor. "Please, come in. My granddaughter is in here."

Beau disappears, and I start pacing. If necessary, we can be up at the Colorado Club in ten minutes. I'm not sure if there's a helicopter pilot on standby, but knowing the standards Byron insists on at the Club, there will be. We can be at the hospital quickly. Unless... maybe there's no landing pad at the hospital. I pull out my phone and search for nearby hospitals. It might be closer by car.

Juniper's mom appears from the bedroom and heads right to the kitchen. She starts searching through cupboards.

"Can I help?" I ask.

"Got it," she calls out. "Ibuprofen," she says to me as she passes me, heading back to the bedroom.

It feels like hours they're in there. I hear the low mumble of voices, but no one else comes out. I figure that must be a good sign.

I check my watch. It's been twenty minutes.

The voices grow louder, and suddenly Juniper appears. She's backing out of the bedroom and moving awkwardly. I step forward to help, and then I realize she's got Riley in her arms.

Oh god. Does this mean we're having to go to the hospital? She doesn't see me and heads into another room across the hall. The sound of running water follows, and I realize she must be going to the loo. I'm not a doctor, but is that a good sign? Unless she's vomiting or... I sit down and take a breath. I'm heading into a tailspin. I need to stay calm. I'll know what's happening when I need to know.

Riley and Juniper head back into the bedroom. The murmur of voices picks up and I get the impression someone's leaving. I stand.

I hear a chorus of thank-yous, and then Beau appears.

"Hey," I say, wondering if he'll tell me anything.

"It all looks fine," he says, and my shoulders drop from up by my ears, where they've been for the last hour. "I've told them I can come down if things escalate, but I don't think they will. It's almost certainly just a virus." I sigh with relief. "Her temperature has come down a little and she's been to the loo, so I think we're good. But she should be monitored. Call me at any time."

"Beau, you're a superstar, man. I'm so grateful."

"It's good to blow off the cobwebs every now and again," he says. "Anything for a fan of my wife." He nods over to the bedroom. "She has quite the poster collection."

I chuckle. "A Vivian Cross fan, huh? Well, isn't everyone?"

"You'll get no argument on that from me. Take care now. I'll catch up with you later."

Juniper appears as Beau drives away. "Thank you so much, Fisher. Having a doctor examine her is so reassuring. I'm sorry if I made the biggest fuss over... nothing." She sighs.

"Don't apologize. Your daughter's sick. You don't have a magic wand to make her better. It must be frustrating and worrying and all these emotions I can't even imagine."

She smiles and presses her hand on my chest. "You're wonderful."

"I'm sitting here drinking coffee. I can't lay claim to wonderful. That's your thing."

She grins up at me. "I'm going to stay here with Riley, though. Do you mind?"

I chuckle. "I'd insist you went to the hospital if you didn't. Do you want me to stay?"

She hesitates. "Maybe."

"How about I stay for a little while?" I suggest. I don't want to leave her. I can't do anything, but abandoning her doesn't seem like the right thing to do.

She steps forward and leans against me, and I envelop her in a hug. She feels so warm and like she fits perfectly. "Thank you."

I press a kiss on her head. "Go be with your daughter. I'll be here if you need anything."

NINETEEN

Juniper

I wake suddenly and sit up. I'm still in my jeans and shirt from last night.

Riley's shifting on her bed. "Mom," she calls out.

"I'm here," I say, getting up from the floor where I've made a makeshift bed out of blankets. Dad came to get Mom after Beau left, and I left Fisher on the couch. I don't know if he's still there. Part of me really hopes he is, but I don't expect him to have stayed. He can't understand how high the stakes are when your child is sick. "How are you feeling, sweet girl?" I ask as I get to my feet.

She pushes up so she's sitting. "I'm really thirsty."

"Here." I reach for her water bottle that's on the nightstand and hand it to her. I put my palm to her head. It feels hot but not scorching like it did last night. I check the clock on my phone. It's 8 a.m. The last round of medicine will have worn off by now. "Let me take your temperature."

I sit next to her on the bed. I take it three times. Each time, it comes out at a cool one hundred. Much better than last night when it went to one oh four when I got home with Fisher. "You feeling a little better than last night?"

She nods. "I'm tired, though." She takes another long drink of water, then says, "I need to pee."

We head out of her bedroom to the bathroom, and I catch sight of Fisher on the sofa, sleeping. He looks so peaceful. I smile to myself. He didn't have to stay last night, but I'm really pleased he did. Maybe I shouldn't be so selfish. It might confuse Riley if he's around, but it was nice having him here last night. Not just because he got a doctor to us, but just knowing there was someone there to give me a hug. It's more than I've had in a long time. Sure, I'll get all the hugs I want from my mom, but that's part of the contract when you're a mother. Fisher didn't have to be here. But he was.

"Mom," Riley says as we head back to the bedroom. "Why's Fisher sleeping on the couch?"

I chuckle. "Well, he drove me home from Grizzly's when Fizzy let me know you were sick."

She nods. "He's too big for that couch," she says. "You should have let him sleep in your bed."

I don't reply. I'm not sure if my daughter's playing matchmaker or just worried about Fisher's back.

"Let's get you back in bed."

"Will Fisher stay and have breakfast with us?"

"Maybe," I say. There's a knock at the door. "You stay there. I'm going to see who that is."

I head out and Fisher's already at the door. He moves to let Beau in, but someone's with him. A woman. She looks familiar. I narrow my eyes.

"Er, hi," I say, as I head over to meet them.

"How is she?" Beau asks.

My gaze flits between him and the woman he's brought

with him. "Much better, thank you. I just took her temperature and it's exactly one hundred degrees. And it's been five hours since she had any Tylenol or ibuprofen."

"Great," Beau says. "This is my wife, Vivian," he says.

Everything clicks into place, and I realize why the woman looks familiar. Her pictures are plastered all over my daughter's bedroom walls. "You're married to Vivian Cross?" I can barely get the words out. I pull my jaw from the floor and glance over at Fisher, and then back at the pop superstar standing in my living room. She might be the most famous woman in America. "You're Fisher's artist at the Colorado Club."

"Guilty," she says. "I thought I'd pop down and say hi. But I don't want to wake up Riley."

"Oh my... Riley's not sleeping. And she's going to perk *all* the way up when she sees you."

"My wife is medicine in human form," Beau says with such pride that it catches me by surprise a little. It's so nice to see someone so proud of his wife. Riley's dad never really liked my art. Told me I needed a real job.

"Maybe I need to..." Should I warn my daughter? "Come on in," I say, leading global megastar Vivian Cross down my cramped, dark hallway to see my virus-ridden daughter.

"Riley, Dr. Beau has come to check on you, and he brought his wife."

Riley watches as we file into her room, and when she sees Vivian, her mouth falls open and she leaps to her feet. "Wait, what? What is happening?"

"Hey, Riley!" Vivian says. "I'm not going to hug you if that's okay. You got something nasty, and I'm busy in the studio up at the Colorado Club recording my new album."

"You're recording your new album in Star Falls? Where I live?"

"Sure am. It's the prettiest place I've ever been to. Totally inspiring." Vivian glances around the room at all the Vivian Cross posters and she elbows her husband. "See, this is me hot rather than covered in baby vomit."

"Did you bring your baby?" Riley asks.

"She's up at the Club sleeping," Vivian says. "I just wanted to drop by and say hi!"

"You're my favorite ever singer," Riley says. "I know all your songs by heart."

"You do?" Vivian looks shocked—the consummate professional. "Which one is your favorite?"

"Oh, I love 'London Love Letter.' Or 'Darling it's You.' Or 'This Time.' All of them really."

"I can vouch for that," I say. "And I'm pretty sure I know most of your lyrics, too."

Vivian laughs. "It's nice to keep it in the family."

"Do you think you might move to Star Falls?" Riley asks.

"We live in London," Vivian says. "That's home. But I'll definitely be visiting Star Falls again."

"Have you been to the Galaxy Grill yet?" Riley asks. "They have the best pancakes. And Fisher likes the waffles, don't you, Fisher?" Riley raises her voice as she talks to Fisher.

He pops his head around the door. "The waffles are incredible. You really should go, Vivian," he says.

She laughs. "Maybe I will. I'm going to leave you with my husband now. He's going to give you a quick checkup. I don't want to disturb him. That okay with you?"

Devastation sweeps over Riley's face.

"But I'll make sure you and your mom get tickets to my next concert."

Riley's face lights up. "Thank you! Mom! Did you hear that?"

I'm not sure how we'd get there, but I figure if she plays Denver, I can probably make it work.

"That's so kind, isn't it?" I turn to Beau. "I don't think there's any point in taking her blood pressure. It will be through the roof."

He grins. "Yeah. But overall, I think she's feeling better."

"I think you just cured her."

"I can't take any credit. My wife does all the magic stuff."

Beau seems like a great guy.

And I know Fisher is.

And now my daughter is glowing, and I couldn't ask for more. I have no right to even dream of more. I know that Vivian Cross will leave, and so will Fisher. And I'll be left picking up the pieces of a life that I didn't get to live—that my daughter doesn't get to live. But I smile and tuck the ache a little deeper inside. Because right now, Riley is okay. And that should be enough.

Right now will have to be enough for today.

TWENTY

Juniper

We're headed to the Galaxy Grill for pancakes. It's usually something we only do once a month, but after Riley getting so sick this week, I just want to treat her. I'm looking forward to some quality mother-daughter time.

"Mom," she says, and I can tell by the tone of her voice she's going to ask me for something that I'm not going to say yes to.

"Yes," I answer back in the same tone, as we pull up in a parking spot.

"I was wondering if we should invite Fisher for pancakes. He was really kind asking Dr. Beau to come check on me."

I'm one hundred percent sure that Fisher facilitating Dr. Beau's visit is not the reason Riley wants him to join us for pancakes. We get out of the car and head to the diner.

"He was really kind," I say. "But he's also really busy." Riley has already suggested that Fisher can be her new dad. She doesn't need encouragement to get attached to him.

"But you could ask," she says. "He might not be busy."

"I'm not going to ask, sweet girl."

"But why?" she asks. "Did he upset you, Mommy?"

"No, of course not. He's busy. And…" I pull in a breath. "He's not going to be in town long. He hasn't moved to Star Falls, honey. He's just here for work. When Vivian has finished her album, he'll be going back to New York."

"But you could ask him."

We pass by Snail Trail, and Marge, the owner, comes out with a cloth. "Morning, Juniper. How are you doing, Riley?" She starts to clean down Marv the Moose.

"Good, Marge, thank you."

"You off for waffles?" she asks.

"Pancakes," Riley corrects her.

"And what about you?" she asks me.

Marge has always been nosey, but I'm not sure why she wants to know my Galaxy Grill order. "Oh, I think I'll probably get eggs."

Marge laughs. "And how about that nice young gentleman who's friends with Byron? You seen him recently?"

"She means Fisher, Mom."

"Thanks, Riley. I know she means Fisher." I nod. "Oh he's fine, I think," I say.

"I just saw him. Came in for some hiking boots. Didn't even ask me the price before he said yes. And I upsold him three pairs of our best hiking socks."

I try to tamp down my smile.

"Mom, that means he's in town. Please call him and ask him to the diner."

"Sounds like he's preparing for a hike."

"Mom. *Please?* I really want to have pancakes with him, and I know he's going back to New York but he's not in

New York *now*, so I don't see why we can't have pancakes with him."

The fact that Riley's so invested in Fisher coming to the diner with us is terrifying. She's started to get attached to this man. The man who is a *fling*. Who lives in New York. Who hasn't got any intention of sticking around. With her dad moving to Orlando, the last thing I wanted was for her to form a relationship with another man who just ups and leaves. It's not fair to her.

"She's making some really good points," Marge says. "I have to say, I can't disagree with any of them."

If I hadn't lived in Star Falls my entire life and known Marge for as long, I might be irritated by someone having any commentary on who I have brunch with. But I learned long ago that if you're going to get irritated by the people of Star Falls having something to say about your private, personal business, this isn't the town for you.

"Thank you, Marge. We're going to give Marv his privacy while he gets his rubdown. See you later."

"Please, Mom!" Riley says, pulling on my arm. "He's funny. And I like him."

Isn't that a reason *not* to call him. But she's right. He is funny, and I like him too. "Riley, he's probably doing something else. We can't expect that he wants to hang out with us."

"If you don't try, we'll never know. Isn't that what you always say, Mommy? You miss one hundred percent of the shots you don't take."

I groan because I know when I'm out-negotiated.

I pull out my phone. "I'll call him," I say. "But don't get your hopes up."

"My hopes are down. Way down on the floor." She grins up at me. "But put it on speaker so I can hear."

I laugh and press call on Fisher's number. He answers right away.

"Hi, you're probably busy, but Riley and I are headed to the Galaxy Grill if you wanted to join us?"

"Love to," he says, without missing a beat. "I just came from town and I'm headed back to the Club, so I'll be five minutes. See you there."

I don't know if I've done the right thing. She's already had one man in her life abandon her for a new life in Florida. I don't want her to think she's not worth sticking around for. But she's excited to see him, and honestly, so am I.

Fisher arrives just as Donna gives us our menus.

For a split second, I worry he'll kiss me in front of Riley and Donna, and I wonder if I can send him a sign. I didn't have to worry. He just slides into the booth, opposite me and Riley, and picks up the menu.

"Hi, you two. Thanks for inviting me. I could eat a cow."

"A cow?" Riley says. "Like really? Are you going to order a cow? I don't even know if they have it on the menu."

"He's not eating a whole cow," I say.

"Also they have four stomachs, and I don't think they'll taste good," Riley says, screwing up her face like someone's suggesting she eat cow stomach.

"Yeah, I'm not going for the cow stomach. But maybe a plate of waffles as tall as a cow?" he suggests.

"That sounds good," she says, her grin back. "I want pancakes but I won't eat a stack as high as a cow." Riley's expression turns serious.

"What about as high as a mouse?" Fisher asks.

"Oh no. I can do more than a mouse but less than a cow."

"Hmmm," Fisher muses, and rubs his hand along his

jaw. He's really good at playing along. It's like I'm hanging out with Riley and one of her friends. It's the kind of weird conversations they have together.

"What about a cat?" he suggests. He raises his hand up over the table to about cat height. "That's at least twenty pancakes. Could you handle it?"

"Yeah," Riley says, nodding enthusiastically. "I'm really hungry. I think I could do twenty."

"Is this helping?" I say, mock glaring at Fisher. "Are you going to clean up the vomit when she eats twenty pancakes?"

"If she vomits, I'll clear it up, but I believe in her. If she thinks she can do it, I think she can do it."

I laugh. This is all I need. "Now I know why you wanted Fisher to join us for brunch—so you two could gang up on me."

Fisher winks at Riley and we're interrupted by Donna.

"Riley would like a stack of pancakes as tall as a cat," Fisher says. "Juniper would like..."

"I'm going to take the scrambled eggs on sourdough."

"And I'll have the waffles, please. And let's get a fruit salad and three Oreo shakes."

Riley grabs the table. "Really? An Oreo shake?"

"Is that okay?" Fisher asks me.

I shrug. What can I say? I'm not going to say no now that Riley's excited. We might be having soup the rest of the week, given each shake is ten dollars.

"I'll just stick with tap water," I say.

Fisher doesn't say anything.

"How are you feeling, Riley?" Fisher asks.

"Good. I have one of my teeth coming through at the back. It's called a molar. Mom, what are the front teeth called if the back teeth are molars?"

"It's a good question," I ask. "I have absolutely no idea. The ones at the side are incisors. But these front teeth... we could do an internet search."

"Anterior," Fisher says.

"Anterior teeth?" Riley asks.

"Yup. And if I wanted to be a tooth pedant, your incisors are also anterior teeth." He glances at me. "I was big into teeth as a kid."

I grimace. "You were into teeth—like in a hobby kind of way?"

Fisher chuckles. "Yeah. It was weird. I was obsessed with oral hygiene. When we came to America, none of the toothpastes tasted the same and I was obsessed with not getting a filling. I read up about stuff and fell into a teeth vortex there for a while. It didn't last long, but here we are. The front teeth are anterior teeth."

"That's cool," Riley says. "Maybe I should be more into teeth."

This brunch is going a whole direction I wasn't expecting.

Luckily we're interrupted by our food arriving at our table.

"Will says you can have half a cat now, and if you eat everything, you can have another half of a cat. That work for you?"

Riley nods. "Thank you, Donna."

"You're welcome, honey. And I'll just get the Oreo shakes."

"You can share mine," Fisher says to me.

Donna comes back and sets one shake in front of Riley and one between Fisher and me, and it has two straws in it. It's like the entire town is trying to get me laid.

"Is Vivian making her album now?" Riley asks.

Fisher puts his finger over his lips. "Remember, it's a big secret that she's up there."

"Oh no it's not," Donna returns with a jug of maple syrup and some whipped butter. "We all know Vivian Cross is up at the Club."

Fisher's mouth falls open. He looks stunned.

"Haven't you learned that you can't keep a secret in Star Falls?" she says, before heading off.

I laugh at Fisher's expression. "I hadn't heard it, if it helps. And the first person who would hear it is Donna. It doesn't mean the entire town knows."

"Oh god. I should inform her security team," Fisher says.

"You really don't need to. The people of Star Falls aren't going to start stalking her and running up to the Colorado Club for autographs. They just like to know what's going on. Especially at the Club. That way it feels more like part of the town."

He shakes his head. And sends off a text.

I reach across the table and squeeze his hand. "Really, you don't need to worry. I know just about everyone in this town. You don't have anything to be concerned about."

He holds my gaze for a beat, and I can't tell what he's thinking. "You really love this place, don't you?"

I smile. "Why wouldn't I?" I glance across at Riley. "Got my sweet girl here and Galaxy Grill makes the best eggs in America."

Star Falls has everything I need.

Well, almost everything.

TWENTY-ONE

Juniper

I'm wearing my best jeans and a blue sweater I got on sale last winter but haven't worn. The sleeves are a little long, and suddenly I'm wondering whether I should have worn a dress or something. Grace Astor sounds like the name of a princess. She'll definitely be wearing a dress. I don't want her to think I'm being disrespectful.

I've agreed to meet Grace down here at the candy store. Fisher's bringing her. She wanted to come to the studio. When I explained that most of my finished work has been bought by the Colorado Club, she said she wants me to give her a tour so I can walk her through the pieces up there. Apparently, Fisher's squared that with the manager at the Club.

The door to my studio creaks, and I spin around to see a blonde woman in jeans and a white shirt enter. She's wearing an ear-to-ear smile. Fisher follows her in, and we exchange a smile.

"Hi," I say, stepping forward and offering her my hand. "My name's Juniper French." I glance at Fisher, and he smiles encouragingly.

"Grace Astor. How do you do?" She glances around the old candy store. "What a great idea to set up a studio in a store that's closed."

"I'll have to move out if Mrs. Peters ever rents it. But it works."

"I see that. The light is perfect here."

"The skylights make a real difference."

"It's really good to meet you," Grace says. "I'm thrilled that I'm going to get to see more of your work. If I'm not mistaken, the lodge I'm staying in has a piece of yours in the dining room."

"Maybe," I say. "I'm not sure where Rosalind decided to put them all."

"They bought a lot, right?" Grace asks.

I nod. "Yeah. Byron's a friend and—"

"But Byron didn't decide to buy them," Fisher interrupts. "His designer did."

"They work perfectly in the space from an aesthetic perspective. Though they're not just decorative. You have a very painterly style. But you didn't go to art school, did you?"

I shake my head. "No. No art school."

"But you got accepted at art school," Fisher interrupts, like he's my full-time PR person.

"I had personal things that kept me from accepting," I explain.

Grace nods and steps toward the work I have set up on the easel.

"I've just finished this piece."

"I love the way you use the light. Who would you say influences your work? I see lots of Turner. Or am I imagining that?"

My body flushes cold and then hot. I feel like I'm under the spotlight. No one's ever seen the Turner influence in my work apart from my old art teacher, who was obsessed with the British romantic painter from the end of the eighteenth century. "He's my favorite painter," I confess. "I've always wanted to see something of his, like for real, but you know..."

"Bizarrely, you know that Indianapolis is the best place to go to see Turner's work in the US?" Grace asks.

I nod. "At the Museum of Art, or the Yale Center for British Art in Connecticut." I switch my weight from foot to foot. "I actually got the book from the Yale Center for Christmas when I was in my early twenties. It has a lot of the paintings in there. I have a couple of other books too..." I take a breath. "But seeing it? I'd just love to see the texture. That's something that's important to me in my work. The texture, and I'm experimenting on ways of using multimedia to build on that textural feel. I don't want to stray too far into that, but I like the way some fabrics look when I incorporate them into a piece."

"Do you have anything you can show me?" Grace asks.

I hesitate. I don't show many people my unfinished work. Of course, Riley sees all my stuff. My mom has lost interest in my painting. And my friends have their own lives. No one comes into this studio apart from me and Riley.

"Okay," I say. "I have a few pieces that the Club didn't want because they were too dark. Then I did a few portraits but abandoned them. I'm not good at people. And I have a couple of pieces I'm working on, but they're not finished."

Fisher's voice is in my head, telling me I'm great, but all I can see is some girl who didn't go to art school, who paints around her job and life as a mother. I'm not an artist. Not really. "Oh, and I have a few pieces at home hanging up, but I didn't think to bring them."

"I'm excited to see everything." Grace is warm and encouraging and not what I expected. I thought she'd be far snootier.

I take another breath, feeling a little more relaxed. Grace seems to like the work, and the fact that she sees the Turner influence is... well, I'm so incredibly flattered.

I bring out two canvases I'm still working on and pull off the sheets from the ones that weren't sold to the Club but remain propped up against the cupboards and walls of the store.

"These are pieces of linen." I indicate to one of the pieces I'm working on at the moment. There's a section at the bottom of the canvas that's raised and lumpy. "I didn't want it to overwhelm the work, but I wanted a more textural feel. Using the linen is a symbol of how the human race can harness nature and make it stronger. How we can work in harmony with the landscape around us. I've also used some of the..."

I pause, I'm not quite sure how Grace will take my confession, but she might as well know all of it, now that she's here.

"I used some of the earth from the mountain. I dried it out and mixed it with my paint. I tried to match the color of the earth at first, and then I moved up and mixed in some green and blues, but still tried to make them earthy. I don't know if that makes sense? Anyway, I was trying to take the physical parts of nature and make them part of the work. That's what gives the painting texture. I wanted to capture nature physically as well as pictorially. You know?"

Grace nods as she examines the work. "I love this direction you're going in, Juniper. You're a very talented painter."

"It's a hobby, really," I say, not quite knowing how to take her praise.

"Do you have ambitions to make it your career?" she asks, straightening and looking at me.

"I certainly did, when I was younger. I wanted to be an artist. I was obsessed with Turner and Rothko and Valasquez, like my friends were obsessed with Rihanna or Justin Timberlake."

"You *are* an artist, Juniper."

The tips of my ears burn hot. I'm not an artist. "I'm a teaching assistant. I just paint in my spare time."

"You're an artist, Juniper," she repeats. It doesn't get any easier to hear. "But you had personal things going on, which meant you didn't go to art school and you had to get a job to pay the bills."

"Yes," I say.

She nods, like she understands completely.

She works her way around the store, looking at my work like she's taking in every last detail. She asks me questions and I tell her anything. She's the first person I've talked about my work with for a long time who seems to really... feel it.

Eventually she turns to me, her demeanor shifting a little. "I'd really like to work with you if it's something you think you'd like to do. We can potentially get you a show at one of my galleries. You'd need to create some more pieces before we can do that. And before *that*, we'd need to start talking about you. I presume you don't have an agent?"

I shake my head. "I just paint for fun."

"I can introduce you to people. You need to find the right person. Do you have plans to come to New York?" she asks. "Meeting some important collectors would be a good first step. Before a show."

"I can't go to New York. I have a kid in school and a job. I can't just up and leave."

Grace smiles. "I understand. The art world is demanding, like any career, but you have real talent. Think about it. If nothing else, you should get an agent who can help you expand your reach a little, now your pieces are on display at the Colorado Club. They can help you get commissions. Help you network with other gallery owners."

My head starts to spin and my mouth goes dry. Everything she's saying is so different to how my life is now. And I like my life how it is now. I'm not sure I'm capable of talking to gallery owners and important collectors. I'd feel like a fraud. I never even made it to art school.

"It's a lot to think about," I say.

"It is. But it's exciting. You just need to keep creating. That's the most important bit."

"Well, that's the bit I can do," I say. In between work, being a mother to an eight-year-old, making sure the house is kept clean and we've got healthy food on the table every night. My plate is full without bringing agents and galleries and everything else that having a second job entails. A second job in a world I know nothing about.

"So we'll talk again. Soon. I'm here for a couple of days. I'm seeing some of the members of the Club. If you want to meet again, I'm happy to get together. I know you have family responsibilities, so I don't want to add more to your plate. I'd love to hear from you when you've had a chance to think about things. You're talented. And I'd like to work with you, but you have to want this, Juniper. I don't want to force you into anything."

I gave up on my dreams of being a painter a long time ago. Maybe Grace's right, maybe I still *am* a painter. But to paint as a career? Those dreams died when Riley came into my life. And now I'm not sure I have room for those same abandoned dreams anymore, now that I'm a mother.

TWENTY-TWO

Fisher

I pull up in front of Juniper's house and kill the engine. She's already on the porch and there's a bottle of wine and two wineglasses in front of her. I can't help but grin. I can't remember a time when a glass of wine on the porch with a woman would have sounded like manna from heaven. In Star Falls, everything hits different.

"Hey, you," I say, as I approach the porch and climb the steps, carrying a gift bag. "How are you feeling? It's been a big day."

"Yeah, I'm exhausted."

"Riley was okay with her grandparents?"

"I mean, she was salty about not being able to meet Grace and tell her about Mommy's art, but she's fine."

I chuckle. "She probably knows it almost as well as you do."

"Not quite," she says. "I do my best work when she's not around."

I lean over her and press a kiss to her lips. "You smell incredible. What is that?"

"Acrylic paint and chicken sausage?" she suggests.

I laugh and sit down next to her. "Wanna drink?" I plonk down the boxed bottle of champagne I brought with me. "I thought we should be celebrating," I say.

"Fisher, you didn't need to do that. I don't even have any proper champagne glasses."

"Tastes the same no matter the glass," I say. "I didn't know if you even drank champagne."

"Well, I don't. It's not on the menu at Grizzly's."

I chuckle. "But you like it?"

I shrug. "I guess. I had it at a wedding once."

Our lives are so different. But I wasn't always living it large in New York. My family wasn't poor, but we weren't living-in-a-penthouse-in-Manhattan wealthy, either. It's not like we don't have things in common.

"How are you feeling about today?" I take the foil off the bottle and untwist the wire holding the cork in place.

"Grace is lovely," she says.

"Very nice. And she loved your work."

Juniper nods. "Yeah. That was good to hear. You think she was just being kind?"

I pour out the champagne into the two wineglasses. "I know for a fact she wasn't. After you'd left the Club, she and I had lunch with Byron and Rosey. It was a shame you couldn't join."

"Yeah, thanks for inviting me. I'm sorry, I had to get back for Riley."

"It's fine." I hand her the glass and raise mine. "To you and all that awaits you."

She smiles, but it's more reserved than I'm used to from

her. "Thank you, Fisher. You've been so kind to introduce me to Grace and to bring her here and... I know you're busy and have a thousand other things to think about. I don't want you to think I don't appreciate it."

"It's fine. I enjoy introducing people who are going to work well with them. And finding talent and helping it soar is my passion. There is nothing to thank me for. I'm getting a kick out of all this." Fact is, helping Juniper is more fulfilling to me than breaking any musical artist before her. There's no pretense with her. No ego. I'm really rooting for her.

She glances down into her lap. "It's just that... the stuff she was saying about my work. It's so flattering. I didn't go to art school, and other than a passionate high school art teacher, I'm self-taught. I just don't know how I'd ever fit into a world where I have to network with important collectors and gallery owners."

"You don't need to fit in with them. You just need to be you."

She presses her lips together in a way that tells me she doesn't believe a word I'm saying.

"I'm serious. That's what agents are for. They can help you find your way, attract the right attention. This is going to be good for you."

She shakes her head and I get a twinge in my gut, like she's hurting and that hurts me.

"What?"

"Fisher, I have a job and a daughter and responsibilities. I can't fit in a pedicure, let alone more time in the studio working on more canvases."

"I get it. But this could be a job, too."

She lets out a half laugh. "Yeah, but it's not paying me a

monthly salary like the one I get at the school, and I don't have a ton to fall back on. Or really anything other than what I got from the Colorado Club, which I'm saving most of for Riley's college."

She's such a good mom. She could take this opportunity for herself, but she wants to keep it for her kid instead.

"I get it. It's a tough decision. You're either willing to bet on yourself or you're not."

"From the guy who came into town on a helicopter."

"I didn't always have money, Juniper. But I knew what I wanted and I went for it."

"Yeah, and you didn't have a kid at the time. Or a mortgage payment."

I can't argue with what she's saying. I don't know what it's like to be responsible for another human being. Priorities must shift. And maybe it makes you less willing to gamble.

"I have a proposition for you," I say. "I'm going to have to go back to New York for a couple of days. I need to have a couple of conversations with people face-to-face. Why don't you come with me? Bring Riley. We can go to the Met and the MoMA. And you can meet up with Grace and maybe have a few meetings with agents."

She starts to shake her head, but I can't let her give up.

"You'll just gather information. Then you can make a more informed decision. There might be answers to your concerns that you're not even aware of."

"I can't, Fisher. You say bring Riley, but what's she going to do while I meet with Grace and agents? Having a kid is the best thing in the world, but from the day you give birth, it means they come first. Before my ambition. Before my choices. Before my life."

"Riley can stay with me at my offices. Or we can bring your mom."

She splutters out a laugh. "My mom would not go to New York City. Hell, she won't go to Denver. It's not happening."

"Then let's find a sitter if you don't think she'd want to stay with me."

"I think she'd want to stay with you a little *too* much. It's another reason I can't go. If we go away together, she's going to become attached. To you. Hell, *I'm* going to get even more attached. And then the next time you fly out to New York City, you'll stay there. And I'll still be sitting here on my porch, and Riley will be snoring in bed. I can handle that. But Riley? Her father moved to Florida. I don't want her to get attached to another man who lives across the country. It's too much for her."

I'm out of arguments. I wouldn't want to do anything that's going to hurt or upset Riley. I understand what Juniper's saying but it kills me to see so much talent stay in Star Falls.

I take a swig of my drink. "I'm sorry if I pushed too much."

She slides her hand onto my knee. "I like that you did. It makes me feel..." She shakes her head, like she doesn't want to say. "I like it."

"Finish that thought?" I say, and I turn to her. "It makes you feel...?"

She smiles and looks up at me under her lashes. "I was going to say 'important,' to you at least."

My stomach lifts in my chest, and I cup my hand around her neck and pull her in for a kiss. She doesn't even see how special she is. And she *is* important. To me. More important than I should have let her become, given I'm leaving Star Falls for good in just a few weeks.

Maybe part of the reason I've been pushing so hard is

because if Juniper was in New York, I'd be able to see her after Vivian has stopped recording. After I've gone back to New York. In real life.

I deepen our kiss and pull her closer. I don't think I've ever felt this way about anybody, and I know I'm not going to want to give her up when I go back to New York.

TWENTY-THREE

Fisher

I expected New York to feel different when I came back from Star Falls, but as a cab hoots its horn at me as I walk over a pedestrian crossing that's on green, I'm faced with the reality that New York is just the same as it ever was. Like it's been on pause while I've been away and someone hit play when I touched down at LaGuardia.

I'm meeting Benny, the manager of The Homecoming Kings, at an Irish bar in Greenwich Village. I've not seen him in a couple of months, which is unusual. He's based in New York and we'd usually grab a drink most months. He's been busy. I've been in Colorado.

I see him by the bar. He's at least fifteen years older than me and has been in the music business a long time. He's old school and I like that about him.

"Fisher," he says, with a nod. "Can I get you a beer?" He beckons over the waitress. He already has a Guiness, but there's no way I can stomach that tonight.

"I'll take a bottle of..."

"Heineken?" she suggests, smiling at me.

"Sure," I reply. "Thanks." I settle onto my stool across the high table from Benny.

"She likes you," Benny says.

I frown, not quite understanding, until I realize he means the waitress. "What can I say? I'm a likeable guy."

"You are that," he says.

"How are things?" I ask. "Any thoughts on the next album? How Right Records can best support the guys?"

"Yeah, the guys are good. Enjoying the downtime after the tour ended."

"We need to wrap things up from a legal perspective, obviously. Where are we with the contracts?" I ask, like I don't know exactly where we are. The new contracts are with Benny, and they have been for weeks now. I made sure they went out before I went to Colorado.

"Yeah, I wanted to talk to you about that," Benny says.

His tone is breezy and it makes my stomach shrivel. Benny is never breezy. He's grumpy and bad tempered, and if he wasn't a music manager, I'm pretty certain he would be doing something that involved hard labor and alcohol.

"I think the guys are looking at their options."

My jaw tenses, and I take a swig of the beer that's in front of me so I appear more relaxed than I am. "Oh yeah? Tell me what they're looking at."

He meets my eye and holds my gaze for a second. "You know I like you, Fisher. You're a good guy. Decent. Straight-forward—unlike lots of people in this business. But the game has changed so much."

"For the record, I like you too, Benny. For the same reasons. And you're right, the business is changing. But it's always been changing. What's great about Right Records is that we're smaller, so we adapt to change quicker. We're nimble."

Benny nods.

"Just level with me, Benny. What's going on?"

Benny sighs and shakes his head. "The guys have been... I don't know how to say it. They've been approached by... Re Records."

He didn't need to tell me.

"There's a new head honcho over there. Talks a very good game."

"Gerry Banks," I say.

"Yeah, that's right. He was a manager before. I knew him from that. Always liked him, although he was a little too polished for me to want to sit in a pub with him."

I know exactly what Benny means. Gerry Banks wears a veneer of affability that's believable if you don't know him well enough.

"I used to work in A&R with him at EMG."

"It's a small world," Benny says. "Anyway, he's been courting the guys pretty hard. Turning up during the last part of the tour. And this was before he landed at Re Records. I thought he was trying to poach them from me."

But no. He was trying to poach them from *me*.

"And he goes to the same gym as Damien. And they've struck up a friendship."

Fuck.

"That's a coincidence. Him being at the same gym as Damien." There's no way it's a coincidence. Gerry is aggressively pursuing The Homecoming Kings and has clearly figured out where Damien goes to the gym.

"Yeah," Benny says and takes a sip of his Guiness. "It is a coincidence."

"Or Gerry's found out which gym Damien goes to and

is stalking him." That would be consistent with what he's done before.

Benny holds my gaze. "Either way, he's still managed to gain Damien's trust."

"And what does that mean, Benny?" I was sick of fucking around. If they're not going to sign with Right Records, I want to know.

"They don't want to re-sign with Right Records. They want to go to Re."

I swallow down the hurt and anger swirling inside me. "I discovered The Homecoming Kings. Fuck, I introduced them to you."

"I know," Benny says. "This isn't my decision."

"But you advise them. You think signing with Re is the best thing for the band?"

Benny pulls in a breath. "I think it might be good."

My stomach falls. The decision is made. If Benny is on board, there's no changing any minds.

"Well, thanks for telling me." My tone is slightly sarcastic because if I hadn't suggested a drink tonight, I wonder when Benny would have told me. "It would have been nice to have had a discussion."

"The decision was made, Fisher. There was no point dicking you about, getting you to jump through hoops. Even I haven't been involved in lots of the discussions. Gerry and Damien's friendship meant it crept up on me. Basically, Damien has been talking to Re every day. Gerry has gained his trust. And you know how the guys are, if Damien's happy, they're all happy."

I let out a cynical laugh. "The irony is that Gerry's engineered a friendship to gain Damien's trust. Damien was never just chatting to a mate. He was talking to the CEO of Re."

"Maybe," Benny says.

I don't say anything. I'm pretty certain that Gerry knew exactly which gym he went to and joined to force a meeting. But what's the point in wasting energy?

What I don't understand is why Gerry can't operate in a straightforward way. Why didn't he just approach the band and suggest a meeting, like every other record company would have done? Through the correct channels. But that's not Gerry's style. He plotted and schemed and pursued The Homecoming Kings relentlessly until he got what he wanted.

And what's worse, I'd bet, he doesn't even want them. He just doesn't want *me* to have them.

The Homecoming Kings. The first band I signed at Right Records. A band I discovered. A band I made. And he's taken them. There's no way he's not targeting me personally.

Well, I'm taking this personally. Very personally.

TWENTY-FOUR

Fisher

I thought a walk would clear my head and allow me to think. But heading to Worth and Sophia's new brownstone on foot hasn't helped at all.

Jack opens the door. "You look terrible," he says.

"Thanks. Are you Worth's butler now?"

Jack chuckles. "I just got here. Everyone's already here."

My body instantly sags with relief. I need to see some friendly faces tonight.

We both head through to the back. This house is only slightly bigger than Worth's last one. I'm not sure why he and Sophia moved. But they did.

As I walk into the back room and see that it's not just my best friends, but some of the wives and girlfriends, too, I can't get the image of Juniper out of my head. It's like she's here without actually being here.

"Hey, Fisher." Sophia holds her arms out to greet me.

I smile and bend for a hug.

We all greet each other, and with every touch and hello, I relax. Thank god for this found family of mine.

"Wasn't expecting to see you for a few weeks," Worth says. "What brought you back so early?"

Typical Worth, figures out that something's off immediately.

"There's stuff going on at work."

He hands me a beer and gestures for me to follow him out to the garden. "Come on, everyone, let's go and sit outside." He lowers his voice. "What kind of stuff?"

The garden is so much prettier than I expected. It's walled, with a huge dining table in the middle with a dozen chairs around it. One for each of us and our significant others. That's no coincidence. Worth and Sophia will have been very deliberate when picking the outdoor dining furniture.

I sigh. "I'm not sure." How do I describe it? I'm being professionally stalked and then sabotaged.

"Use your words," Jack says, like he's talking to a toddler as he takes a seat opposite me.

"Ha. You're funny."

"It's an affliction. But I'm at peace with it," he deadpans. "Tell us your woes, Fisher, my friend."

"Oh, no biggie, someone's trying to professionally destroy me. That's all."

Jack nods. "Okay then. Who's next? Worth, what's going on with you?"

Worth shoots him a don't-be-an-asshole look, but I don't mind. I need the levity that Jack's providing. I've been in my head too much, ever since last night and my meeting with Benny.

"The Homecoming Kings are signing with Re Records."

"Can they do that?" Bennett asks. "Legally?"

"Yup. They're out of contract. Stupidly, I assumed they were going to sign back up with Right Records. I knew other labels would try and get them to switch but..."

"But you found those guys," Leo says. "You made them. They can't just sign with someone else."

"Well, they can," I say. "And what's worse is that... do you remember me telling you about Gerry Banks?"

"The one you thought was stealing your artists when you were still at EMG?" Worth asks.

"That's the one."

"Wait, who? What? I feel like I missed something," Jack says.

Worth relays the story to the rest of the table as if I'd told him yesterday. How I always thought Gerry was targeting me personally but I could never be sure.

"This all happened before we were at business school. Before I knew any of you guys," I say. "Maybe I'm just being paranoid—"

Jack cuts me off. "Trust your gut. And as if he would just find the lead singer at his gym. There's no way that's a coincidence. I think you're right. He's targeting you."

"But why?"

"Because you're the best at what you do," Worth says.

"I'm small fry in comparison to the major labels."

"But you just signed Vivian Cross," Bennett says. "You're not small fry. Actually, was Vivian signed to Re Records before? Is this payback for that?"

I shake my head. "No. She was at Universal."

"Is it worth you asking him for a meeting? Like a lunch or something? See if you can figure out what's going on?"

"I've thought about it. But he won't give anything away. He never did, even when we were in our early twenties. He's got this strange... he's always been a popular guy.

Everyone liked him. But I just couldn't connect with him somehow."

"Probably because he was stealing your artists," Worth says.

"Maybe," I say. "I don't know what it is, I just think it's more than just about the artists. It feels personal."

"Have you looked into his background?" Jack asks.

Immediately, I think of Juniper and her quoting *The Art of War*. "A little," I confess. "I found out that he's also from Pennsylvania. He's slightly younger than me."

"Did you know him? Cross paths with him when you were younger?"

I shake my head. "No. Not as far as I'm aware."

"Did you fuck his wife or something?" Jack asks.

Now it's my turn to give him a don't-be-an-asshole look.

"What?" Jack exclaims. "I'm being realistic. Is anyone saying Fisher is still a virgin?"

"I haven't fucked his wife," I say. "He's been married since I've known him. I've met his wife. We definitely haven't fucked."

"I can get my people on it," Jack says. "There must be a reason why he's targeting you."

"Your people? What does that mean? Are you part of the Mafia now?" I ask.

"Uh, yes. The Mafia otherwise known as the establishment of New York City."

I laugh. Jack's not wrong. Being from the Alden family means Jack's grown up in a world I know nothing about. He's got generational connections with anyone worth knowing in America and probably the entire world. The six of us are all wealthy. We're all successful. But Jack's from old New York money. And there's *nothing* so powerful.

"So who exactly are your people?" I ask.

"Just the security people my family uses," Jack responds.

"Well, if you let me have a number, I can contact them."

Jack narrows his eyes slightly. "It doesn't work like that. They're not going to take your call. But it doesn't matter. I'll speak to them and one of them will call you."

"What are they going to do?"

Jack shrugs. "Probably pick him up outside his apartment. Bundle him into a van. Take him to an abandoned warehouse in Jersey and ask him some questions."

I pause, waiting for Jack to crack a smile and tell me he's kidding, but he doesn't say anything. I glance over at Bennett and Worth, but their expressions are blank. He's got to be kidding. I don't want Gerry Banks kidnapped, for crying out loud.

"Jack," I say. "I don't want—"

"I'm kidding. They'll just poke around. No one's getting taken to Jersey. Dad won't work with anyone who's ever set foot in that state."

"Okay, but no kidnapping either."

"Scout's honor." He puts up his three fingers. "Not unless we really need to."

I roll my eyes. "So how's the hotel coming, Worth?" I want to change the subject. I want to feel a little lighter. More hopeful. I can't shake the feeling that Gerry won't stop at The Homecoming Kings. He wants more.

"It's good. Poppy and Avril are running the show. I'm just along for the ride," he says. "What about your place?" he asks.

"Actually, I'm thinking of selling it." I *hadn't* been thinking about it until just now. I get offers on the hotel all the time. It's in a great location, and I really don't make the best of it. I love my five best friends but I don't love the hotel business.

"What?" everyone around the table choruses.

"I get offers all the time. It was a great idea when we left business school. It bound us together. But for me? It's not my passion. And I like the idea of a simpler life."

"Are you serious?" Bennett asks.

"Yeah. The reason for us having those hotels was to maintain our bond, but we don't need hotels to do that. Not anymore. I'm not sure if we ever did. There's no way any of you are drifting away from me. I wouldn't allow it. And anyway, it's not like I ever win, anyway. You always win, Bennett. You're *always* going to win."

"Not true," Bennett says. "Byron's always going to win. If we allow the Colorado Club to qualify for our little competition, that is. It's a controversial topic. Is the Club really a hotel? I would argue it's not really within the original scope of what was agreed."

I chuckle, shaking my head. "Sounds to me like you don't wanna be a loser. Maybe you need to up your game."

"Are you going to buy something else?" Worth asks. "You know I had the Boston hotel before Ninth Street. It's much better having something in the city. But I guess that's not your problem."

"Right. It's not the actual hotel or the location that's an issue. It's the fact I don't want a hotel. Life is... I know I have people to run it, but... life in Star Falls is really simple, and it's made me realize how complicated things are back here."

Jack gasps. "Fisher! You're not thinking of moving there permanently, are you?"

"You're moving to Colorado?" Sophia appears, carrying a plate of cheese and meats and sets it down on the table.

"No, I didn't say that."

"I'm not losing you too," Jack says. "Not you and Byron. No way will you survive in Colorado."

I roll my eyes. "You haven't lost Byron. He and Rosey spend most of their time in New York."

"But he's in Colorado a lot. He's got a choice between Colorado and New York, and Byron picks Colorado. *A lot.*"

"It's where he grew up," Worth says. "And it's beautiful."

"Yeah. The Grand Canyon's beautiful. I don't see any of you moving there."

"He's got the Club there," I say. "And Worth's right, it *is* beautiful. That's partly because life is slower. Less complicated."

"New York is energy. It's life. And it's different to everyone. You can set your own pace in New York." It sounds like Jack's defending his honor. As if New York is his town and I'm personally insulting him by saying something nice about another part of the US.

"I agree with you," I say. "I'm not saying I'm moving. I'm just saying, it's nice getting back to basics sometimes."

Sophia splutters into her drink. "Don't let Byron catch you saying the Club is basic."

"I don't mean the Club. I mean..." I can see Juniper on the bench on her porch, two glasses in front of her and a bottle of wine. Some of the best evenings of my life have been spent sitting there with her. Sharing our thoughts and lives. Having her nestled in my arms. Feeling her lips on mine. There's nothing better. Not even in New York.

"You mean what?" Jack says. "The fresh mountain air?"

"Well, yes, now you mention it. But also, I've been going into the studio with Vivian. I've enjoyed it. I haven't done it in a long time. There's always other stuff to be dealt with that seems more important when I'm in New York. Being in Star Falls with Vivian... well, it's forced me to slow down."

"It's good to get a fresh perspective," Worth says.

"I like the authenticity of the place," I say. "No one's trying to get ahead. No one's trying to make a connection with you so they can get in front of someone you know. Life is very simple. I'd forgotten how peaceful that is. You know?"

"Ahh," Jack says. "Who wants peaceful?"

Everyone laughs, and I raise my glass and Jack clinks his against it.

"Did you meet anyone, Fisher?" Sophia asks. "A woman, maybe?"

"What makes you say that?" I ask. "I just like how life is simpler there. It forces you to think about what really makes you happy."

"Well, if there's no one in Colorado, then I have a friend you might like."

I chuckle. "Thanks, Sophia."

"I'm serious. She's super cute. Just your type. She's a lawyer. A real ballbuster."

"You think I like ballbusters?"

"You like strong women," Sophia says. "And Samia is gorgeous and powerful. I think you two would be perfect together. I'm going to do a dinner when you're back in New York for good. I'll play a little matchmaker."

I smile but don't tell her my stomach is churning at the thought of being set up. I can't remember the last time I was exclusive with a woman, but I don't even want to sit opposite someone at a dinner if that person isn't Juniper.

Worth and Bennett start talking about how being with the women in their lives made everything better, and I want to listen, but I'm interrupted by Jack.

"But seriously, you're not moving to Colorado, are you?" he asks in a whisper.

"No plans," I say. It's true. I'm moving back to New York in three weeks. But I can't help thinking that something inside me will have shifted by then. "But I'm going to reprioritize. I want to get into producing more. I might even start training up a successor. I can see myself stepping away from the CEO role. Maybe I can be chairman and then go back to discovering artists. I loved doing that. It felt like I was creating something. I've seen the way Juniper looks when she's painting, and I want to love something that much."

"Juniper?" asks Jack.

"Oh, one of Byron's old school friends. I introduced her to Grace Astor."

Jack nods. "And did you also introduce her to your penis?" he asks formally.

I can't stop a laugh from erupting. "You're ridiculous."

"You're hypnotized by pussy."

"I am not!"

Jack shakes his head. "You gotta get her out of your system. Make the rest of your time in Colorado count, and then come back and do business the way you want."

He says it like I'm considering an alternative. I'm not. It's not like I can move to Colorado. My business is in New York. My business that needs my attention. My friends. My life. Everything I've ever known. Except Juniper.

TWENTY-FIVE

I haven't heard from Fisher for three days. He's been in New York City the entire time. And it's not like we're dating. I didn't expect him to call. Or even text. Except... I miss him.

He's supposed to be back today. But maybe he won't come back. Maybe that will be that and I'll never see him again. I huddle under my blanket, despite the heat. I just can't get warm, but I can't bear being inside because it's too stuffy.

Riley is over at my parents', batch cooking. Hopefully she'll bring some home with her. Our freezer could do with a restock.

My phone buzzes on the table beside me and my stomach lurches. Is it stupid to hope that's a text from Fisher?

I scoop up my phone and see Mom appear on the screen.

Riley wants to stay over. That okay?

It's nice she's having fun. I love the bond Riley has with her grandparents. I'm lucky they're both alive, and they've been so supportive of me and Riley.

I reply that of course it's fine, and I slide the phone back onto the table. Evenings on my own don't happen very often. It's precious free time that I should be reveling in.

My phone buzzes again and I stand the butterflies down. It's probably just Mom asking if she has to wash Riley's hair. I open the message.

It's from Bill, Riley's dad, confirming the date when he's going to be coming to Star Falls next month.

As I'm staring at his text, wondering if he'll actually make it this time, another text comes through telling me he's leaving a day earlier than we'd discussed because of a ballet recital for his youngest daughter.

Typical. Riley definitely comes bottom of his list these days.

As I'm mentally handing my ex his ass, headlights illuminate the porch.

My breath catches in my chest. I can't make out who it is right away. And then the headlights go dark and I can see that it's Byron's truck.

It's Fisher.

I stand, fighting the urge to toss off my blanket and run to him. I want to feel his arms around me. I want to smell that expensive whatever-it-is he wears. I've missed him. It's been three goddamn days and I've missed him.

"Hey," he calls as he gets out of the truck, like he just saw me yesterday.

I can't help but smile. He's had his hair cut and he looks younger than he did before. He pushes his hand through the side of his hair like he's self-conscious or something. I can't believe Fisher could ever be self-conscious. He's the most confident man I've ever met.

"Hey, stranger," I call back. "You had your hair cut. What else is new?"

He bounds up the stairs and heads right to me. "Fuck, Juniper, it's good to see you."

My stomach tilts at his words.

I've missed you, I think.

He lifts me up, and I wrap my legs around his waist.

"What's new?" he asks. "Tell me everything I missed."

I tip my head back and laugh. "Nothing's new. We're in Star Falls, remember?"

He laughs. "You know, I thought the same about New York when I went back. It's exactly the same as it was when I left." Our eyes lock, and instantly I'm weak for him. I don't know how a man managed to go from perfect stranger to making me weak just looking at me in a few short weeks. But Fisher's managed it. "Kiss me," he says.

I slide down from his arms, take his face in my hands, and stand on tiptoes. "There's nothing I want to do more."

He presses his lips to mine and my entire body buzzes, like it's being woken from a deep sleep. He pulls me against him so there's no space between my body and his.

He's hard, and the thought that he wants me makes my knees weaken. Makes my heart weaken.

He pulls back. "You okay?"

He must feel how much I've missed him. I'm not okay that he's been gone but I'm better now that he's here.

I shake my head. "Come inside and... come inside me."

He groans. "Juniper. I don't want to wake Riley and—"

I place a finger over his lips. "She's at my parents' for the night. My mom just messaged to ask me if it was okay."

"I really like your mom," he says, stepping so close to me, sweeping his lips over mine.

"Let's go inside," I say. As much as I loved it down by the falls, I want to see him in my bed.

He scoops me up and takes me inside.

"I don't even know where you sleep," he says.

"The door next to Riley's."

He kicks my bedroom door open and puts me down softly on my feet. His fingers go straight to the buttons of my blouse.

"I've been thinking about this for so long," Fisher whispers, pressing a kiss between my breasts. He pushes my shirt off my shoulders and kneels at my feet, unbuttoning my jeans and lifting each leg to take them off. He presses a kiss just above my knee, and I shiver. When he sweeps his hands down my thighs, my back arches. He's barely touched me and all my nerve endings are standing to attention, waiting for what's next, wanting more but knowing more will be too much.

He hooks his thumbs into the sides of my underwear and pulls them down. He groans at the sight of my bare pussy—like it's the most erotic thing he's ever seen. Fisher being turned on by me makes me feel like a goddess. If I can turn on a man like Fisher, anything is possible. My nipples stand to attention, scraping the lace of my bra and desperate for his touch.

He places kisses over my lower belly, from one hip to the other, teasing me, making me wait. It's delicious torture. I push my hands through his hair, needing to feel him, wanting more of him.

He pulls away and maneuvers me so I'm lying on my back on the bed, my ass on the edge of the mattress.

"I've dreamed about this. Two nights in New York and all I've thought about is how you taste."

I sigh. Could that even be true? Is it possible that he's thought of me as often as I've thought about him? I've been counting down the hours until he was back here. It's terrifying to think how it's going to feel when he's gone for good. I don't know how I'll cope.

But I can't think about that now.

Fisher's tongue slides down my folds. He flicks and presses, circles and coaxes me into a frenzy.

I can't take any more but I never want it to stop. I never want to stop feeling this.

Wetness pools between my thighs, and if I wasn't so worked up, I'd be embarrassed about how responsive my body is to him. But there's no room in my brain for embarrassment. There's too much else in my body to feel. And it's all pleasure.

All of a sudden, his fingers slide over my breasts as his tongue works my clit, and I arch my back.

"Fisher!" I scream.

He stills, and I feel the loss of his tongue. "You know the rule," he growls. "No coming without my permission."

The tone of his voice is almost enough to push me over the edge. Fisher is such an affable, easygoing guy. But in bed?

In bed, he's in charge.

"Fisher," I whimper.

"You taste so good," he says. His fingers start to move again, moving in circles over me.

My breathing comes in short, sharp bursts and I grip the sheets, trying to hold on. I don't want to disappoint him.

"Please, Fisher. Please can I come?"

He groans. "Open your eyes. Let me see you."

I do what he says, desperate to please him. He gazes at me like I'm the most beautiful, sexy woman he's ever seen.

With a small nod, he says, "Now come."

His thumb circling my clit and our eyes locked, I break into pieces, my entire body floating up, up, up.

He looks at me with such reverence, like he's never seen anything so spectacular.

"Fisher," I say on a sigh.

He rearranges me on the bed and rolls on a condom.

"I have to be inside you," he grunts. "I've waited too long."

He kneels between my legs. My entire body is floppy, exhausted with the effort of orgasm. But as soon as I feel his crown at my entrance, my body comes alive again. I don't know how it's possible.

"Jesus, you're so wet," he grunts.

"I want you," I whisper. "All the time." It's a confession I never thought I'd make. I want the same as he does—to keep this light and airy, but something about him makes me want to tell him the truth. Like the secret's too big to keep to myself.

"I want you all the time, too." He ends on a gasp as he slides into me.

He's so big, and I'm so full, but when he's inside me like this, I feel complete, like he's the key to my lock.

"Is it too much?" he asks.

"You will never be too much," I say. It's exactly enough. He's exactly enough.

His eyes flutter shut as he begins to move over me. The tendons in his neck tighten and I trace them with my fingers.

I widen my legs, wanting him deeper, more. Wanting him to be part of me. "You're so incredible," I whisper, sliding my fingers into his hair. He catches my arms and pushes them over my head.

"I'm going to come if you touch me," he says, his fingers tightening around my wrists as he thrusts into me.

He dips and presses a kiss to my lips. His forehead is sheened with sweat, and I know it's all the effort it's taking him not to come.

Inside me.

I groan at the thought of him being so worked up that just touching him will send him over the edge. This beautiful man who's surrounded by beautiful, glossy women in New York is fucking me. Is so worked up that he can't handle me touching him without coming.

I do that to him.

The thought sends a pulse through my entire body and Fisher cries out.

"I'm going to come," I say, breathlessly. My body is tightening in that familiar way that it does with Fisher. Like I'm being wound over and over and I'm about to snap.

"No!" he bellows. His thrusts grow sharper, needier, less controlled. He must be so close, but he's not willing to let go. Why?

"Fisher!" I call out. "Please. Please. Please let me come."

"Come," he bellows. "Come now!"

The coil snaps and I dissolve under him. He thrusts up and I feel his orgasm blend into mine.

He collapses over me, and I want him to stay there forever.

I wrap my arms around him and our breaths come heavy and labored. He rolls to his side, and I cling to him so we're still connected, not wanting to let him go. I can't.

He starts to move, but I try to hold him in place. I don't

want to lose this moment. I don't want him to pull out of me. It feels like I'll lose a part of him.

"Don't move," I say. But that's not what I'm saying. Not really. I'm saying don't leave. Don't go back to New York. I'm asking him to stay. Stay with me.

"I have to. I need to deal with the condom."

He pulls away and I'm empty.

I roll to my back as he takes off the condom. I know he's right. I don't want to get pregnant. We need to be sensible. But at the same time, I never want him to leave.

He pads back from the bathroom and crawls into bed, pulling me into his arms.

"You okay?" he asks.

I nod.

"You don't seem okay."

"I'm always okay when you're here," I say. All I can think about is the contrast between when he's here and when he's not. It's all I can think about.

"How was Star Falls when I was gone?" he says.

"The same," I reply. "I told you, nothing ever changes in Star Falls."

"Have you spoken to Grace?"

I don't want to talk about Grace right now. I don't want to think about anything. If I start thinking, all that will fill my head are thoughts of what life will be like once Fisher is gone. I slide my hands down and circle my fingers around the base of his cock. I sweep my hands up his velvety smoothness, and he groans.

I try not to smile.

"Juniper," he says, through gritted teeth. "What are you doing?"

"I'm making you hard," I say. "I want you to fuck me again."

He groans and lengthens in my hands. "You can't get enough, can you?"

I shake my head. I want more of him. I want to take everything I can get.

He takes my breast in his hand and massages it, pulling at my nipple. I squeeze my legs together, trying to stop the wetness that starts as soon as he touches me.

He's hard and heavy in my hands, and I lean over him for a condom. I tear open the packet and hand it to him.

While he's rolling on the condom, I arrange myself so I'm facing the headboard, my hands clinging to the top while I kneel on the mattress.

"You want to get fucked from behind?" he asks, his voice dark.

"I want you to fuck me from behind," I correct him.

He comes behind me and I can't see what he's doing, so I drop my hands and turn.

"Put your hands back on the headboard and don't move unless I tell you to." His tone is a warning.

I moan. What is it about Fisher telling me what to do that makes me like it so much? I half want to find out the consequences of disobeying. But more than that, I want to please him, so I resume my position.

He presses his palm against my back, urging me lower, and I do my best to comply. "I can see everything from here," he says. "Your pussy's so wet, Juniper. It's like it's begging for my cock."

I whimper, desperate to feel him.

"Is that what it's doing, Juney? Begging for my cock?"

"Please, Fisher. I need you. *Please.*"

He groans, victorious. He's gotten what he wants—my compliance, my need, my desperation.

The tip of him enters me, and I squirm and push back, trying to get him deeper, but he pulls away.

"You don't decide. Haven't you learned that yet? I know your body. I know what you need. I will decide."

"Please, Fisher! I'll do anything." I'm so desperate for him it actually hurts. It feels like if I don't get him inside me soon, a piece of me will break.

But I don't have to wait too much longer. In one deep thrust, he's inside me.

I'm breathless, unable to think straight because all I can do is feel.

"That's what you want, isn't it?"

I nod my head, and he pulls out and slams into me again. I whimper at how good it feels. How right. How I've never felt need for a man like I do for Fisher.

His front presses against my back and his hands roam my body as he thrusts in and out. His hands go to my breasts, squeezing, pinching, pressing. His arm around my waist keeps me in place. Keeps me in the perfect position for his relentless cock, driving into me over and over. I can barely catch my breath as he slams into me.

I know I'm going to be sore in the morning. I'm thankful. I'll be able to feel him despite him not being with me. That's what I want. A constant reminder of him. It's what I need.

He anchors his hands on my shoulders and pushes into me, and it's so deep and so perfect, my orgasm twists awake at the bottom of my spine.

"I'm going to come," I choke out in panic.

He pulls out and his hands leave my body. "No coming," he snaps. "Not until I tell you."

"Fisher!" I cry out at the loss of his body over mine.

"Take a deep breath. You're not to come."

I cling to the headboard, desperate to let go and pull him back over me, but he's told me not to move, so I don't.

"You think you can take my cock again without coming?" he asks.

I nod my head.

His breath is hot on the back of my neck and my muscles unlock as I feel him close to me again.

His cock nudges at my entrance and slides in again.

Instantly, I'm close to orgasm.

I shake my head. I don't think I can do this. He feels too good. Too perfect. "Fisher," I cry out, helpless.

"Breathe," he says. "Don't come. Breathe."

I try and do what he says. I pull in a breath and try to pull back from the edge of my orgasm. It helps a little, but my entire body starts to vibrate, like my climax is threatening to spill over in every cell of my body.

"I'm going to fuck you now, Juniper. And you're going to keep taking deep breaths and you're not going to come until I tell you. Okay?"

I pull in a deep breath because just his words are enough to send convulsions of pleasure through my body.

I nod, unsure if I'll actually be able to stop myself. He pulls out and I exhale.

"Relax your body," he says. "It will be so much more intense when you do come."

I don't think I can take more intensity. Being with Fisher is already the most intense sex I've ever had. I'm not sure I can survive more.

I do my best to unlock my shoulders and release my tightened muscles, and then he slams into me and it pushes the breath from my lungs and my orgasm flicks her tail like she's lying in wait, ready to be unleashed.

"Fisher!" I cry.

"Don't you dare come," he says, slamming into me again. He pushes so hard, I almost lose my grip. He pulls me up, his arm around my waist. My muscles are weak now. I don't know how long I'll be able to hang on.

"I'm going to make you come so hard, you're never going to forget it."

For a fleeting second, I wonder if he's trying to fuck me so I don't forget *him*. He doesn't realize that I could never forget him.

"Now come," he says, and his fingers find my clit. It's like he's pressed a release button and I'm exploding around him. My body quivers as he holds me, still fucking me relentlessly and without mercy. My orgasm stretches on and on and on, and it's like roses are blooming over and over in my body. As I float back down, Fisher's arms are around me and he's fucking me still. It's like he thinks I might disappear if he stops.

My entire body is limp and lifeless, and finally he explodes behind me, calling my name. He pulls me back onto his lap and I tip my head back so it's resting on his shoulder.

His chest is heaving. My stomach is still rippling. I'm raw and exhausted and happy.

Fisher's made sure I will never forget him.

TWENTY-SIX

Fisher

Vivian's already at her usual table when I arrive to meet her for breakfast. I check my watch. I'm ten minutes earlier than our agreed time. She's not usually late. But she's not usually early, either. The hairs at the back of my neck stand up. Something's wrong.

"Hey," I say, sliding into the chair opposite her.

"Hi, Fisher." She looks a little surprised to see me.

"Were you not expecting me?"

She shrugs. "Of course."

"Is everything okay?" I ask her.

"Yeah. Rough night with the little one. And... you know, I think we're coming to the end of the album. Things will shift again."

The end of the album. That's a good thing for Right Records. But it means I'll have no reason to be in Colorado.

"It's sounding spectacular."

Finally, she smiles. "Yeah, I'm really happy with it. I really worried about recording after the baby. You change in so many ways after a child. I thought maybe I'd be so focused on motherhood that I wouldn't be able to be a musician anymore."

"You've proved yourself wrong."

She nods. "Yeah, I think I have. I really want to finish off 'Dear Husband' today. We're so close. There's something missing though. You want to come into the studio? You've already earned a producer credit on this album. You may as well."

She didn't have to mention the producer credit, but I appreciate it. I've enjoyed working with her. "It would be a pleasure. I've really loved this time in the studio."

"I thought I'd better put you to work, seeing as you insisted on coming out to babysit me."

"Not babysit," I say. "Just to make sure you're happy. And anyway, I've enjoyed it. The break from New York has been..."

"How is Juniper?" she asks.

I chuckle. "She's going to be hard to leave."

"You wouldn't think about splitting your time between here and New York?"

I have thought about it. I've thought about it a lot. Especially since going back to New York. "I'm away five minutes and Gerry Banks is already trying to destroy my business." I grin at her but instead of smiling back, she winces. My stomach turns over. "What?" I ask.

"Well... speaking of Gerry. He called me again yesterday. He asked if he could take me to dinner. I told him I was away recording my album and he..." She shakes her head, like she can't quite believe what she's about to say. "He said, 'I know you're in Colorado.'"

It's like I've taken a punch to the stomach. "How did he know?"

"It gets worse. He says he's staying here. Arriving in two days."

I sit back in my seat. How is that possible? This is my best friend's place. "Is he a member?"

Vivian shrugs. "I have no idea. He just said he was arriving with some friends and that he wanted to take me and Beau to dinner. I told him we already had plans but..."

"He's not going to give up. He's followed you out here to Colorado, for crying out loud."

"You think he's followed me?" she asks. "Maybe it's just a coincidence."

I'm angry, but I'm also stunned. Why would he think he could follow Vivian out to a place like this? It's so remote. And she's with her family. "It's not a coincidence. No way. He wants to get you to sign with Re Records."

"That's what Beau says. But I'm signed with you."

"He'll probably tell you that he can get you out of it, or will ask you the terms... and you're only signed for one album. He'll probably want the next one."

She wrinkles her nose. "Maybe some people would take it as a compliment, but I think it's creepy that he'd follow me out here."

"He'll stop at nothing," I say, almost to myself.

"I've told him I'm not interested. And I'm really not. But I just wanted you to know that he's about to show up."

"He probably doesn't know I'm here." Or maybe he does. He seems to know everything about my artists. Most likely he thinks he can steal Vivian right from under my nose.

"Well, I'm busy. Beau and I are eating in our lodge, like we do every night. I want to sleep and work and hang out with my husband and kid. That's why this place is perfect."

"I'm glad it's worked for you," I say. "And don't worry about Gerry. I'll deal with him."

She sighs. "He can't force me to have a conversation with him."

"I'll arrange for more security on your lodge and the recording studio."

"I'm not frightened."

"No, but you shouldn't have your peace disturbed. We thought you'd avoid fans and paparazzi by coming here. We hadn't thought we'd have to protect against stalker record company executives."

Vivian laughs. "It's true. Maybe he's just a superfan. He probably wants tickets to my next show or something."

"Thanks for telling me," I say.

"I have nothing to hide. I'm really enjoying working with you. I have no desire to move anywhere."

"Thanks for saying that. If you don't mind, I'm going to talk to a few people. Get some things in place." I look up, and Byron is coming through the entrance to the breakfast room.

"Yeah, go do whatever it is you need to do. I've eaten already, so I'm going to go off and start for the day."

We both get up and Vivian heads out, saying a quick hello to Byron on her way out.

"Can we talk?" I ask him.

"Can I eat while I listen?" He orders breakfast from a waitress who's standing nearby, and we go and grab a table in the corner of the room. I explain that Gerry's coming to stay at the Colorado Club.

Before he says anything in response, he picks up his phone, taps out a message, presses send and turns back to me. "No one comes to the Club without full details being provided. It's possible he's staying with a member. They're allowed to bring a limited number of guests per year, but we'll have full details."

The manager of the Club, Hart, heads toward our table and greets us with a relaxed smile. "Can I invite you gentlemen to our private dining suite?" he says.

Byron stands, and we follow Hart to the other end of the restaurant, through a door I've never noticed, and then through a second door into a small dining room with an oval table with twelve chairs. It overlooks the same view as Blossom, with the same floor-to-ceiling windows. Byron takes a seat at the head of the table and the manager and I sit opposite each other.

"We're aware that Mr. Banks will be arriving in two days," Hart says. "He's a guest of Mr. and Mrs. Franklin."

Byron nods his head. "They were one of the first members to sign up, is that right?"

"Correct. They've never brought a guest before."

"And was Mr. Banks always due to be one of their party on this trip?" Byron asks.

There's a knock at the door and the three of us fall silent. One of the waitresses from Blossom arrives with Byron's breakfast and sets it in front of him, complete with coffee and orange juice.

"Do you want anything?" Byron asks me.

My appetite died as soon as Vivian mentioned Gerry. I shake my head.

The waitress leaves.

"He was added two days ago," Hart says. "Provided all the details we asked for and we ran him through all the normal checks. Everything cleared, so we proceeded as usual."

"Two days ago. So that's when he found out where she was staying."

"Security around Ms. Cross has been watertight," Hart says.

"Yes, I've been in contact with her manager, who's delighted there's nothing leaked to the press about her whereabouts or even that she's away recording."

"I don't think the Club has leaked anything," Byron says.

I think about whether Vivian coming to see Riley after she'd been sick had been a wise move. But honestly, if it had leaked that way, the press would have it. It wouldn't just be Gerry Banks.

"This is Gerry digging," I say. "He probably bribed someone. It doesn't really matter who. I don't think he'd target the Club. He wouldn't know this is the place to start. It's probably someone on her team. These things get out."

"So what do you want us to do about it?" Byron asks. "We can inform him he's no longer able to be accommodated."

Hart nearly chokes. "Obviously, Mr. and Mrs. Franklin won't be happy."

"Then I'll give them a refund of their membership. The important thing is you get what you need, Fisher."

I sigh, grateful to Byron for his loyalty. The problem is, it doesn't solve the issue with Gerry. He'll just find Vivian when she leaves this place. He's going to keep coming after her. "I don't know *what* I need."

Byron glances at Hart. "I'll let you know my decision."

With that, the manager excuses himself.

"I'm happy to uninvite him," Byron says. "But you're just putting off the inevitable. If he doesn't meet with Vivian here, it will be somewhere else. Better he wastes his time where we can all witness it rather than back in New York."

I nod. "I know. This isn't about Vivian. At least, I don't think it is."

"You don't think the CEO of one of the biggest record labels in the business wants to sign the biggest star in the business?" Byron asks, like I'm an idiot.

"Well, of course he does, but it's more than that. It's the fact that she's signed with Right Records. With *me*. That's the issue for Gerry."

"Then you need to find out why."

I nod. I have to confront him. I have to find out what his problem is. And I want to solve it. I'm done spending time and energy on Gerry Banks. I need to speak to him. Why he's so intent on having me fail.

"Is he staying in the same lodge as your members?"

"I can check."

I don't want to have this showdown in public. But I need a witness.

"I'm going to be right by your side," Byron says. "You're not having this conversation without me." He offers before I even need to ask.

Of course. That's what we do for each other.

That's why I know I can handle Gerry Banks. Because I have five brothers who have my back. No matter what.

TWENTY-SEVEN

Juniper

It feels like it's been raining for a month straight. It's only been three days, but there's a feeling of damp everywhere I go in Star Falls at the moment.

"Mommy, can we go to the playground?" Riley asks as she tucks into her cereal at our small dining table. "You said yourself that we're not made of sugar."

I laugh. When Riley was little, she was like a cat. She never wanted to go out in the rain. I used to coax her outside, telling her she wasn't made of sugar, so she wouldn't melt in the rain. I only have myself to blame for her wanting to go to the playground in this downpour.

"You're as sweet as sugar," I say. "But no, we can't go to the playground, Riley. It's just too wet."

"But I'm bored, Mommy. We spent all day yesterday inside, too."

She's right. We spent yesterday getting caught up with chores and sorting through Riley's wardrobe. It was immensely satisfying, but not very fun for Riley.

"Let's go to the studio," she suggests.

It's a perfect day for the studio. Okay, the sun isn't out, but the skylights make it possible to paint, whatever the weather. I just can't face going in there at the moment.

I tried last week to go, but I got nothing done. All I could think about was Grace and the possibilities I'm giving up if I say no to her. It's paralyzing. Usually, I can immerse myself in my work, whatever is going on in my personal life. Even when I gave up art school because I was pregnant, even when I lost that baby, even when Riley's dad and I were splitting up.

At the worst times in my life, art has been my salvation. But now? Now, all I can think about is that I'm being offered a chance at my dreams again, and I can't take it.

Can't or... won't.

"No studio today," I say. "I'm waiting for some paint to come in." As soon as I say it, I know Riley will find holes in my logic. She's a smart kid, and sometimes I'm guilty of treating her like she's still a baby.

"You have a ton of paint, Mom. Use what's in the studio."

"But I'm at a crucial bit and the paint I'm waiting on is metallic. I don't have any in the studio." It's a lie, but as soon as I say it, it occurs to me that metallic on my current piece would actually look really cool. A deep, dirty bronze beneath some of the darker colors might look really effective, and I don't have any. I make a mental note to do some online shopping tonight when Riley's in bed.

There was a time when the idea of buying metallic paint would have been out of the question, but with the money from my sale of paintings to the Colorado Club, I can afford it and still not dip into Riley's college fund. Most of it is earmarked for her, but I've managed to establish a small emergency fund, and I also put aside a few hundred dollars for fun stuff. Metallic paint qualifies.

And what Riley doesn't know is that she's getting a ninth birthday party at Pizza Meet Ya.

"What does metallic mean?" she asks.

"Paint that looks like metal. Let me show you." I pull up on my phone a picture of a metallic paint. It sure looks pretty.

"Oooh, Mommy, it looks like it has glitter in it." Her eyes light up and it fills my heart that paint can get her as excited as it gets me. Maybe Riley will want to go to art school. If she does, the money from the Club will make her dreams a reality. What mother doesn't want to do that for their kid?

"Right. You think it would look nice on the piece I'm working on at the moment?" I ask.

"I think it would look amazing on all your pictures!"

"Yeah, so I'm going to wait for that. We'll have to make non-studio fun today."

She sighs and releases her spoon. "No more chores. My room is clean. The laundry is folded. I don't want to do anything else."

"I agree. No more chores today."

Riley's eyes widen, and she stares at me, waiting for me to change my mind.

"What do you want to do?" I ask. "We could always decorate for Christmas?"

"Really?" she asks, sitting forward in her chair. "Like put the tree up?"

"Why not?" I ask.

She thinks about it for a moment, then shakes her head. "It's summer. We'd just have to take it down again and that would make me sad."

"Doesn't mean we can't have fun in the meantime. You love decorating for Christmas."

She shakes her head solemnly. "It rubs out all the fun," she says. "I don't want to do that."

"But that's like saying that if we don't get dressed, we won't get our clothes dirty so we won't have to wash them and fold the laundry."

"Right. That's actually a pretty smart idea, Mommy. Let's just wear our PJs today."

"Well, I'm already dressed," I say. "But you can't not do things just because there'll be some clearing up or some laundry after. I'd never paint if I didn't want to screw back on paint caps and wash my brushes."

Riley just shrugs, and I take her bowl from in front of her and place it in the sink. Maybe I went a bit overboard with the chores yesterday. The last thing I want to do is encourage her to limit herself from having fun or exploring new opportunities because of the small possibility of the downside of cleaning up after. It's just part of life. The A on your English paper requires the sacrifice of study. Painting a picture means you have to wash your brushes.

And then the thought hits me like a sucker punch—a career in art requires me letting go of things I currently have in my life.

Is it the same? The sacrifice is bigger, isn't it? But the potential upside is too.

I shake my head. No, it's not the same. It's not like I can give up my job. I have a mortgage to pay and food to put on the table. The sacrifice isn't worth it. Plus, Riley's in school. It's not like I can uproot her and move to New York. I'm pretty sure they don't have many abandoned sweet shops that only charge a homemade pecan pie and a bottle of wine for rent every month.

My phone bleeps on the table next to Riley.

"It's Fisher!" she says. "Can he come over? He's fun, and I bet he'd have a lot of ideas of what to do in a rainstorm."

I roll my eyes, deliberately not saying no, because then we'll just get into a debate about why Fisher can't come over, and I don't think I can stand it. I want to see him, but I don't want my daughter growing attached.

I swipe open the message as Riley continues to ask me about Fisher.

Fisher: Hey, what are you doing this rainy day?

I grin helplessly at the message. I have no idea why. It's not a particularly sweet or romantic message. It's just good to hear from him. It's nice to know he's thinking about me.

Me: We're just deciding. Riley's bored and balked at the idea of putting up the Christmas tree in May. No idea why.

"Who are you messaging, Mommy? Tell me! Is it Fisher?"

"Yes, sweet girl, it's Fisher."

"Can he come over? Please, Mommy! We could all watch a movie together. It would be so much fun! We could even get the popcorn machine out. We have corn!"

My phone beeps again.

Fisher: The Christmas tree? Am I missing something? Sometimes Star Falls feels like a far-off planet I just landed on.

I can't help but grin again. He can make me smile like no other man.

Me: We're just trying to find something fun to do on such a rainy day. She wants you to come over.

I don't know why I add the last bit. I've been completely clear about not wanting Riley to become attached to him, but I'm basically leaving him an opening to say he can come over. Why? So I can tell him no? Again?

Three dots appear, and I stare at the phone as Riley tries to figure out on the calendar how many days there are until we can put our Christmas decorations up for real.

I stare at the phone and realize it was no accident that I mentioned Riley wants Fisher to come over. I want Fisher to say he's free. I want to see him. I want him here.

Maybe Riley will be upset when Fisher leaves. But it's not like we've been dating two years and he's living with us. I'm being overprotective. And she likes Fisher.

I start to type.

Me: If you're free, and you don't mind a day watching movies and listening to an eight-year-old talk about Christmas, we'd both love to see you.

I take a deep breath and press send.

Fisher responds in seconds.

I'm on my way and I'm bringing snacks. What are Riley's favorites?

I bite back a smile.

Me: Anything with too much sugar and not enough nutrition.

"Fisher's coming over," I announce.

Riley whips her head around. "Really?"

"We can watch movies. Set up the popcorn machine. It'll be fun."

"It *will* be fun, Mommy. I promise! Do you think Fisher likes Disney movies?"

He doesn't know what he's let himself in for. "Maybe," I say.

We're still trying to find the perfect movie when Fisher raps on the door.

"I'll get it!!" Riley yells, jumping up from the couch and running to the door.

"Hey, Riley," Fisher says. "Thanks for inviting me over. I was so bored today."

I take him in as he and Riley greet each other. He looks so tall next to her. He's tall anyway, but next to Riley, he looks like and giant and she looks tiny. His hair's wet and I wonder if it's from the rain. It looks darker than it usually does, and suddenly I have a vision of him fucking me in the shower. How his chest would look covered with water droplets, how I'd want to sink to my knees in front of him and take him—

"Mom!" Riley yells, despite me standing right next to her. "Fisher brought games!"

I snap out of my shower fantasies and focus on what's actually in front of me.

"Hey, that's great," I say, as I peer into the gigantic duffle bag Fisher's brought with him. "Looks like you have every single game imaginable in there."

"Well, I didn't know which ones you already had, and they had a ton at the Club," Fisher says, grinning at me. I can't help but smile back. It's so good to see him.

"Do we need an agenda?" Fisher asks as I shut the door behind him. "You talked about a movie. Do you want to do that or the games first?"

Riley purses her lips and takes in a breath like a sage old woman about to give some important advice. "I think we need to make snacks a priority. Mommy, can we make popcorn?"

"Homemade popcorn?" Fisher says with a groan. "That's my actual favorite. I've brought some snacks too, but maybe we can get to them later."

Riley's eyes light up. "You brought snacks? Let me see."

"Riley," I say. "Mind your manners."

"Snacks are important," Fisher says. He pulls out a smaller bag from the duffle. It's stacked with candy, marshmallows, chips—everything Riley and all other eight-year-olds love.

I shake my head. I don't think she'll sleep for a week just from being in close proximity to that many snacks.

Fisher slides the snack bag onto the counter and I pull out the popcorn machine. Riley collects the popping corn from the cupboard. I then set to work on melting some butter while Riley and Fisher figure out the popcorn.

I steal glances at them from where I'm cutting off a chunk of butter. They're cute together. Fisher doesn't try to dominate the situation. He feigns ignorance at all the appropriate times and encourages her every step of the way. I sigh and think that if anyone was looking at the three of us now, they'd think this was a pretty perfect family.

Except we're not a family and Fisher is leaving soon.

Too soon.

"That crunchy chocolate is Mom's favorite," Riley says as she pours the melted butter over the gigantic bowl of popcorn. "We have to save that one for her."

"Which one?" Fisher asks, shooting me a glance.

"The blue one. The one that's got cereal in the chocolate."

"Oh, that's a good one. But you're right, we should save that one for your mom."

"Right. Because we have the rest. And the popcorn."

Fisher laughs. "Right."

"Did we decide on a movie?" I ask.

Riley glances at Fisher. "I really like Disney movies. Is that too babyish for you?"

"Babyish?" he asks. "Movies aren't for babies. And do

you know that Disney makes those movies so adults will like them too?"

"Really?" Riley asks.

"Really. What one were you thinking?"

She glances at me. "I was thinking *Brave*. Would that be good?"

I nod encouragingly. "I think that sounds perfect."

I find the movie, Riley and Fisher grab the snacks, along with water for everyone, and we all head to the couch.

"Mommy, we need a blanket," Riley says.

"I'm on it," I say, and head to my bedroom to get the one from my bed.

When I come back, Riley and Fisher have arranged themselves so Riley's in the middle, Fisher is on one side, and there's a space for me on the other side of Riley. They look so comfortable together, like hanging out like this is something we do every Sunday.

"Blanket is ready. Should I get two?" I ask.

"No, it's better if we all huddle under one," Riley says. "It's cozier."

I can't help but think that my daughter is trying to create a family out of the three of us. Maybe I'm reading too much into it. We were going to end up watching a movie, even if Fisher wasn't here.

But he *is* here.

I take a seat next to Riley, and I can feel Fisher watching me. It's strange having him here with me and my daughter together. And at the same time, it's entirely comfortable.

Fisher's resting his arm on the back of the couch, and he reaches out his hand like I should hold it. I lean back, resting my head in his palm, wanting the connection but unable to hold hands with him in front of Riley. We're already at complicated. We don't need to shoot straight past it.

After an hour and a half of *Brave*, all the popcorn has been eaten, plus too much of my favorite chocolate and half a bag of marshmallows. Fisher and I have shared at least a dozen smiles and glances, and I'm one glass of wine away from asking him to move in.

"What next, Mom?" Riley asks, throwing the blanket off us all.

"Well… what about one of the games Fisher brought?" I suggest.

"Let's see." She heads off to nose through the bag.

"You okay?" I ask him. He's probably hating this. People without kids usually max out of kid-friendly activities pretty quickly, no matter how enthusiastic they are to start with.

"I know," Riley says, holding a Monopoly box. "We should have a kitchen disco and then a board game."

Fisher looks horrified, and I can't help but laugh.

"Great idea," I say. "You figure out the music. I'll clear the furniture. Can you get the other end of the couch, Fisher?"

He leaps off the couch. "Where are we clearing it to?" He glances around at our small open living area. There are not many places it will go, but we don't need a big space.

"Just over there a bit. It gives us a dance floor."

Vivan Cross' latest, "But Baby, I Love You," starts up, and I grab Riley's hand and we dance. We've been doing this since she was a toddler. Sometimes I needed a reset when the day was a flurry of diapers and crying. Sometimes she needed to burn off some energy. And as she's gotten older, it's become a way we have fun together. Riley gets to play her favorite music and it's something we share. A continuing bond as she grows.

I spin her around, and then we shimmy before rocking out with some tap stepping.

Fisher's just watching us, grinning, like he's not quite sure what he's looking at.

"Come on, Fisher," I call. "Come and dance!"

Riley goes and grabs his hand and pulls him onto the dance floor. I don't think for a moment he'll join us, but he does. He spins Riley around and around until she's dizzy, then totally geeks out with the hitchhiker and the twist, like he's some kind of grandad.

Riley insists on teaching him some moves, and then like magic, he's dancing along normally. Although "normal" isn't a word I'd associate with Fisher. He's fun and kind and sexy as hell. Plus, the man can move. But I knew that already.

The track ends and "Single Ladies" comes on. It's a favorite of Riley's and mine.

"Mom," Riley calls over the music. "I don't know if you can dance to this anymore. Not while Fisher's in town."

My heart stops for a second and my jaw hangs open. I don't know how to react.

Of course, Fisher comes to my rescue. He grabs my hand and spins me around, pulling me out of my shocked trance.

"Riley, it's illegal not to dance to this song, even if you're not single. And even if you're not a lady." He thrusts his left hand in the air and twists it in time to the music and for a second I wonder if he has the entire routine memorized.

After a couple more songs, I'm exhausted, and I collapse on the couch and watch as Fisher and Riley continue the kitchen disco.

I've never seen my daughter look so happy, and I've never felt more complete.

TWENTY-EIGHT

Fisher

Today is the day. I've spent long enough trying to explain away Gerry Banks' behavior. Today, I'm going to look him in the eye and tell him I'm onto him.

I'm pacing in my lodge, waiting for the call from Byron. To occupy myself, I think about dancing around Juniper's living area with her and Riley yesterday. I have plenty of fun in New York, but I can't remember ever feeling so completely free and unselfconscious. Not in a long time. I've had a relatively high profile for a number of years in New York and I run a business connected to a lot of even more high-profile people. I have to be cautious. I don't want anything I do to impact the artists I work with. But there's no one to take any notice in Star Falls, let alone when it's just me, Juniper, and Riley.

I've always prided myself on being authentic and open, but hanging out with Juniper and her daughter makes me realize that even I have a game face. And I wear it most of the time.

A hammering at the door pulls me out of my thoughts. I swing the door open and come face-to-face with Byron.

"He arrived about an hour ago," he says, without introduction. "He and Mr. and Mrs. Franklin are having coffee and snacks in the upper lounge area."

"Is it busy up there?" I planned to bump into him and then put him under some pressure. I want him to know I'm onto him and there'll be no more Mr. Nice Guy, no more ignoring the way he's trying to steal the artists I've discovered and nurtured. I'm going to tell him if it doesn't stop, I'm going to target him right back.

"There are always people up there."

I nod. That's understandable. The views from up there are the best in the Club. "I want to seize the moment. But at the same time, I don't want a big public showdown."

Byron steps over the threshold of my lodge and closes the door. "Grab your key and your phone and let's go. You're not going to have a big public showdown. You're simply going to let him know he's not going to fuck with you anymore."

Byron's right. Neither Gerry nor I are the type to make a scene. We're both far too focused on our business.

"You need to seize the day. Do this now. I'll walk you up there and I'll keep Mr. and Mrs. Franklin talking while you speak to Gerry."

We head over to the main building and my heart begins to race. If this was just one record executive being competitive with another about an artist, there would be no conversation to have at all, but this is different. Gerry's been coming after me, on and off, for years, and I just don't know why. But he needs to back off.

I see the back of his head as we enter the lounge. Having Byron to occupy Gerry's friends means that I can speak with him privately without pulling him to one side. It will look fairly friendly, but I'll be able to tell him exactly what I want to.

"Byron." Two people who I presume are Mr. and Mrs. Franklin stand as soon as they spot us. "How wonderful to see you. We didn't know if we'd get to see you on this trip." I study Gerry out of the corner of my eye, still sitting on the couch. I can tell he's just realized I'm there and is working out how to play it when we're introduced.

Byron shakes both of their hands and then introduces me. "This is one of my closest friends, Fisher Right."

I shake their hands, grinning.

"And this is our good friend, Gerry Banks," Mrs. Franklin says, as Gerry stands.

"Oh, Gerry, this is a coincidence," I say. "Gerry and I go way back."

Gerry gives a faltering smile. "Fisher!" he says, as he composes himself. "So great to see you. You were the last person I was expecting to run into up here." He's been watching Vivian closely, but judging by his expression, he truly wasn't aware that I was here, too.

"It's a small world," Mrs. Franklin says. "Gerry found out we were coming and said he's wanted to visit since he saw the opening-night pictures."

"It's a beautiful place," Gerry says. "A real retreat. It surpasses all expectations."

"That's what we're aiming for," Byron says. "I wanted to ask you about your lodge," he says to Mr. and Mrs. Franklin. "How are you finding the access to the hot tub..."

As Byron engages the Franklins, I turn my attention to Gerry. "So, you're here to see if you can run into one of my artists, is that it?" I ask him. We might as well get directly to the point.

He narrows his eyes in mock confusion. "I'm sorry, what are you talking about?"

"You know exactly what I'm talking about," I say, my voice low. "You've done this to me ever since we met back at EMG. You're intent on stealing my artists."

Gerry guffaws, but slides a glance toward the Franklins, confirming that he's faking his laughter. "I'm just doing my job."

"But you don't do it to others," I say. "Just me. What is it? If you're trying to get my attention, Gerry, you have it. But this weird obsession with the artists I work with has got to stop."

He's silent for a beat. "This is business. I want to work with great artists. If I'm interested in your artists, you should be flattered."

Neither of us is mentioning Vivian. If he does, he'll give away that she's the reason he's here. And there's no way I'm going to betray Vivian's trust. Even if she's probably on her way to the helicopter by now. Vivian wrapped up the album a little earlier than planned and decided to head back to London, given her location has started to leak. She said she wanted to quit while she was ahead. She's a woman who knows what she wants and isn't afraid to go after it.

I shake my head. "This isn't about the artists. You know that. I know that. For some reason, you want to take what's mine."

He holds my gaze. It's like we're playing chicken. Is he going to admit what's going on or am I going to have to go further, cut deeper?

"I think you've got things the wrong way around. You had what's *mine*, and I'm just leveling the playing field."

"What?" I say. "Which artist that had any connection to you have I ever worked with?"

"I didn't say you worked with one of my artists."

"Right," I say. "Because I haven't. Deliberately so. I don't want anything to do with you. So what's your problem?"

When I look at him for answers, it's suddenly clear to me that this has nothing to do with business.

He pushes his hands into his pockets and shakes his head. "I think I'm going to go and finish unpacking. I'm feeling the altitude. Maybe I need to lie down," he announces in a louder voice, which catches Mrs. Franklin's attention.

"Gerry, are you okay?" she asks.

"I'm fine. I just need to get used to the altitude."

The whir of helicopter blades in the distance makes me smile. Vivian's gone now. Gerry's not even going to catch a glimpse of her. I know her departure isn't a complete victory for me. He won't give up on trying to poach Vivian and my other artists... but now he knows I'm going to be watching. I won't just stand by, trying to be the bigger person anymore.

Now, I'm fighting back.

TWENTY-NINE

Fisher

I hand Juniper a glass of wine and she pats the space next to her on the bench. "You look like you have a lot on your mind."

"Yeah, I just can't shake something Gerry said to me. It's probably bluster, but he said something about how I've taken something that's his, and how he's trying to level the playing field."

"He's trying to make things equal between you?" she asks, and leans her head on my shoulder.

"I suppose that's what he means by levelling the playing field, but why? What does he think I've done to him?"

"Have there ever been any romantic entanglements?" she asks. "Like maybe—and I'm not saying you knew—but maybe you dated his girlfriend, or maybe a girlfriend left him for you?"

I shake my head. "Gerry's been married since before I knew him."

"Huh. I thought for sure that would be it. Did you go to college together? Like, was he at your college and you didn't know? Maybe something happened there?"

"I was a geek at college," I say. "My mom and dad went through a really bad divorce just before I left for college, and I spent my college years a little dazed. Their divorce came out of nowhere, as far as I was concerned."

"I'm sorry, Fisher," she says, and slides her hand into mine.

"It was a long time ago," I say. "But it had lasting effects. I went off to college determined that I wasn't ever going to fake anything."

"What do you mean?" she asks.

I sigh and set down my wineglass. "I spent my entire childhood thinking my mom and dad were the happiest parents of all my friends. Some of my other friends used to have parents who argued all the time. Others never spent any time together. But my mom and dad seemed to genuinely love each other. We'd spend the weekends as a family doing stuff. Even as a teenager, my favorite thing to do was to hang out with my parents. How geeky was that? They were just so much fun. I look back on those days, and I just remember laughing and... like you and Riley when we were having the kitchen disco. Every day was like that."

"Sounds wonderful," Juniper says.

"It really was," I reply. "They made it wonderful."

"Do you know why they decided to divorce?"

Darkness gathers in my chest at the memories of the conversation around the kitchen table. "When they told me, it was as if they were telling me that we were moving house or something. Mom was still full of smiles. Dad was cracking jokes. It was all so... fake."

She squeezes my hand, like she wants to transfer her strength to me.

"I stopped believing what I saw from then on. I learned to read what was under the surface in people's words and actions."

"You stopped trusting people," she says. "Because if you can't trust your parents, who *can* you trust?"

"Exactly. So I was a bit of a loner in college. I kept to myself until I learned to operate in this new world where no one was who they said they were. Music was my sole companion."

"Oh, Fisher," she says. "That sounds terribly lonely."

It *was* lonely. It felt like when I left home, I took nothing with me. No sense of security. No understanding of what was right and wrong. No real ability to cope with the world. I didn't trust anyone and I didn't trust myself.

"It was at first. I grieved the old world through music and created a new one. At first, I couldn't listen to anything I associated with my parents, and that was everything I listened to before I got to college. It pushed me to look for new artists and new types of music. I became a musical gannet," I say on a laugh. "Looking for salvation through new music. And I found it. Music became my therapy." I blow out a breath. Thinking back to that time still stings.

"It wasn't until after college that things started to change," I say. "I figured out that I could be authentic, and so there must be others in the world capable of not faking it. I learned that I had to keep my circle of trust small, but still interact with the world knowing it was full of bullshitters who were pretending to be happy, competent, capable."

"But you work in the music industry. Isn't that all about image?"

"Right. But I know that. I learned how to keep my

distance from all the pretense. Emotional distance, anyway. I try and focus on the music. Because that's what I love. The rest of it... I have my shields up. The industry is full of people pretending to be someone they're not. And I don't just mean the artists. People are so desperate to ingratiate themselves with the artists that they'll bend and change depending on who they're talking to and what those people want."

"Sounds awful."

"It's actually okay, because it's so easy to spot. At least it is for me. It's so obvious. All I can control is myself. I know I'm authentic. And I expect nothing of anyone else."

"Fisher," she says, shifting and looking up at me. "That's still a very lonely place to be."

"Is it?" I ask. "I have great friends. It's not that I isolate myself. I'm just careful."

"And when we were dancing in the kitchen, having fun with Riley and me, like you did with your parents, did you think that was real?"

I sigh. "That's about as real as it gets. Kids can't fake stuff like that. And you?" I look into her trusting, open blue eyes. "You're exactly who you say you are." I press a kiss to her lips and her warmth travels through my body.

I pull back, and she snuggles in closer to me.

"I'm going to miss you," she says, echoing my thoughts.

"Me too." I don't know what else to say. Our lives are so different, lived at almost different ends of the country. I can't offer a compromise or any kind of long-distance connection. It just wouldn't work. And I won't lie to her. I refuse to pretend.

"If you're ever in New York, you should let me know," I say.

She lets out a laugh, because what I'm saying is ludicrous. We both know it, but I said it anyway. I said it because I mean it. I don't know why, but the idea of leaving without any possibility of ever seeing her again creates a slice of sadness that lodges in my gut. It doesn't feel right.

She doesn't ask me to call if I'm back in Star Falls, and I understand why. She doesn't want to be waiting for me to ride back into town. I get that. She needs to get on with her life, and I need to get on with mine.

"You never know," I say teasingly. "Grace Astor might tempt you to New York yet."

She doesn't say anything. Riley is her priority and Star Falls is her home. I get it all. I'm just pissed, honestly. Why did a woman I enjoy so much, the first woman I've ever been able to be one hundred percent myself with, turn out to have roots in a small town in Colorado? Why couldn't she be in an apartment in the East Village or even a walk-up in Brooklyn.

"How's Vivian?" she asks, changing the subject to safer ground.

"She left this morning. As I was talking to Gerry."

She lets out a half laugh. "That must have been satisfying."

"More than it should be. It's not like I can keep him away from her forever."

"She seems lovely. Not the kind of person who would go behind your back to talk to another label."

I let out a cynical laugh. "You're right. She doesn't seem like that kind of person. But most people will take a call or a meeting if it might mean it could earn them more money. That's just human nature."

"Well, it's not how we do things in Star Falls," she says.

I press a kiss to the top of her head. "I think that's probably true."

I think Rosey was right. Star Falls is a magical place. It's a place I'll be sad to leave, but I'll be forever grateful I got to spend some time here.

THIRTY

Juniper

Fisher told me I got the choose what we did tonight, our last night together. He suggested we take a helicopter ride over the mountains and he could arrange a dinner for us somewhere special.

The way I see it, there's nowhere as special as Star Falls.

"Really?" Fisher says as he pulls up outside Grizzly's. "This is where you want to go?"

"Are you saying there's something wrong with Grizzly's?" I ask, arching an eyebrow at him.

"Absolutely not. Best wings on earth."

"Right," I say. "Your favorite. You need to have the full Star Falls experience tonight. Who knows if you'll ever experience its magic again."

He grins at me like I'm the most thoughtful woman on the planet when all I've done is bring him to the local bar. "But this isn't the final destination tonight," I say. "So don't get too comfortable."

We head into the bar and Byron and Rosey are already

seated. "First, on your Star Falls experience: Wings, pool, and your best friend. What more could you want?"

He slides his hands around my waist and presses a kiss to my head. "You know a way to a man's heart."

My stomach flips when he says heart. Have I reached his heart? He's definitely in mine. I think he has been since the moment I laid eyes on him in Grizzly's all those months ago.

We're not just reliving Fisher's Star Falls experience. I'm reliving my Fisher experience.

"Did I ever tell you that I first saw you in Grizzly's? It was just around the time of the opening of the Club."

"You said," he says. "I still don't know how I didn't see you and hit on you immediately."

"Oh, I kept my distance. I wasn't... this is a small town, and I wasn't used to seeing a man I... seeing a man like you."

"Like me?" he asks.

I shrug, and Rosey runs over and pulls us both into a hug. "Hey, guys. You ready for pool?"

"I guess so," Fisher says. I don't know if there's a tinge of disappointment in his voice, but I hope not. This isn't the only place we're going to stop by tonight.

"We're going to beat you," Rosey says, pulling me along by the hand. "Boys against girls," she calls out.

I groan. I don't want to be in any game where I'm not on the same team as Fisher. I glance behind me to see Byron slapping Fisher on the back in commiseration, and then they follow us into the back.

"So, Fisher," Rosey says. "When are you next back in Colorado?"

"Rosey," I say. "Please, can we not talk about Fisher coming back to Colorado or me going to New York? Not tonight. Fisher and I have always been clear about what we are to each other. I want to just enjoy the evening. I want to have fun."

"What she said," Fisher says, and holds out his hand.

Byron chuckles at the frustrated expression on Rosey's face.

"It's just that you're so good together. And Byron said he's never seen Fisher so happy with a woman."

I pull in a breath and shake my head. I don't want to do this. I don't want to spend the evening telling Rosey all the reasons Fisher and I can't be together. It's too depressing. It's too much.

Rosey starts to say something else, and Byron steps between the two of us and walks her back to the other side of the room, whispering in her ear.

Fisher raises his eyebrows. I can't tell whether he's exasperated with Rosey or disappointed in me. Does he want to be convinced we can work?

"For the record," I say to him, so no one else can hear. "It's not because I'm looking forward to you leaving. We both just know the reality of the situation."

He pulls in a breath and pulls me into a hug. "Unfortunately, we do."

His body envelops me. He's so big and reassuring. It makes me feel like it's going to be okay. But I'm not sure if it is. Fisher's only been in my life a few weeks, but I can't even begin to think about the hole he'll leave when he's gone.

"Let's just try and stay in the moment." He releases me from his arms.

But I don't let go of him. I can't. I want to take each embrace, kiss, and touch and commit them to memory. I know when Fisher leaves, life's never going to be the same, and I'm going to want to bring out my memories of this time together for the rest of my life.

Eventually I let him go.

"Pool," I say.

"Don't forget wings."

I laugh. "How could I forget the wings."

After we win the two games, Rosey comes up to me and slings an arm around my shoulder. "I'm sorry for being a pain in the ass."

"That's okay. I know you only have good intentions."

"Honestly, I'm so happy I met Byron, and it's so completely unbelievable that I did. It shouldn't have worked and we had the odds stacked against us. It just makes me want the same thing for everyone in the world."

"I get that."

"Wanna meet me at Grizzly's again on Friday?" she asks. "Donna, Beth, Marge, and I are having a girls' night. Wanna join?"

I want to say yes. I like Rosey, and hell, I know I'll need a distraction. Mom will babysit. I'm just not sure I'll want to do much in the days following Fisher leaving. "That's so kind of you to invite me. I'll see if I can get a sitter."

"It's been great getting to know you while Fisher's been here."

"You too, Rosey."

I look over at Fisher chatting to Byron, and he turns to meet my gaze as if he could tell I was looking at him.

"Okay, we need to go now," I say. For a second, I expect him to suggest we stay for one more drink, but as soon as he starts in my direction, I wonder why I doubted he'd want to leave.

We head out and back into the truck. Fisher looks at me expectantly.

"Where else to go but the falls?" I ask.

"I was hoping you would say that," he replies.

"You must have guessed, given the cooler I had you load into the truck."

"I had a tiny inkling," he says, grinning as he puts Byron's truck into drive.

I roll down the window and the breeze that fills the cab is warm and full of summer.

"It's a perfect night," he says.

Is it, I think, but I don't say anything.

"Tell me what you're thinking?" he says.

I glance across at him and realize that me not saying how I'm feeling is what he fears most: people not showing him exactly who they are.

"What are *you* thinking?" I counter.

"I asked first." He smiles but there's a nervousness about it I'm not used to with Fisher. What's he scared of? That I'll tell him that I want him to stay? That I won't?

"I'm thinking that I wish AC in cars was never invented," I say, as we pull up to the parking area by the falls. "I think we should always have to wind our windows down in summer. I think it's good for the soul or something."

"Oh, yeah. I agree. Except not if you live in New York City. Then when you're stuck in traffic on Broadway, an open window is the last thing you need."

Immediately I start to wonder if he's saying more than his words. Is he telling me New York City isn't a place I'd want to go? Or is he saying he doesn't want to go back and needs a reason to say?

Maybe he's just thinking he doesn't want the windows down on a busy street.

He pulls out the cooler from the back of the truck and we head up the falls in thoughtful silence.

"Can I tell you something?" I ask him, as we take a seat on the blue checkered blanket I packed.

"Anything," he answers.

I hold his gaze as I speak, because I want these words to count. "I was also thinking that I'm really sad you're leaving. I was thinking how you've woken up a part of me I didn't realize was sleeping. I think you're a really good man. You're kind and funny. I'm proud to have known you these last few weeks. Grateful to have called you a friend. And flattered to have had you as my lover."

He reaches for my face and sweeps his thumb over my cheek. "I wish things were different," he says. "Not because I've regretted these last few weeks, but because things are going to end, and I'm not sure I'm ready."

A fist tightens around my heart. It's not just me.

He sighs. "I've been trying to think of ways—"

I press a finger over his lips. "Don't do that." I shake my head. "Don't give me hope."

He takes my hand from his lips and presses a kiss to my palm. "All we have is hope."

I shake my head. "After you leave, I have to bury every morsel of hope I have that you might come back. I don't think I can survive any other way."

"Oh, Juniper," he says, his voice a mixture of pity and longing.

He presses his lips against mine and I push my tongue against his. I want all of him. Now. I want to take as much as I can get, in the hopes that it will be too much and I'll wear it out, whatever this is between us. Because it has to be fleeting. It has to run out. I have to get to the end of it. The alternative is way too heartbreaking. If there is no end to what we have. If it were to go on indefinitely, then what I'm giving up is far more than I can cope with. It's a life I know I'd be forever happy in. A man who's perfect for me.

It would mean Fisher is the love of my life. And that's just unacceptable.

Our kisses are urgent and frantic, as we fumble to undress each other and ourselves. When we're finally naked, he gently guides me to my back and crawls over me. The warmth of the sun still rests in the ground below us. He presses kisses across my collarbones, one after another, like he wants to give me every last kiss he has.

I'll take them all.

I try and block out the sound of the falls behind us. It's a constant reminder of where we are and where he's going to leave. It's a ticking clock. A countdown to a time without him.

"Fisher, I need—"

He cuts me off. "I know," he says. He's not going to make me beg. Not now. He needs this as much as I do. He rolls on a condom and pushes into me. He doesn't need to check if I'm wet. I always am for him. He just needs to fuck me. We both need this.

He moves in and out, above me, our eyes locked. I want to stay like this forever but my body has other ideas. It's like he has some kind of manual on how to make my body respond. It's mental, but it's also physical. Sometimes when I'm with him, it feels like I'm not in control of the sensations inside my body. Like I'm a vessel for Fisher to do with what he wants.

"You feel so good," he whispers, as he thrusts into me so deep, the air leaves my lungs. "And I'm going to miss you so much. You feel like home," he whispers, voice rough as he sinks into me, like he's trying to memorize the way I feel from the inside out. "And I don't know how I'm supposed to walk away from that."

The words hit harder than any goodbye could. They crack something open in me.

I swallow the sob threatening to rise. I wanted this to be simple. Fun. Temporary. But he never played by those rules, and now I'm drowning in all the things we'll never get to be.

"Why couldn't this just have been about sex and a good time?" I whisper, my voice breaking. "Why couldn't this be easier?"

His forehead presses to mine, breath catching. "Because then it wouldn't have meant anything."

And it did. It means everything. Which is exactly why it hurts so much.

I reach around him and pull him toward me, his chest against mine, our skin pressed together, nothing between us.

This is the last time I'll feel him like this. I can't allow myself to think about how he might come back to the Colorado Club again. I won't do that to myself. Because once tonight is over, Fisher and I are done. If I find out he's in town, I'll be avoiding Grizzly's and his call. I know that it's going to be tough to watch him leave this time. I'm not going to get through it twice. Once will be torture enough.

THIRTY-ONE

My entire body is buzzing. It's half pleasure, half pain. Juniper beneath me is all curves and softness. Her skin feels like silk, and sliding inside her, pure heaven.

I've never had a woman own me physically in the way Juniper does. It's like every sense is multiplied by a hundred. Every move a thousand times more pleasurable because she's under me.

But it's too good. I don't think I can take any more.

Like she senses it, she shifts and nudges me over, so I'm on my back. She straddles me.

I think this is worse. Underneath her long hair, her breasts sway as she moves, her body is lit up by the moonlight. I squeeze my eyes shut in the hopes that I can keep a grip on what I'm feeling, but it's hopeless. It's as if an invisible thread is being wound around us and each second we're bonded closer and closer.

She grips my cock around the base and whimpers as it finds her entrance.

"Juniper," I choke out, my eyes flashing open because I can't *not* watch her sink onto my cock.

She sighs as she lowers herself, and I think I might explode right here and now, filling her up, making her mine.

But she already is mine. She's said as much. I don't know if it's because we've both known what we have is time limited, but we've formed a connection that feels years... decades deep. Maybe even lifetimes.

From the moment I met her, I've known there's no guard up, there's no game face, no façade. I don't think I've ever felt so sure of anyone.

She lifts her hands to her head, sweeping back her hair, the tendrils revealing her naked breasts like the lifting of a curtain. Somehow, she secures her hair behind her.

"Fuck," I spit out. "Thanks for that."

She smiles, cupping her breasts in her hands, then taking my hands and replacing hers. They're heavy and firm and her nipples are red, sharp, and greedy, desperate for attention.

I flick them with my thumbs and she moans, sinking lower as she widens her legs.

She starts to shift, small intense movements, my dick deep inside her, like she's milking me. Her walls tighten as she pulses over and over, and I can see my orgasm in front of me like a sheet of glass and I'm about to drive headlong into it.

I'm not ready.

Not this quickly. Not tonight. Not now.

I grip her waist and still her.

She tilts her head like she's questioning me.

"It feels too good," I say. "I don't want to come. Not yet."

She groans, twisting her hips.

"Fuck," I splutter out on a laugh. "You're incredible."

"You make me feel incredible," she says.

I push her up, slowly, gently, trying to take back control of this situation so I don't come too quickly. She twists and flicks her hips, sliding me deep within her again.

"I want you to come," she says in a breathy whisper. "I want to know you feel as helpless against the pleasure I can give you. Just the way I feel whenever you touch me."

"Juniper," I groan, my arms flopping down beside me in surrender.

She slides her palms over my chest and starts to move in a relentless rhythm, her hips slide and circle, and all I can do is lie there as she rides my cock. Her hair begins to escape a little as she moves, the strands falling, stroking her body. All of a sudden I'm jealous. When I'm gone, they'll still be able to touch her.

My jaw tightens at the thought.

And then her movements get faster, like she's trying to get to the end of the race.

"Juniper," I call out.

"I want you to come, Fisher." Her tone is desperate and needy and I want to give her anything she wants.

My entire body tenses, I smash into the wall of my orgasm, and unable to stop myself, I thrust up, up, up into her.

She's shaking above me, her orgasm set off by mine, her head's back as she cries my name over and over.

"Don't stop," she calls out. "Please don't stop!"

I know what she needs. It's the same thing I need. More. She needs to know she's gotten all that she possibly can.

I pull her off me, and lay her down next to me while I dispose of one condom and roll on the next. I don't know how I'm hard enough, but Juniper makes anything possible. Settling down beside her, I pull her back toward me so we're on our sides and her back is against my front. I push her top leg forward and press my cock against her. She shakes as I circle my tip around the entrance.

"You want more?" I ask her in a whisper.

"Yes. Everything," she pants back in response.

I slide into her, long and slow. She groans like she's feeling me for the first time and she's never felt anything so good. I'm so hard, I'm dizzy from lack of blood flow to my brain. I lean back slightly and I can see where we join, where she surrenders to my cock. The condom glistens with her wetness as I pull out.

I hook my hands over her shoulders and I drive up into her.

"Yes," she pants. "Like that."

I slide my hands around her waist now, one finding her pussy. She's all wetness. All over her. As my fingers find her clit, she calls out and tries to pull my hand away.

"No," I chastise her. "You're going to come now. But you don't need to worry. I'm not going to stop fucking you. I'm going to keep going until you're begging me to let you come again."

I push into her and she dissolves, shuddering on my cock. I do exactly what I say I'm going to do and I keep fucking her. I keep playing with her clit, even though she tries to move away, I hold her firmly in place. "You're not going anywhere."

"Yes," she chokes out. "Yes. Yes. Yes."

Fuck. Her words. The desperate tinge to her voice. It's too much. The pull of her around me, the slipperiness of her clit. It's sheer perfection.

"Fisher!" she whimpers. "I'm—"

"No coming," I snap. "You greedy girl."

I thrust up into her, harder now, wanting to push her right to the brink.

"Please," she says.

"Breathe deeply," I say as I slam into her. "No coming."

I feel her insides shudder as she tries to pull in a full breath. "Fisher. I'm trying."

"You're such a good girl." My voice is low and tight as the words slip out from my clenched jaw.

It's as if I've located my autopilot switch, and I'm no longer in control of my own body. I lift her knee up, trying to get deeper, wanting to take everything from her, hoping tonight might last me a lifetime.

"Fisher," she calls out.

"You can come for me now."

She cries out in gratitude and her orgasm tears through her body like it's the last time she'll ever come. At the same time, my orgasm appears like the roar of an escaped dragon, thrashing its tail, knowing it's finally free.

Except I don't feel free. I feel bound. To her.

I wrap my arms around her, our breaths sharp as we pant, desperate for air.

Her body rises and falls with mine as we both try to descend back into reality.

"Make me a promise," she says as our breathing returns to normal.

"Anything," I say, and in that moment, I mean it.

"Promise me that at the end of tonight, we can pretend that I'll see you tomorrow. I don't want to say goodbye."

I tighten my arms around her. "I promise. You're incredible. You've changed me forever," I confess. "I didn't realize I'd ever be able to feel... like this." She's asked me not to give her hope. I get that. There's no point. And I don't want to make our situation feel more biting than it already does, but I owe her the truth. I want her to know that she's come to mean more to me in a few weeks than any woman ever has. "You are talented and kind and I'm... you're the kind of woman—"

She shifts, and it stops me in my tracks. She turns in my arms and we lock eyes. She shakes her head and presses her lips against mine, stopping me from saying any more. Stopping me from telling her how my heart feels like it's cracking in two at the thought of leaving. Stopping me from telling her that I think I'm in love with her.

I don't know what's worse—having to live with knowing I love someone I can't be with or never having met them in the first place.

There's no point in railing against inevitability. I press my lips against hers and allow myself to melt into the moment.

THIRTY-TWO

Juniper

I can't get myself together today. The morning routine usually runs like a well-oiled machine, but today I feel like I'm trying to catch water in a colander. All I can think about is Fisher driving off in Byron's truck after he'd dropped me home last night, and he yelled out the window, "See you tomorrow."

We promised each other no goodbyes. And he fulfilled his promise.

His words still hit like a sucker punch to my gut, and I collapsed on the porch crying.

I've just got to get through the next few days. I need to put on a brave face for Riley until the weekend and then I can retreat and... regroup. Rebuild myself.

"Do you have your backpack?" I yell. "And did you brush your teeth?"

Riley bounds out of her bedroom, baring her teeth. "Teeth are clean and backpack is by the door." She skirts around me, heading into the kitchen.

I turn, following her. "And what about your lunch—"

She's already at the refrigerator. "Got it, Mom. What's with you this morning?"

I shake my head and grab my keys and sunglasses. "Nothing. I just didn't sleep very well."

"You'll be able to sleep in this weekend." Riley's excited that her dad is back in Star Falls, starting on Saturday for the start of Riley's summer vacation. It couldn't have come at a better time. I need to get into the studio and let out all my feelings onto the canvas. Then maybe all these conflicting feelings I'm having about Fisher will stop churning inside me. "Are you going to paint?" she asks.

"Come on," I say, heading out the door. "We need to leave for school."

"But, Mom, are you going to paint?" She looks a little distressed.

"Yeah. I guess. Why?"

"I'm going to be with Dad for nearly two whole weeks when school is closed. You won't have work to keep you busy, and I don't want you to be lonely. Especially now that Fisher's gone."

My heart snags at her concern for me. I ruffle her hair and nod toward the car.

Riley said her goodbyes to Fisher when he came to pick me up for our final date last night. He handled it expertly, just telling her that he'd see her around. I think she expects that he'll be back next week. But he won't, and I need to come to terms with that.

"I'll be fine," I say reassuringly. "It's not like tidying up this place is going to take me an hour. I have plenty to do. Don't you worry about that."

She grins at me as she gets into the back seat. "Dad says we can go fishing."

"He's taking you to the lake?"

"Yeah, and he says we can camp and stay overnight and stuff."

Shit. He should have discussed that with me. He's not exactly a mountain man. I'm not sure if he's capable of spending the night in a tent. He was always very particular about his bedtime routine.

"Wow," I say. "That sounds like fun. So long as it doesn't rain."

"It won't rain."

I laugh. There's nothing that beats a child's optimism. If her dad has promised her a camping trip, then he's going to have to follow through. I've seen that expression in Riley's eyes before. She'll be staying in a tent on her own if she has to.

I make a mental note to order a few things that might make an overnight stay a little more child friendly. And also to talk to Riley's dad about the location of this proposed trip. I need to understand if he's properly thought this through.

"You know how much I've wanted to camp."

Did I? I've never heard Riley mention camping before. There are a thousand new obsessions every week, it seems.

I put the car into drive and we head out in the direction of the school. "Did you remember your lunch, Mom?" she asks from the back seat.

I sigh. It's still in the refrigerator. "I'm grabbing something with Miss Peters today," I lie, referring to another of the teaching assistants. She doesn't need to know her mother's a mess this morning.

"Oh. Cool. Wouldn't it be good if Dad came to Star Falls during school one time? Then I could show him my classroom. He's never seen inside. Not even last year."

"Yeah. That would be fun. But you know he doesn't

want to share you with school," I say. Fact is, her dad could come to Star Falls more often. Frankly, if Riley's schooling was important to him, he could have arrived a few days early and arranged a meeting with her teacher. But he leaves all that to me. He always has. At least this way, I'm on top of everything.

"Did he send you his flight details yet?" Riley asks.

"Not yet, sweet girl. But he will."

"I just don't know if he's going to be here in the morning, or will I have to wait until the afternoon?"

Last time Riley's dad visited, I picked him up from the airport. It was Riley's idea. She wanted to meet him with a banner. I agreed her father coming into town should be an exciting event. I hoped that it would help mitigate the fact that his visits are so infrequent.

My phone buzzes and my stomach turns inside out. For a split second, I think it might be Fisher. But of course it won't be. We agreed that when he left Star Falls, we'd have a clean break. There was no way of continuing our relationship, and I didn't want to have false hope or be disappointed when he said he was coming to town and then didn't, or said he'd call and then got caught up with his life back in New York. A clean break is better. For both of us. It won't be Fisher that's texting me, even though a part of me wants to hear from him.

It will be lunchtime in New York City soon. I wonder if he eats lunch in his office. Or maybe he eats out a lot? Maybe even every day. I think that's common in New York. Or maybe he prefers to have lunch at his desk. Or with his team? I have so many unanswered questions. Things I'll never know now.

"Mom," Riley yells, pulling me out of my thoughts.

"Sorry, what did you say?"

"I said do you think we'll have to memorize spelling during the vacation? Because if we do, I don't think I should take them to Dad's. I don't think we'll have time to do them."

"Right," I say. "We can just do them when you come back."

"We'll have plenty of time. I'll be able to spend the entire rest of the summer with you."

"I know, sweet girl. I want you to have fun with your dad." I turn into the school grounds and find my normal parking space.

Riley spots the message on my phone. "Mom, Dad sent you a message. Please can I see it?" she asks. "I bet it's the time of his flight."

"It probably is," I say, opening the text as Riley looks over my shoulder.

But it's not the time he's going to land tomorrow.

I scan the text, taking in snippets.

I'm not going to make it.

Fiona's sick.

Tell Riley I'll make it up to her.

I press the side button on my phone to make the screen go blank, but I'm pretty sure I'm too late.

I turn, and the expression on her face crumbles my broken heart into pieces.

"Mom?" she says. "Dad's not coming?" Her tone is hopeless and dripping with disappointment.

I clamber out of the car and slide into the back seat next to Riley. I undo her seat belt and pull her onto my lap. "I don't know. Let me read it properly."

With Riley sitting on my lap, I open the phone and read the text in full. She's seen the worst of it. There's no point hiding it now.

It's even worse than I first thought. He's not coming, and he's not going to be able to reschedule because of prior commitments. Wasn't *Riley* his ultimate prior commitment? Everything else in his life seems to come before her since he moved to Florida.

"Mom, that means I won't see him all summer. I'll be nine before I see him again!"

I pull her against me, trying to provide a little comfort. There's nothing I can say that's going to make this better. Nothing I can do. Her father doesn't put her first. I have no idea what that must feel like, what that must do to her brain. To her heart. But it breaks mine.

"I'm so sorry, sweet girl." I press a kiss to the top of her head and I don't let go, even though it means we're both going to be late to class. It's on days like this that I wish I had a different job. One where I wasn't in the same school as Riley. I could take the day off and keep Riley home with me. I'm inches away from getting back in the driver's seat, driving us both home and putting on a movie.

This isn't fair to her.

Life isn't fair.

"Mommy, I don't want to go to school. And I don't want to see Daddy ever again! You can't make me."

I close my eyes. I wish I could take away the pain she feels. If she hadn't seen the text, maybe I could have called him and given him hell. Told him he needed to step it up or he'd lose his daughter's love and respect. He's going to get that call from me anyway. But it won't take away the disappointment Riley feels now. That's what I want to do. Scoop up her pain and bury it deep in the mountainside, where it will never surface again. Riley deserves better.

This is exactly why I didn't want to date after Riley's dad and I broke up. I didn't want another man in her life to let her down. One is plenty. My heart breaks for her, and I hope against hope that she doesn't learn to love men who let her down and leave her. I don't want her to have to go through this any more than once. With her dad.

In that moment, I'm grateful Fisher left when he did. I'm pleased there's no hope that he's ever coming back. That way, he can't hurt Riley. He can't hurt me.

THIRTY-THREE

Fisher

I used to spend a lot of time in the Met, but as I take the steps from the exit, I realize it's been years since I've visited. And after my tour today, I wonder why.

The three days since I've landed back in New York have been miserable. I've become an expert at putting on a happy face, but all I think about is Juniper. I hoped the Met might help somehow. I thought that maybe I'd feel closer to her. But all I thought about as I made my way around is how I wished she and Riley were here. How we could have had brunch and then spent the entire afternoon wandering around. Juniper would be able to tell me about the works. I'd see her light up in the way that she does when she's around art or talking about art.

But she's not here. Neither is Riley.

I hail a cab and the knot in my stomach intensifies. A New York cab has always brought me a weird sense of freedom. When I first arrived in the city, I took a cab up Broadway and I felt like I was finally home after feeling out of place during my college years—probably because my mom and dad's divorce threw me for such a loop, I didn't know which way was up. But today, it's just me and this huge city that has been home for so many years... and for the first time ever, I feel like I don't belong here.

Thankfully, I'm meeting Bennett, Worth, and Jack tonight. They'll help me take my mind off things. I always belong with them.

My phone buzzes. It's a message from Jack.

Change of plans. We're going to my club. See you there.

I tell the driver of the change in destination. We're only a few blocks away. The sooner I get there, the better. I'm clinging to the hope that when I see my friends, I'll start to feel better. I'll start to heal.

Jack's club is like something out of the start of the twentieth century. It's all tall columns and gold leaf. I've been to a lot of private members clubs all over Manhattan. The artists I work for have belonged to every single one in the city. Except for Jack's. You don't get into this place without lineage and old money. Both things Jack has in spades.

I climb the steps, give my name at the reception desk, and I'm shown to one of the lounges. Jack and Bennett are already there.

They stand and we hug. It feels like forever since I've seen them. I know it's only been a few weeks since I've seen Jack, but so much has happened since it feels like a lifetime.

"You look like shit," Bennett says.

I force a grin. "Thanks, mate."

"I mean it. Are you sleeping?"

"Why wouldn't I be sleeping?" I ask, glancing over at the bar. In seconds, someone is taking my drinks order. Thank god. I need a beer—something to take the edge off.

I glance back at my friends and they're both staring at me, concern in their expressions.

"We know you really enjoyed your time in Star Falls," Bennett says.

"Right," I reply. "But it was always temporary and now I'm back home."

An unfamiliar silence passes between us.

"How's Juniper?" Jack asks.

"No idea," I say, as if the words don't cut into me like the sharpest of blades.

"You can talk to us," Jack says. "We're here for you."

Thankfully, Worth arrives, taking the attention from me. But my reprieve doesn't last long.

"How are you?" he asks, slapping me on the back. "Missing Juniper?"

"Guys, you're acting like I just lost my dog or something. I'm fine." I take a deep breath. I'm talking bullshit. These guys are my best friends in the world. Why am I putting on a brave face with them? They're here to support me. To listen to me. To help. "I'm *going* to be fine. I'm just... I didn't expect to... Juniper was special, and it's going to take me a minute to adjust."

"Did you and Juniper ever talk about maybe continuing things long distance?" Bennett asks.

"No point. Her entire life is in Star Falls. Her kid. Her family. Her job. And my life is here. It's not like we could ever be... anything." I blow out a breath and take a swig of my beer. The logical response that I've had in my arsenal for all these weeks sounds less and less convincing. Not because our circumstances have changed. But because of who she became to me. They say love conquers all. But whoever said that is a bullshitter.

"There are plenty of people who date long distance and

then the compromises are easier to make further down the road," Worth suggests.

"I can see that," I concede. "But not for Juniper and me. She's lived her entire life in Star Falls. She's never going to leave. Hell, I suggested she and Riley join me when I came back to New York for a couple of nights, and she wouldn't come. And as much as Star Falls is a beautiful place, I can't run my business from there."

I know what they're thinking. I don't need to work. It's true. I've made my money, but business isn't always about making money. It's about purpose. It's about direction.

"And it's not just about my company. It's also New York." I sigh. Except right now, I feel like New York doesn't fit somehow. Like I don't belong. But I know if I were away too long, I'd miss it. I'd miss the energy and the life. The possibilities.

"Rosey and Byron seem to have found a good compromise," Worth says. "Spending time in Star Falls and New York."

"It's different. Byron grew up in Star Falls. He has roots there. And anyway, Juniper has never even visited New York. She wouldn't even come here for two nights. Let alone split her time between here and Star Falls." I shake my head. "Anyway, we weren't even close to talking about stuff like this. We always knew we had a shelf life. It wasn't ever meant to be some great love affair for six weeks."

Worth starts to speak, but before he can get the words out, we all groan.

"We know, Worth," Jack says. "You fell in love with Sophia the first moment you met her and married her as quickly as you could."

I'd never thought Worth ever did anything that wasn't meticulously considered and planned before he married

Sophia. When they announced they were married, I thought he might have a brain tumor or something, it was so out of character. He was so convinced that he loved her from the moment he'd met her. And now? Having spent nearly six weeks with Juniper? Worth marrying Sophia when he hardly knew her doesn't seem so crazy.

Juniper and I connected in a way where I felt like I could see into her soul, and I let her into mine.

"I'm not trying to be insensitive," Worth says. "Only encouraging. If you love Juniper, isn't it worth trying to figure it out?"

I groan again. I can't deny loving her. Not to these guys.

"If it's meant to happen, it will," Worth says. "Maybe you need to take a week or two and see how you feel."

I nod. That's the best advice I've had yet. I'm not sure I've ever had my heart broken. Maybe this is what it feels like. I've not been on this journey, and I don't know where to turn, but maybe things will feel easier as the days and weeks pass. I can't imagine how, but I have to cling to the possibility that there will come a day when I don't yearn for Juniper like I do at this moment.

THIRTY-FOUR

I think I have the sweetest, most empathetic little girl in the world. She insisted on joining one of her friends at a day camp today. She said she wanted me to paint. I told her I wanted to hang out with *her*, but she said the day camp was amazing when some kids from her school went during spring break. Apparently, they spend the entire day outside, building forts and I don't know what else. Even though I think she somehow feels guilty for not being with her father, almost like she was some kind of burden to me when nothing could be further from the truth, I let her go. It might take her mind off her dad.

Riley has lost some of her spark since her father announced he was postponing his visit to see her. He's dodged my calls and hasn't responded to my texts. I hate it when she's faced with the truth—that she's not her father's priority. It's heartbreaking to see her be let down over and over.

I see her head among the kids coming out of camp to

greet their parents, and then I hear her laugh. It's so full of life, so clear and joyous, I can almost catch it with both hands.

She bounds toward me, grinning. "Mommy." She turns to a girl beside her and whispers and then giggles. I can't remember having seen this girl before.

Her mood is infectious and I can't help but be lifted up by her. Today in the studio has been more difficult than usual. I never have to muster up creativity, but today, it felt like all my limbs were coated in tar and my brain was stuck.

Riley's father.

Fisher.

It's just too much swirling around in my head. Seeing my daughter so happy pushes everything else to the side.

"Hey, sweet girl. How was your day?"

"We had so much fun," she says. "This is Emma. She's my best friend now. We're probably going to go to college together."

I nod. "Good to know."

"Can I come again tomorrow?" she says. "Emma is here all week. I know it's a lot of money, but, Mommy, we made a fire. Tomorrow they're learning how to fish."

"I don't know if they have a place," I say, glancing around to see if I can spot the supervisor.

"Please, Mommy! I'm sure they have a place. They had one today."

I don't waste time telling her that's not the way these things work. I just head over to the woman in charge and ask.

There's a spare slot, and I put Riley's name down. Another little girl I don't recognize with beautiful dark brown eyes comes over to her and they talk excitedly about how they're going to catch a huge fish tomorrow and how that will look great on college applications.

What's the obsession with college? She's got a minute before I become an empty nester.

When we get in the car, Riley straps herself in and announces, "Emma's brother just went to college."

"Ahh," I say, things falling into place. I pull out of the parking lot and head back home.

"He's in college in New York. So that's where Emma and I are going."

"New York, huh?" My stomach aches a little at her mention of the place where Fisher is right now. I thought I'd be over it by now. If I had any inkling that him leaving would hurt this bad, I'd never have had that first pool game with him.

I just have to give it time. The pain and longing is bound to fade. It has to.

"Yeah. NYU," Riley says. "That stands for 'New York University.' You see, Mommy? NYU—New York University."

"Super cool," I say. "But you've never been to New York. It's a big city. Maybe you won't like it."

"I've seen it on the TV. It looks very... all the women have really nice clothes and their hair is very pretty."

And Fisher is surrounded by them all, every day.

"Yeah. And there's lots of traffic and no lakes to fish in."

"No lakes? Or mountains?"

"No, you have to drive a long way to find a lake or a mountain if you live in New York."

I watch her in the rearview mirror. Her brow is furrowed. "That's okay," she says. "Star Falls will always be home. I can come back here if I want to fish."

I smile at her perfect solution. "Don't you forget it. You gotta promise you'll come back and visit me."

Riley laughs. "Don't be silly, Mommy. You'll be in New York, too. You'll move with me when I go to college, won't you?" She stares into the mirror, waiting for my response.

"Sure, honey." She's got a decade to change her mind, but in this moment, I'm very grateful Byron's designer bought so many of my paintings for the Colorado Club and I have the money from that tucked away in a college fund for Riley. I'm going to need it if she sets her sights on NYU.

"It will be an exciting adventure," she says. "Dad left Star Falls, and he likes it a lot where he lives. We're going to have the best time in New York!"

My heart crumples a little at her mention of her father. Is that part of why she's talking about college in New York? She wants to know what's so exciting past the mountains of Colorado that would keep a father away from a daughter? Maybe. Maybe she's just caught up with the fantasies of a new friend. Either way, it's good to see her happy.

"Fisher's in New York too, right?" she asks, and my stomach falls through the floor.

"Right," I say, trying to fake a breezy tone.

"We could see him then."

"Who knows," I reply, trying to keep my voice light.

"And they have a lot of concerts there. And there's a big park and I'm sure there are trees to climb. Maybe even a lake."

I sigh as she chatters on about New York. I've never heard her even mention a place outside of Star Falls. This place has been her world for her entire life. It's strange to hear her talking about spreading her wings. She's still so little. I still have the desire to shelter her and keep her safe. But maybe that will never change. Maybe this is the next stage of pretend play. She's moved on from baby dolls and is seeing herself walking down Fifth Avenue with pretty hair and fancy clothes.

"When we get home, can I tell Grandma that we're going to live in New York? If she's upset, we can tell her we'll visit. We'll come back every holiday."

"Right," I say. "Every holiday."

Star Falls will always be her home, no matter how far away she is.

THIRTY-FIVE

Fisher

Listening parties are part of the drill as a record company executive. But I haven't ever enjoyed a listening party like I have tonight's. Vivian's new album—her first with Right Records—has been played in public tonight for the first time. Kinda. There have been a couple of "leaks" on YouTube to try to create buzz. People have gone wild for what they've heard so far. My gut tells me it's only going to get better. I think this is the album of the decade. Tonight will only fuel the buzz.

The party should have finished an hour ago, but it's still in full swing. The excitement in the air is palpable. I've been to a number of listening parties where you know from people's reaction that the album is going to bomb. Tonight has been the exact opposite of that. Judging by people's reactions, this is going to be the album of her career. And that's saying something. Vivian's already a global superstar.

"Hey, Fisher." Tommy, Vivian's manager, comes up and

slaps me on the back. "I heard you got a producer credit on this album?"

I chuckle. "Maybe. I was in the studio a little. Couldn't resist giving a little bit of input here and there." I don't know if it was something in the air in Star Falls. Maybe it was spending time with Juniper. But I really enjoyed getting back into the creative side of the music industry. That was the part I always loved, but over the years, as I've gotten more and more successful, that side of things has become further and further away. This album brought me back to my roots.

"Well, it sounds great. It's a more mature sound from Vivian," he says. "It suits her, and I think she'll widen her audience with it."

"Her audience is pretty wide already," I say, as I spot Jack on the other side of the room. I didn't realize he was coming tonight. All my friends were invited, but Jack never comes to these sorts of things. He's standing with Byron and Rosey. It's nice to have them here, supporting me. Just like they always do.

Someone taps me on the shoulder, and I snap my head around.

"Hey, super-producer," Vivian says, grinning at me.

"Congratulations, Vivian," Tommy says.

"Thanks, Tommy. As you know, I had a blast recording this album. I think it shows."

"It feels very authentic," he says. "It's going to be huge."

She smiles, and I can tell it's forced. I don't think Vivian cares much what people think of her music. She knows she enjoys writing, recording, and performing.

Someone approaches Tommy, leaving Vivian and I to speak. "You should be proud of yourself. It's a great achievement. I think you're going to see critical and commercial success with this one. Tommy's right."

She smiles again, and this time it's genuine. "Yeah, I hope so. Although, you know, getting to make the record that I want to make, with good people. The fact that these lyrics are lyrics I've written—sometimes with help, but even so... It feels so good. I finally get to have the career *I* want. And you know what? That only happened when I met Beau. He gave me the confidence to go for what I wanted."

"Sounds like husband material," I joke.

"He's a good one."

"Wasn't it such a shock to move to England?"

She shrugs. "Not really. His family is the best. They're almost as much of a draw for me as Beau himself." She laughs. "But I love London. And I get to come back to the US all the time. I'm living the best of both worlds, so I can't complain."

"I'm happy *you're* happy."

"Oh, and you know Gerry called me the other day."

My stomach churns at the mention of my nemesis. "Really?"

"I know. He's relentless. Anyway, I told him I wouldn't meet him for lunch. I also told him I'm happy at Right Records."

"That's good to hear. That you're happy with us." I pause. "And that you wouldn't meet him for lunch."

She laughs. "Why would I waste my time? Speaking of, let's start talking about the next album."

"We should definitely do that," I reply.

Before I can tell her that I'll talk to Tommy and get the ball rolling, we're interrupted by Efa and Bennett. Efa and Vivian squeal and pull each other into a hug.

"It's been too long," Efa says. "I miss you. I miss everyone in London. Tell me everything? Where's Beau?"

"Remind me how you two are connected," I say.

"We're family," Vivian says. "Beau's brother Jacob is married to Efa's sister, Eira."

"I think I'm more confused now," I confess.

"My brother-in-law is also Efa's brother-in-law." Vivian turns to Efa. "Is that right?"

Efa narrows her eyes like she's thinking. "Maybe. It's complicated."

"It gets worse during the holidays."

"And now I'm your sister-in-law, Fisher, you're basically family with Vivian, too."

I grin at Efa's assertion that Bennett's my brother. She gets it.

Jack and Bennett come over and join us, with Vivian's husband, Beau. Jack pulls me to one side. "You know I said I'd get my family's security team to look into Gerry," he says. "Well, they've found a few things I thought you should know." He holds up a flash drive.

"You want to email it to me?"

He shakes his head. "I always assume if I email something, it's going to get into the public domain. This file is encrypted. I'm not sure if you'll want this getting out."

Jack's acting like he's part of the CIA, but he looks serious.

"What is it?" I ask him. I glance around. The party's finally winding down. The place is less busy than it was even ten minutes ago.

"I wouldn't have mentioned it here if I didn't think you'd want to know right away. I want you to enjoy your night. But I don't want to keep this from you, either."

"What *is* it, Jack?"

He pulls in a breath. "I have a laptop in the car if you want to see it now?"

I expect to come back into the party, so I don't say any goodbyes before I leave. I just follow Jack down to the limo that's waiting at the bottom of the stairs to the hotel. Of *course* Jack has a limo idling at the curb. He's Jack Alden.

I slide into the back on one side and he gets in the other side. Without saying a word, he plugs the flash drive into the laptop, puts in the various passwords, and then brings up the file on the drive.

He hands the laptop to me.

The file is headed "Alden Family Security," and underneath are the words "Gerry Banks."

The first page is full of stuff I already know. Where he works. His career history. I skim down to the section of the report subtitled "Family Background."

It says how he was raised by a single mother. For years, he thought his father had died. Later, he found out that he was the result of an affair his mother had with a married man whom she'd worked with briefly.

Inexplicably, my heart begins to race and my palms slick with sweat. I pull in a breath, trying to steady myself. I read on.

Name of father: David Grant

That's my father's name.

My mouth goes dry and my heart stops. I can't hear anything. I don't know if I'm still breathing. I glance up at Jack as if to say, is this what I think it is? He's wearing a concerned expression.

It's exactly what I think it is.

"My fucking father is *his* father?" I spit out.

"It would seem so."

"And he's known? All this time?" I hand the laptop back to Jack. "So he hates me because he hates my... our dad?"

Jack swallows. "Your father never took responsibility for him. He refused to acknowledge paternity and wouldn't submit to a test. You got him. He didn't. Your father chose you."

I try to make sense of what Jack's saying. My father chose me? I certainly never felt that way. Since the divorce, he'd never made much effort with me.

"So how do we know he's Gerry's father?" Maybe Gerry's mistaken. My thoughts start to race. If I can convince my dad to take the test, we can prove it once and for all.

"I don't think Ms. Banks, Gerry's mother, ever had a doubt. And anyway, your father *did* submit his DNA eventually. After Ms. Banks served him with court papers."

Does my mom know? Is that why they ended up divorcing. "When did that happen?"

"Gerry was fifteen when she launched the lawsuit." I scan the screen and nausea rises in my belly.

I was eighteen. That's when my parents divorced. I wonder if my mom knew all along.

He was someone's father and tried to pretend he wasn't. He was worse than I ever thought he was. I thought he was faking being a happy family man. I just didn't know how deep his deceit went.

"It doesn't say if your dad paid anything," Jack says. "Gerry got a full scholarship to Penn State."

"What year did he go?" I ask, trying to find the answer in the text in front of me.

Jack recites the dates. It's a question he's already asked himself. Gerry started the year as I entered my final year.

"So he turned eighteen just before I graduated from

college. That tracks. Maybe Gerry's mom told him then." I turn to Jack. "You think he followed me into the music business or do you think that was a coincidence?"

Jack shrugs. "Seems like a *big* coincidence."

"He's still coming after me for my father's mistakes," I say. "When is it ever going to stop?"

"I don't know, Fisher. But at least you know what you're up against. It's definitely personal for him."

"He probably thinks I had a charmed upbringing." I sigh. "I suppose I did in a lot of ways. But it was *too* perfect. And it was all a lie."

I've always given my mom equal blame with Father for portraying the charade of being a happy, loving family. But maybe she was blindsided by the other side of my father just like I was. "I should call my mom."

"Tread carefully. It may not be something she wants to discuss. Not now after all this time."

I need to know when she found out. I need to know how long she was pretending. Was this all my father's doing?

"Thanks, Jack. I could never have put all this together."

He pulls out the flash drive and hands it to me. "What are you going to do?" he asks. "Will you confront Gerry?"

I pull in a breath and a sense of calm comes over me. My muscles loosen and my surroundings come back into focus. "I'm not sure confront is the right term. But we need to talk."

"We're here for you," Jack says. "Whatever you need."

I'm so lucky. Biology means nothing. I have the best brothers a man could ever wish for.

THIRTY-SIX

Juniper

There's an unexpected knock at the door, and even though this is my house, my mom, who's batch cooking Bolognese sauce for us for the next decade, asks me to get it.

"Okay, Mom," I say, humoring her. "I'll get on that."

"I can do it," Riley says.

We both arrive at the front door at the same time. We open it to a guy from a courier company, wearing brown shorts and a gummy smile. He thrusts a white square package at me.

"Mrs. French?"

"Miss," I mutter. Everyone always assumes I'm married. But as I've proved to myself by staying single, there's no one in Star Falls I'd ever *want* to marry.

I sign for the package and then scan both sides looking for a sender, but it's blank apart from our address. I wasn't expecting anything. What could it be?

"What is it?" Riley asks.

"Hang on. Let me click to X-ray vision and I'll tell you."

"Ha ha," Riley says. "Open it. You got a special man to deliver it. It must be something amazing."

My mind immediately goes to Fisher. But why would he be sending me anything? I haven't heard from him since he left. And I won't. That was our agreement. No dragging things out. A clean break.

I peel open the cardboard envelope and peer in. It seems like papers. My heart starts to thud. Surely it's not from Riley's dad. He's not suing me for custody or something, is he? Why are my thoughts even going there. He can't even make it back to Star Falls for a week at the beginning of summer to see his kid. He's not going to want her full-time.

I empty the papers onto the dining room table and Riley spreads them out, turning them over. It looks like... what's... The name Vivian Cross catches my attention, and then I pick up notepaper that has Vivian's name across the top.

It's handwritten. Why would we be getting mail from Vivian Cross?

"Dear Juniper and Riley," it starts.

"Mom, Vivian sent us concert tickets! She said she would and she did!"

I look up, and Riley is bouncing up and down holding the two tickets. She has a grin from here to Aspen.

"Where is it?" I ask, looking at the tickets. "Oh, sweet girl, it's at Radio City Music Hall. That's in New York City. We can't go all the way there for a concert."

My stomach turns over as I say New York. It's where Fisher is. If we went, we'd be in the same city, breathing the same air. I could call him.

No. I can't call him. Clean break. Clean break. Clean break. It's easier this way. It *will* get easier. I'm sure of it. I have to be.

"Mommy, we *have* to go! You know I've always wanted to go to New York. Please, Mommy?"

"You've always wanted to go to New York for the last five seconds since you met Emma."

"Oh, Mommy, can Emma come too?" she asks.

I shake my head. "We can't go, Riley. We'd have to get a flight, pay for a hotel. It's way too expensive. You know we can't afford it."

Tears gather in Riley's eyes, and she runs off to her bedroom.

She's had so many disappointments lately. I wish I could make things better for her.

"What about that money you earned from selling your paintings?" my mom says from where she's stirring the sauce on the stove.

"What?" I ask.

"You know, I thought you made a nice amount of money from the Colorado Club buying all of those paintings of yours."

"Yes, I've put it into Riley's college fund. I've kept a little aside for fun stuff. It's paying for camp this week. But it's not enough for a trip to New York."

Mom turns to face me. "I'm not suggesting you blow her entire college fund. But you could take a trip to New York. Didn't you say that nice gallery lady that came to visit you was in New York? You could meet with her. That might turn into something for your painting."

I laugh. "She'll have long forgotten about me," I say.

"Well, be that as it may. But you don't lose anything by reaching out to her to tell her you'll be in town."

If I was going to New York City, it would make sense to call Grace. She may even be able to introduce me to some people, like she said she would. But I'm not going to New

York City. There's no way. "I can't fritter away Riley's college fund because of some unrealistic dream I have."

"Well, first, you wouldn't be frittering it away. It's potentially an investment in both of your futures."

"Yeah, and it might be nothing. It might be a lot of money down the drain just to chase after something that's never going to happen."

"Maybe. Maybe not. You'll never know unless you go. I heard a man talking on the TV the other day, and he said something that stuck with me. He was talking about... I don't know what, I wasn't really listening. But he said something that did catch my attention. He said, you miss one hundred percent of the shots you don't take."

My stomach falls to the floor.

She looks me dead in the eye. "He wasn't wrong. You have to take opportunities when they're given to you, Juniper." She turns back to the pan and sets the lid on. "And worst-case scenario, your daughter gets to have an experience of a lifetime. Seeing Vivian Cross in concert is a dream come true for her. But also, visiting a city like New York. Showing her more of the world like that, expanding her young mind? It's good for her. I wish I'd been able to do that for you."

"You do? You wanted to take me to New York?"

"Well, not New York, necessarily. But I wanted you to know about the world outside of Star Falls. It's important to have roots, Juniper. But it's magical to have wings." She looks at me. "I wanted you to soar."

I glance at the floor, trying to keep the tears at bay. "I let you down," I say. Getting pregnant at eighteen isn't what any mother wants for her daughter. I understand that now in a way I couldn't comprehend when I was younger.

Mom turns off the stove and crosses the room to gather

me in her arms. "You could never let me down. If anything, it was the other way around. I never really showed you what life might be like beyond Star Falls. And maybe on some level, you were scared to leave. Getting pregnant allowed you to stay here."

She sighs as she pulls me into a hug. "We all do the best we can. There's no looking backwards. Only to the future. Riley is the greatest blessing. You're a wonderful mother and having a child was the most important thing to you. But you don't have to sacrifice your wings for Riley. You may even be able to show her how to fly."

I squeeze my mom tight, tears gathering in my throat.

"Take her to New York, sweet girl," my mom says. "See how you both can fly."

THIRTY-SEVEN

Fisher

If I'd scheduled a meeting with Gerry Banks, he'd have probably dodged me for weeks. Enough time has been wasted. So I'm taking a leaf out of his book and being underhanded to get what I want. Sometimes the ends justify the means.

Lucky for me, Vivian sees me as family because of the connection to Efa and Bennett, and when I asked if I could arrange a meeting with Gerry and pretend it was a meeting with *her*, she didn't even ask why. She just agreed.

I've requested a private room in the restaurant. I'm not sure how Gerry's going to react. He's hated me for years and has covered it up. Now I'm going to reveal I know who he really is.

When I arrive at the restaurant, I'm ten minutes late. I want to make sure he's situated so it's less easy for him to walk out when he realizes Vivian's not coming, and he's stuck with me.

The hostess assures me Gerry has already arrived and

leads me to the back of the restaurant to the private dining room.

"Gerry," I say. "Good to see you."

His mouth falls open, but he recovers quickly. "What a surprise. Is the lovely Vivian with you?"

I turn to the waitress. "We're going to need a bottle of your finest tequila and two shot glasses. You drink tequila, don't you?"

Gerry's wearing a tense smile, but he nods.

"And a selection of appetizers. Unless there's anything in particular you were looking to order?"

Gerry's smile falters. "Anything works for me."

I take a seat opposite Gerry, and we stare at each other until the hostess closes the door.

"You've hated me for a long time, Gerry," I say. "And I've always wondered why. At first, I thought it was just the way you did business, but over the years, it's become clear that you do business differently when it involves *me*. You try to undermine me. Undercut me. Steal artists. Take credit for things I did."

He stares at me blankly.

"I let it go mostly. Avoided you when I could. When you got into management, I deliberately swerved doing business with your artists, ducked out of parties when you arrived. But when you turned up at the Colorado Club, I realized that this game of cat and mouse was never going to stop. It got me thinking."

I stop as the door to the dining room opens and a waiter appears with a bottle of tequila and two glasses. Before he can offer to pour us some shots, I take the bottle. I need something to take the edge off of this terrible conversation.

The waiter leaves and I pour us out a shot each. I slide one across the table toward Gerry and pick the other one up. I knock it back. The burn at the back of my throat feels good, like a grazed fist after a deserved punch. It fits. Feels right.

Gerry doesn't touch his. I get it. He wants a clear head. He might suspect, but he doesn't know what's coming.

"It got me wondering why?" I say. "I realized this was more than professional rivalry. It was more than I just irritated you, or I reminded you of a guy back in high school. But what?"

The corner of Gerry's eye twitches.

I pour myself another shot and sit back. "So I did some digging. You're not the only one who can track people down at remote locations in the way you did with Vivian."

I'm grateful he doesn't deny it. We both know it would be ridiculous, and I admire him in a way for just staying silent.

"For a long time, I had a very happy childhood. I thought my mom was thirty percent cookies and my dad hung the moon. They were loving parents to me and, I thought, in love. Our house looked just like my friends' houses. My backyard the same as theirs, complete with water pistols and Slip 'N Slides and a barbeque when the weather allowed. I don't know why or how, but even though my life looked a lot like my friends', something told me I was lucky. That I'd hit the jackpot. Maybe it was the way my friend Jonny's mom used to yell at us when we trailed mud into their house. Or if we got too excited, the way Jody's dad used to grab him by the arm and whisper in his ear with his jaw clenched, like he was threatening to murder him. My mom rarely yelled. My dad always joined in the fun."

Gerry's mouth is set in a straight line, his jaw clenching tighter and tighter as I speak.

"And then, just before I left for college, my parents announced they were divorcing."

I exhale. Every time I think of that day, I always get a little unsteady on my feet. It's a hint of the feeling I got that day—that the earth I stood on was no longer solid.

"No big deal, right?" I ask him, not expecting an answer. "Plenty of couples get divorced. And I was technically an adult. But to me, they might as well have told me they were Russian spies, or that they weren't my real parents and they were just looking after me for the couple next door. It was as if they'd revealed a fundamental lie about my life up to that point."

Gerry takes the shot of tequila I poured him and downs it. He wipes his mouth with the back of his hand and replaces the glass on the table. I pour him another shot and then, together, we both take our second.

It doesn't burn as much this second time. I wish it did. I wish the discomfort in my throat could make me think of something else other than the lies my parents told me.

"From that moment, I trusted nothing and no one. If my own parents could lie to me so easily, if they could pretend so well that their own son believed them, then there was *no one* who wasn't capable of lying to me."

I swallow at how fucking lonely my next confession feels.

"In that moment, our relationship was fractured forever. All I could think about was how I wished I was Jonny, having a mom who yelled, or Jody, who had to put up with his dad's temper, because at least those parents weren't liars."

We sit in silence, my thoughts loud in my head. I'd been so angry. So let down. So altered from that moment.

"And then," I say eventually, "when I did some digging

on you, I found out that about the same time my parents told me they were divorcing, your mom had finally gotten the courage to file for child support from my father."

Gerry nods, slowly. Solemnly.

"I don't know if my mom just found out he'd cheated then. Or she'd lived with it since it happened. Maybe it happened throughout their marriage, and she just didn't know what to do. She didn't work. I think she would have been too frightened to divorce my father when I was a kid, even if she had found out."

I pull in a breath and feel lighter for it. "I have compassion for my mother that I haven't felt in a long time. Maybe ever. I think she did the best she could in the circumstances. It took me a long time to trust my gut, but actually, ever since that day when they told me they were divorcing, my gut's never been wrong. I think my mom was a victim of my father's bad behavior..." I pause. "And so were you." I want him to believe me when I tell him the next bit. "I didn't know."

Gerry finally speaks. "He denied my existence my entire life."

I pour out two more glasses of tequila, ready to hear his story.

"I hated you," he says. It must feel good to admit it. And I can't blame him. I would have hated me too. "I wanted what you'd had. I wanted a dad who wanted me. I wanted the perfect family. Growing up, my lack of father just wasn't talked about. I craved him, though. I wanted a dad to throw a ball with, to have water fights with. My mom was a good mom. She worked two jobs. She loved me.

"Then things shifted when I was thirteen. My mom lost her job and she got really stressed. She told me later that that's when she reached out to..." He grimaces, unable to even refer to our father. "When she'd told him she was pregnant, he fled. She never saw him again. And when she reached out, he wouldn't take her calls. It wasn't until she lost her job that she got lawyers involved."

Since I was eighteen, I've thought my dad was a liar. But now I can add coward to his character description. And all this time, my mom has never told me what happened. Maybe she's been trying to save face. Or maybe she's been trying to protect me.

"She got another job, so she dropped the lawsuit for a couple of years. At that point, I knew what had happened. I knew I had a father and that he had another family. I guess it was just my age—I didn't understand how the world worked. I just accepted things. I think she wanted to give him an opportunity to know me." He lets out a cynical half laugh. "He didn't take it, of course. I overheard them on the phone. My mom told him that he had two sons. Not one, and that you had a brother. He hung up."

My stomach churns at the lies. At the cowardice. At the lack of fucking character. The guy I idolized for so long. The man who called me his sidekick. The man I thought hung the moon was nothing like the man he'd pretended to be.

"Before then, I'd never really pictured him or you. I accepted he wasn't in our life without question. But from that day, I couldn't get you out of my head. You were easy to find on social media, after I learned your last name from the court papers my mom had." He sighs as if he's finally given up the fight, like he realizes there's been too much misplaced bitterness. "I went to the same college. Even managed to get myself in the same dorm. I was sick of missing out, and I was determined not to anymore. I wanted what you had."

It all makes sense now. I wish we'd had this conversation earlier.

"Turns out we both like music. I'm not sure if it was my passion before I started in the business, but it is now. I love it. And managing the bands—that's what I loved most. Spotting potential in artists and delicately shaping it so they fulfill their potential..." He nods and smiles for the first time since I ordered the tequila. "I should be grateful to you. My job is genuinely my calling. Anyway, when we both ended up working at EMG, I thought my time had come. I could take what you thought was yours. Make sure you had less to make up for all the time when you had far too much. Much more than I had.

"And after EMG, you set up your own fucking label. Man, I was *pissed* about that. You were going to get to work for yourself and not have to put up with asshole managers who didn't give a fuck about anything but being spotted out with the latest singers."

I chuckle at his frustration. The music business is full of people whose only ambition is to be seen as close to the talent. I've never understood it.

"That's why I became a manager. I didn't want to have someone telling me what to do when *you* didn't have to put up with that shit, either."

Jesus, even when I thought we'd followed different paths, he'd chosen his because of me. I've never felt so sorry for a man as I do for the one sitting in front of me.

"Anyway, I'm good at what I do," he says. "I got the opportunity at Re because of my own merits." He sounds slightly defensive.

"I know," I reassure him. "There's never been any doubt about that in my mind."

He nods, his eyes flitting around the room, like he can't quite take the compliment.

"Our father is an asshole," I say, pouring out another shot of tequila. "But I'm not him."

"I don't know what's worse," he says. "Never having the perfect family, or thinking you've got it and discovering it's all been a lie."

"Pick your poison," I say. He looks at me, and I don't know if I'm imagining it, but I swear there's something I see that wasn't there before. A softness... or maybe a lack of bitterness.

We both reach for our glasses and raise them in the air and tip them back. It feels like the beginning of a truce or something.

THIRTY-EIGHT

Juniper

New York couldn't be more different than Star Falls. And yet, somehow, it still feels like home. Fisher was right about everyone belonging in New York. There's an energy that makes me feel like there's a place for Riley and me here.

Fisher. God, I miss him. I close my eyes in a long blink in a futile attempt to wipe him from my thoughts.

Riley squeezes my hand a little tighter as people come toward us on the sidewalk of Park Avenue. "There's just so many people!"

I laugh. That's an understatement. "You're right. A little more than Star Falls, right?"

I made sure our hotel is within walking distance of Radio City Music Hall and Grace's gallery. I didn't want to negotiate the subway for the first time with Riley. I'm sure it would have been fine, but I wasn't going to take any chances with my daughter. Yes, I want her to fly, but that doesn't mean I want her to break her wings trying.

"Yeah. A lot more," she says. "And it really smells bad, Mom."

I laugh. "I can't argue with that."

"But it's cool." She gazes up as we come to a stop at the crossing at 59th Street. "The buildings are so tall. They block out the sky. It looks even more New York than in the movies."

As ever, my daughter knows exactly how to encapsulate a feeling. "I like that. I agree, it's more New York than it is in the movies."

"Can we go to the top of the Empire State Building?" she asks.

We're not here for long. Just two nights and one full day. First, we're stopping at Grace Astor Fine Art to meet with Grace. She seemed really pleased to hear from me, and when I said I was coming to New York, she said she'd love to meet.

It's not that she'd ever been cold or unenthusiastic about my work. The opposite, in fact. It's just that reaching out to her and hearing how excited she seemed gave me... confidence. Maybe she really saw something in me. It's not like Riley and I can come to New York on a regular basis, but maybe there's some kind of way where she could help me get my art seen by more people. Like Mom said, I've got nothing to lose by going to see her.

"We're going to the gallery first."

"But not the Met?"

"No, this is to a gallery of a friend of—" I nearly say Fisher's name but I stop myself just in time. "Of mine. She wanted me to stop by if I was ever in New York. Then I thought we could go through the park on our way to the Met and..." I haven't had a chance to check the price of going to the top of the Empire State Building, but I bet it's not cheap. The tickets to the Met are expensive, and Riley said she really wanted to go together, but maybe she's humoring me. Before bed, I used to talk to her about the paintings in that museum like I used to work there.

"Oh yeah, I definitely want to go through Central Park. And definitely want to go to the Met with you. I'll be right there with you when your dream comes true, Mama."

"You will?" I ask her.

"You always say it's your dream to go to the Met. And today you get to go."

"But if you want to go up the Empire State Building, I can check the price of tickets." I should have thought about it before now. Maybe if I'd booked them earlier, I might have gotten them cheaper.

"I want to go to the Met more than I want to go up the Empire State Building."

"Really?" I ask.

She nods her head.

"Are you sure, because, like you said, the Met is my dream, not yours."

"I'm sure. I can see the Empire State Building from the outside anyway. My dream is coming to New York and seeing Vivian Cross in concert. I'm literally having two dreams come true in one day! And I want your dream to come true, too. And I also really, really want to go to the Met. Do you think we can get a selfie outside—the two of us?"

"I think we can arrange that." I can't help but let my mind wander to what might have happened if we'd have come with Fisher when he'd asked us. He said he'd take us to the Met. I still miss him like he left Star Falls two days ago. It doesn't make any sense. He wasn't in town long enough for me to feel like I do. It's like he took a part of me with him when he left, and I can't function properly without it.

We come to another crossing and I pull out my phone with the screenshot of the gallery's address. "I think this is it. Except I don't know which part of the street it's on. Let me pull it up on a map."

We stand on the corner of the street as I try to figure out which direction we're heading. "Ahh, it's right," I say. "Just down here." I scoop up Riley's hand again. "You think you'll be okay looking at the art while I talk to Grace?"

"Sure," she says. "I'll be even better if you give me your phone."

"Not happening."

"Really?"

"Really."

"I promise I'll be really good, Mom. I won't—"

"It's not happening, Riley. The gallery will be full of beautiful art, and I brought your book. If you finish looking at the art, you can read."

"You did?" Her eyes light up like I just told her she could eat candy all day. "I didn't know that."

I pat my handbag and chuckle to myself at her excitement about reading. Let's hope it stays like that.

"I see the sign," she says as we continue up the street.

My stomach flips as I see where Riley's pointing across the street at a simple white sign with black lettering. This is it. I'm in New York. About to talk to a gallery owner about my paintings.

The door is all glass, but when I try to enter it, it doesn't open. My heart starts to race. Did I get the wrong time? The wrong day? Has she changed her mind and decided to keep the place closed to avoid me.

"You need to ring the bell," Riley says, as she presses the buzzer on the doorframe. "It's for security," she says, sagely.

Grace appears in a few seconds, beaming at us both as she approaches the door.

"She's really pretty," Riley mutters.

"Yeah. She really is."

"Riley, Juniper!" Grace says as she opens the door. "Thank you so much for coming. How is your first trip to New York?"

"Awesome," says Riley.

"Awesome is good," Grace says. "And you're going to see Vivian Cross tonight, I hear?"

Riley nods. "She's my favorite singer," she says.

"Mine too," Grace says, offering her a high five.

"Riley's brought her book so we can talk."

"Great," Grace says. "My assistant has Connect 4 in the back if you're interested? I'm warning you though, she always beats me."

Riley grins. "I like that game."

"Good," Grace says. "Tanya, come and meet Riley." She turns to me. "She'll be perfectly safe. The door is locked, and if we get anyone in the gallery, Tanya can bring her in to sit with us, if you'd prefer."

"Thank you."

"Tanya, show Riley around the gallery. If she wants, she can read her book in the chair over there. That way she can see us while we're in my office. Or you two can play Connect 4."

"Got it. Gallery tour first?" Tanya asks.

Riley glances at me and then nods.

"I know what a worry it can be. When I bring my children into the city, I always get nervous, even though I've lived here my entire life. Anyway, enough about me. Come on back. I hope you don't mind, but I invited a friend of mine to join us."

My breath catches in my chest, and I brace myself. She's told Fisher I'm here. I'm going to see him. I won't be able to hold it together.

"She's an agent," she says. "I think you might like her."

I grin at Grace like I haven't just done an emotional loop the loop. Okay, so not Fisher. That's good, isn't it? Good that I won't see him. Good that the door is still firmly closed. That's how it should be. How it has to be.

I follow Grace to the glass office at the back of the gallery. It doesn't seem like much of an office to me. Just a room with a table and four chairs. And a tall blonde woman in a white suit.

She smiles as Grace opens the door. "Juniper French? I'm Rachel Grint." We shake hands, and I try not to feel like the country bumpkin I so clearly am. I'm in jeans and a white shirt. I'm wearing sneakers and big panties. I bet these women don't own a pair of sneakers. Or waist-high underwear.

"I'm very excited about your work," Rachel says, as we all take a seat around the table. Grace guides me to the seat opposite the window, and I relax slightly because I can see Riley chatting away to Tanya as they both look at one of the paintings. "Grace has shown me some pictures, and then of course I've taken a look at your website. You're very talented."

"Thank you," I say. "I never made it to art school or anything though. I don't know if that means people aren't going to like my work or—"

"Art school isn't a requirement to produce thoughtful, beautiful work. You've proven that. Like I said, you're very talented."

I smile. "Thank you."

"I've been talking to Rachel about you being based in Star Falls, and how your trips to New York would be infrequent. I presume any foreign travel would be even more difficult."

"Foreign travel?" I say, like I didn't hear completely clearly. "Why would I need to travel…"

"We can work around it," Rachel says. "A number of my artists have shows in the Middle East and China. But we can figure this out. If that's what you want. But you have to want it."

"The Middle—yeah, no, that would be… impossible."

My mind starts racing as I realize that when I told Grace before that making trips to New York would be impossible, it wasn't because of Riley. It wasn't because I didn't have the money.

It was because I was scared.

Maybe my mom was right, and my fear was part of the reason I never went to art school in the first place. New York felt like a foreign country to me, just like China or the Middle East does now.

"I just want to take this one step at a time," I say, correcting myself.

Maybe Riley needs to see China, just as much as she needed to see New York. It's good for her to experience all the people and the smells, as well as the Met and Radio City Music Hall. My mom was right. Star Falls is a beautiful place, but there's an entire world out there, and I don't want Riley to be afraid to spread her wings and experience all that life has to offer. Then she'll *know*, not just believe, that Star Falls is the best place on the planet.

"But I do want it." As soon as I say the words, I understand how true they are. I don't have to give up on my dreams just because I'm a mother. I want to be an artist. That's where my heart has always been.

"That's good to hear," Rachel says. "One step at a time is how these things work. I don't want to push you to do anything you're not comfortable with."

I pull in a breath, feeling a new sense of confidence. "Great. But I'm going to do my best to be as flexible as possible," I say.

"Good," Grace says, nodding enthusiastically. "It's good to know you're keen."

"And if you decide you want to work with me, I see my job as to protect you, as well as promote you," Rachel says.

"This is why Rachel's perfect as your agent," Grace adds.

I nod. If Grace thinks Rachel's the right person, then she's the right person. Fisher trusts Grace. I trust Fisher.

"Tell us what you're working on," Rachel says.

"Space," I say. "Not astronaut-space. Space and negative space," I say. It's the easiest way I know how to describe what I've been trying to paint in the last few weeks since Fisher. Any of my unfinished works have been set aside, and I've been trying to paint what I feel: loneliness. "I'm trying to communicate loss," I say.

Rachel and Grace both nod at me, willing me to say more, but I'm not sure if I can.

"Oh wait. I took some photographs. Nothing's finished yet."

"Wow!" Rachel says as I pull up the first image. It's a lapis lazuli blue circle. And around the outside is a similar blue with a tiny amount of white added. It's almost the same color, but not quite. The paint around the edges of the circle is thicker, and you can see the paint strokes all heading toward the circle like it's trying to get the circle to stay. "It's a little different to what I've done more recently."

"It's very bold," Rachel says. "And very interesting."

"I haven't shown it to anyone before. Not that I show my paintings to many people anyway. I don't get many visitors on my website. Although, I did have someone call me the other day. Someone who stayed at the Colorado Club wants to buy a piece from me for their apartment. That's really nice, right?"

"For them," Rachel says, and Grace laughs. "They're lucky to be getting you when you've not been exhibited yet. I'm willing to bet they know a little about art and see your potential."

I shrug. I'm just pleased to be making another sale. I can top up Riley's college fund with most of the money this trip cost. It will make me feel less anxious.

"This feels like a good place to start for your first exhibition," Rachel says. "It's fresh and different from your other work, but not so different that we couldn't display some of the pieces the Colorado Club didn't buy alongside it."

"I agree," Grace says. "It makes sense to use the historic stuff. It's slightly softer, but still impactful. And we'll do the first show in New York."

The pulse in my neck starts to throb, and I swallow, trying to keep my panic at bay. "My first show?" I ask. "When are you thinking?"

"We can be guided by you. Makes sense to have the opening during a school vacation. That way you and Riley will both be able to come to New York."

My mom will want to come, I think to myself. And my dad. They're not art lovers, but they'll be proud. I think.

"Are you thinking soon?" I ask.

"We can do some planning, but we don't have to set a

deadline," Rachel says. "But we *will* need to see some of your newer pieces sooner rather than later."

I take a couple of breaths, trying to calm my body. Energy has started to fizz through me, and I realize that actually, I want a date in the calendar. I'm excited. I want people to see my work. Maybe it will be a complete disaster, but an exhibition at a New York gallery is what I used to dream about as a kid. This is what I've been waiting for my entire life.

"I want to work toward an exhibition," I splutter out. "I have the entire summer where I can paint. Riley can come to the studio or can be with my parents." I want this. I want this for me. I want this to show Riley that you can follow your dreams no matter your age. I want to be a painter.

"Good!" Grace says, beaming at me. "In the meantime, I'm going to reach out to my network and see if I can arrange some influential collectors to see some of your pieces. If we can get a sale from them, it will help us build buzz going into an exhibition. I think I might have someone for one of the pieces you just showed me in your studio—the blue piece."

"Oh right," I say, nodding. "So if that piece is sold before the exhibition, then you'll need more—"

"Not at all," Rachel says. "Any buyer would be more than happy to lend it to us for the exhibition, and we can mark it as sold. And before you reach out to anyone, Grace, we'll revisit Juniper's pricing."

Grace smiles. "Of course you will." She nods toward Rachel. "Told you she was good." My anxiety must show on my face, because her smile drops when she looks at me. "But there's no pressure," she says. "We'll work with whatever timeline works for you. If it takes two years, it takes two years."

"I'll have all summer. But things get busy when Riley and I go back to school. Once the semester starts, if I just had some time in the week, it would be easier. If I worked part-time and Riley was at school, I'd have a lot more hours in the studio." I do have that money from the Colorado Club that I've put aside for Riley's college fund. But I really don't want to spend it on living expenses. If I was certain I could replenish it, then maybe that would be an option. "When you say you think you have someone who might be interested in buying the blue piece, can we talk numbers? I'm just wondering if maybe if I sold some pieces before the show, I might be able to reduce my hours a little."

"That sounds like an interesting idea," Rachel says. "What kind of salary would you be looking to replace?" she asks.

"I make twenty-five thousand six hundred a year."

Rachel and Grace exchange a look. And I feel like I've overstepped.

"Obviously, I would still work, so I'm not saying I'd need to replace that entire amount. And we could cut back. Although, I'm not sure where—"

Rachel interrupts me. "Grace is going to sell that blue piece you're working on, and what you get from that will cover your salary for an entire year, along with any amount you're going to have to pay for materials."

I swallow, trying to take in what she's saying. "Twenty-five thousand, just for one painting?" I ask. "Are you serious?"

Grace and Rachel both nod, like what they're telling me is no big deal.

"And you think I'd definitely sell one? I wouldn't want to give up my job entirely in case I didn't... It's a lot to think about."

"And no one is pressuring you to give up your job," Rachel says.

"You should do what you're comfortable with," Grace says. "Going from being surrounded by children all day to being in your studio alone might be too big of a change to make all in one step."

I can't believe I'm even considering giving up my job. It's been the only thing keeping Riley and me afloat all these years. Bill has always done the bare minimum. But they're right, I don't need to give it up completely. Maybe I just need to test these new wings over the summer and see if they work. See if being an artist feels like me. I have a feeling it will.

THIRTY-NINE

Juniper

I have a sense of optimism about the future that I haven't felt in... I don't know how long. I don't know if it's something in the New York air or because of my meeting with Grace and Rachel, but it feels like my insides have shifted around and I'm different somehow. Fundamentally changed by this trip.

"I wish we didn't have to fly home tomorrow," Riley says as we head west on 51st Street.

"Yeah, me too," I reply. "I've enjoyed out girls' trip."

"And it's not just been any girls' trip. We didn't go to Colorado Springs, Mom. We're in New York City."

I laugh. "No, we go a little farther afield than Colorado Springs, don't we."

"We like to spread our wings!" Riley says, taking her hand from mine and holding out her arms. She drops her arms to her sides and slides her hand against mine again. It's the start of what's to come. She'll need to hold my hand less while she goes out into the world. I'll always be here when she needs me. My mom was right, Riley needed this as much as I did. She needed to see that you can be a long way from home and still feel connected to the people you love. We both needed to see that it wasn't so scary to leave Star Falls. Even if it was just for two nights.

"Mom!" Riley yells, pointing ahead of us. "There it is. That's Radio City Music Hall." The familiar façade of the venue comes into view—the star-spangled banners hanging side by side next door, the illuminated red lights. "I can't believe we're here."

I laugh. "Neither can I," I say.

"Do you think we'll meet Vivian again? She did send us the tickets."

"Oh, honey, she'll be super busy getting ready to sing beforehand and likely she'll be exhausted afterwards. I don't think we'll see her." I brace myself for Riley's disappointment, which still has the ability to grip me by the heart. We have VIP tickets, but there was no mention of a meet and greet.

"Yeah, that makes sense. This is her job. She's not on vacation like she was in Star Falls."

My little girl. She's growing up. I don't bother to tell her she wasn't on vacation in Star Falls.

"But I did get to meet her. Not many people can say that. No one else in my class has met her."

"I bet they haven't."

We show our tickets to the staff member on the door.

"Welcome," they say. "Please make your way to the VIP lounge up the stairs and to your right. One of my colleagues up there will direct you."

"VIP lounge?" I mumble, as we head toward the stairs.

"It means very important person," Riley says.

"Thanks," I say, rolling my eyes on a smile. Riley doesn't

quite understand the implications of being directed into the VIP lounge. I'm not sure I do. It's not like we're actual VIPs. Maybe it's not a big deal.

"Please, may I see your tickets," a uniformed man says at the top of the stairs. I pull out the tickets again.

"Just this way." He indicates we should go through a door. "There is direct entry to your box from here."

Our box?

We push through the door into a bar area. It's a fairly small space, with a glass window overlooking the auditorium. There are a few people on one side of the window talking. They've all got suits on and look quite a lot older than Vivian's average fan. I thought I was going to be the oldest one here tonight. And we're not dressed up. Riley has her Vivian Cross t-shirt on with plain leggings. I'm in jeans and a white shirt. I'm not sure how long we'll last in this VIP lounge.

"Drink, madam?" a waiter with a tray of drinks asks.

"Is this alcoholic?" I ask, pointing to a champagne glass that looks like it's holding orange juice.

"Yes. Or if you want something non-alcoholic, we have virgin mojitos over at the bar."

"Mommy, can I have a mojito? Frankie said she had one when she went to Miami last year and they were the best."

I swallow, wondering how much a virgin cocktail will set me back at Radio City Music Hall. Probably a week's worth of groceries. "I think we'll stick to water," I say. "Mojitos are too much sugar on top of an already exciting evening."

Riley shrugs. "Boring."

"Water is available at the bar," the waiter says.

I'm going to have to ask for tap water. They probably only have bottled. We head over to the bar and I ask for water, and as predicted, the bartender opens a fresh bottle and pours two glasses. I pull out my wallet, where I've stuffed my dollar bills. He slides two glasses over to us. He doesn't ask for any money.

"How much is that?" I ask.

He grins at me. "It's no charge, ma'am."

"Oh," I say, a little surprised. I pull out a couple of bills and set them on the bar. "Thank you."

"Thank *you*," he says.

I pick up both glasses and hand one to Riley, before heading across the room to look at the auditorium.

"Is that the stage where she'll be performing, Mom?" Riley asks.

"I think so," I say. I wish we could just go to our seats. I feel awkward and uncomfortable. Like we're hillbillies who've come up to the big city. New York has felt like home until right now.

"Shall we go and find our seats?" I say to Riley. "We can figure out where the restrooms are and get situated."

We get directed down a corridor and through some more doors. "You're Orchestra 4, Row CC," the usher says to us as we arrive at another set of doors. "Best seats in the house," he says with a grin.

"Thank you," I say, as he directs us into the auditorium.

We find our seats eventually and I have to triple-check. The seats are three rows from the front and right in the middle. Riley's going to have the time of her life.

"Mom, you have to take a picture of me!" she says.

There aren't many people in the auditorium yet, and Riley poses in front of the stage and I take at least three hundred pictures.

We're posing for a selfie when Riley says, "You think Fisher will be here?"

I almost lose my balance, I'm so distracted by her question, it's like my brain can't process which way is up. "No," I reply. "Why would you think that?"

"Well, he works with her, doesn't he? Why wouldn't he be at her concert."

Call me naïve, but I didn't even contemplate Fisher being here. Maybe it's because I associate him so strongly with Star Falls. "Lots of people work with her, honey. Fisher doesn't go to all her concerts."

She looks downcast. "I really thought we'd run into him. I didn't realize how big New York was." My stomach churns at her disappointment. I really didn't realize how attached she'd gotten to him in such a short space of time. It was what I'd tried to avoid, and I thought I'd been successful.

I press a kiss on her head. "Yeah, it's even bigger than I imagined too."

"Fisher!" Riley screams, and pulls out of my arms.

I look up—and see the man whose name she's screaming.

My heart soars in my chest and my body starts to shake. And my entire world grinds to a halt.

Fisher.

My Fisher.

All tousled hair and broad shoulders. He's right here, coming toward me.

Riley jumps into his arms and he lifts her up, grinning. Pulling her into a hug. Then he looks up and our eyes lock. Even though I know it's impossible, it feels like the ground is shaking. Like I'm going to topple over. I grab on to the back of the seat where I'm standing so I don't fall.

I've missed him so much.

Did he know we'd be here? Did he ask Vivian to invite

us? Maybe he'd been the one to offer the tickets. I don't know how these things work.

"Hey, Juniper," he says, in his easy-breezy British way as he comes closer. "I wasn't expecting to see you guys tonight."

"I just knew we'd run into you!" Riley says. "I've been telling her all day we'd see you."

"You have," I say. "And you were right. Honestly, I wasn't expecting to see you, either."

"You got tickets?" he asks. "They're pretty hard to come by." He leans forward and places a kiss on my cheek. Maybe I'm imagining it, but he seems to linger a little longer than he needs to.

"Vivian sent them," I explain.

"Oh," he replies. "That makes sense. That's nice of her."

So he didn't arrange this? Does that make this awkward for him? I know we'd agreed to a clean break, but it's so good to see him.

"She's really nice," Riley says. "I really like her."

Fisher grins at her. "You could have called. I could have given you a city tour."

I smile. "We're only in town one more night. We came in yesterday and... I thought you'd be busy."

He sighs. He looks a little bit like the spark has gone from his eyes.

"Everything okay?" I ask.

He searches my eyes as he pulls in a breath, and it's like he wants to say something but he can't. Riley's dancing around at our feet, and here we are in public, Vivian Cross about to come onstage. It's not exactly the time to chat.

Except, it feels like he's telling me he misses me. And I want to tell him that right back. But what's the point? Maybe we do both miss each other. Maybe Fisher didn't come back to New York and forget about me right away, like I've assumed he's done. But where does that leave us? No further forward. His life is here and my life is in Star Falls. It's an impossible situation.

"Are you coming back to Star Falls soon?" Riley asks.

He pulls his mouth into a smile. "I'm not sure," he says. "Probably when Vivian records her next album."

"My mom misses you," Riley says. "And so do I."

My stomach lurches, but I don't correct her. She's not lying. She's obviously picked up on my heartache, however much I've tried to hide it.

Fisher and I smile sadly at each other. He doesn't tell us he misses us too. Maybe he does. Maybe he doesn't. Either way, it doesn't change anything.

"I spoke to Grace," I say, in an effort to change the subject.

"You did? While you were in town?"

"Yeah, earlier today. We went to the gallery."

"I read my book," Riley says.

There's an announcement off in the distance, and more people start to fill the seats. People pass by and slap Fisher on the back. He's dressed in a navy-blue sweater and jeans, but this must be work for him. We're probably keeping him from it.

"How did it go?" he asks, just as a woman with red hair and glasses approaches us.

"I'm sorry to interrupt, but can I grab you for a second, Fisher?" she whispers in his ear, and he nods.

He turns to us. "I'm sorry, I'm going to have to go. There's something... someone I have to—"

"It's fine," I say. "It was good to see you," I say.

He looks into my eyes like he wants to say more again,

but I look away. We've said it all. There's no need for an epilogue in this story.

"It was really good to see you," he says. "Maybe we can catch up later. Have you eaten?"

I nod. "We grabbed a slice of pizza on our way over here," I say. "You go and enjoy your evening."

The woman with the red hair calls him, and he glances between us. "Pizza. Yeah, good. Well, enjoy."

"Good to see you, Fisher," I say, and I manage to get the words out before my voice cracks. He heads over to the seats in front of us to the side. My throat tightens, and it feels like I'm not going to be able to breathe unless I get outside or have a drink or something.

I can't stay here all evening and focus on anything but Fisher, ten yards away from me. This entire evening is going to be complete torture for me.

"You okay?" Riley asks.

"Sure," I say on a smile. "I think the show's going to start any moment now. Let's get in our seats." I deliberately don't look across at Fisher. I can't. I'm going to do my best to pretend he's not there. I can still feel his cheek against mine as he kissed me. I can still smell his cologne that smells like expensive, freshly ironed linen.

The lights of the auditorium dim, and I'm hopeful that Fisher will fade into the blackness and I'll be able to focus on Vivian Cross.

Something tells me there isn't a show on earth that will be able to pull my attention at the moment.

FORTY

Fisher

I know Vivian's assistant is saying something, but I can't focus on anything at the moment other than Juniper's scent of honey blossom that still swirls in the air even though she's yards away.

"So shall I put a plus-one down for the party?" Hailey says.

"Sure," I say.

She makes a note on her phone. "Great. I'll tell Vivian." She scurries off, and I snap my head back toward where I last saw Juniper and Riley. I scan the rows near where they were standing, but I can't make them out. The lights have already dimmed. Vivian's due out on stage at any moment.

Seeing Juniper was the last thing I expected tonight. I'd half considered sending them some tickets. It's the only performance of the album in the US for the public, and I knew Riley would want to see her. I didn't think there was any point. It never occurred to me that Juniper would leave Star Falls. Not even to take Riley to a Vivian Cross concert.

Now I feel like a prick. But she told me she wanted a clean break. That's what I've been trying to do. To forget her.

It's impossible.

Seeing her has brought everything into focus. I spent years thinking I had everyone figured out. I helped people discover their dreams yet kept everyone at arm's length. In all honesty, that's why Gerry was probably able to steal talent from me. I kept people close but not too close. I demanded authenticity without giving it.

Gerry. My brother. He hated me so much, he built a whole empire just to tear mine down. And I get it now. I understand his pain. I have the same hole our father left in him. We both carry it. We both push people away.

I've done the same damn thing with Juniper. Expected her to give more than I'm offering.

Juniper.

She makes everything complicated in the most beautiful way. I kept telling myself we were from different worlds— me with my skyline and contracts, her with mountains and morning sunlight. But the truth is, I kept her at arm's length because I didn't want her to be another person who could leave me with a hole.

Because if I let myself fall for her, she has the power to undo me.

But there's no one I want more.

I wish we'd had more time to talk. I thought she'd decided she didn't want to pursue anything with Grace. She thought it would be too much pressure with everything else that she had going on with Riley and her job. I can't help but wonder what changed her mind. Or maybe the catch-up with Grace was just a social thing. Maybe she's not working with her.

I have so many questions.

I want to know whether she likes New York. Somehow, it's important that she doesn't hate the place I call home. I want to know if they've been to the Met. Did they do a tour? Have they had an ice cream at Serendipity? Have they been to FAO Schwarz? Where are they staying? When are they leaving?

There's so much I want to say. So many things to talk about. So much of me I want to show her.

Maybe Juniper's right. Maybe there's no point. We know that we each have to go back to our corners of the world in the end. Maybe it's just reopening a wound. I understand why she wanted to walk away and not look back. I thought I wanted that too. But seeing her? Here? Now? I can't think of anything worse than her and Riley going back to Star Falls and me not having had the chance to see more of them.

I want whatever I can get of Juniper, however painful it might be to leave her when the time comes. However big the hole. *If* the time comes.

"Hey." Jack nudges me. He's sitting beside me. I didn't even notice him arrive. "Hi."

"Hi," I mumble, and glance back over my shoulder. I remember that Jack's here with his niece. I lean forward so I can see Felicity. "Hi, Felicity. Are you excited about the show?"

She gives me a high-five and nods. "Really excited," she says.

"You okay?" Jack asks.

"Not really," I admit.

"Not looking forward to the show?" he asks, his tone sarcastic.

"Juniper's here."

"She is?" he asks, scanning the faces behind us. "I thought you weren't going to see each other after you left."

"I didn't know she'd be here. Vivian sent her and Riley tickets."

"And you're pissed?"

"Uncle Jack, you can't say pissed," Felicity says. "I'm a child."

Jack sighs. "Just don't tell your mom."

"What's in it for me?" Felicity asks.

"You get to come to Vivian Cross concerts." Jack turns back to me. "You're upset that Vivian sent her tickets?"

I shake my head. "No, I'm not upset. No, I *am* upset. I just..."

"You're a mess," Jack says. "Did you speak to Juniper?"

"I did. And I miss her." I can't say this to Jack because he won't understand. How can anyone understand? But I say it anyway. "I think I'll miss her for the rest of my life."

He regards me with a frown. "I'm not very good at giving advice. Certainly not about women who you might miss the rest of your life. Most of the women in my life I've known for as long as I've been alive. The last girl I dated I was at preschool with." He sighs. "New York is a very small place. I don't get the chance to miss anyone. But if I thought I'd miss a woman my entire life... I'm not sure what I'd do, but I'd do something. I don't think I could just walk away."

"You're right, you're a terrible advice giver. Knowing I should do something doesn't help when I don't know what I should do." Music starts to play from behind the curtain and the crowd starts to go wild, screaming, clapping, and trampling the floor. "It's not like I can just leave New York and my business and move to Star Falls. You wouldn't even dream about doing that. Would you?"

"Yes, but that's me. You can do anything you damn well

please. If you think you'll miss her forever, you need to be with her."

More unhelpful advice from Jack. I need Worth.

"She lives two thousand miles away," I say.

"Make it happen," he says simply, like all I have to do is cross Fifth Avenue and she'll be there, ready and waiting.

"But how?" I ask.

"Fisher, you've done hard things your entire life. You've been practically estranged from your parents since college. You've discovered hundreds of talented artists, set up a successful independent record label that's signed the biggest artists in the world. Figuring out how you and Juniper can be together isn't even on your top ten list of the most difficult things you've done in your life. Figure it out."

"I'm in love with her," I splutter out, and I clutch my chest, not sure if my heart's still beating.

"I can tell. I'm not an expert when it comes to these things, but I know that losing a woman has never caused me to miss a gym session, let alone given me the miserable face you've been wearing for the last few weeks."

"I keep thinking it's going to get better, but it keeps getting worse. She's all I think about. She's all I want."

"Then what the hell are you playing at? You know how to go after what you want. Make it happen."

There's a smash of drums and the start of the intro to the song Vivian and I wrote together. I can't take credit for any of the lyrics. But the melody is mine. I produced this one, too. It's one of the later tracks that only just made it on the album.

I glance over to where I last saw Juniper and Riley, but I still can't see where they are.

I just don't want them to leave before I get a chance to speak to them.

FORTY-ONE

Juniper

I haven't heard a single song Vivian has performed the entire night. She's just finished her encore, and I swear it feels like it's her first song.

"She's so amazing!" Riley shouts beside me.

I grin at her and nod. My daughter's so happy. Everything feels worth it. The cost of flying here. The hotel. Even seeing Fisher, despite how painful it was. I can't decide if I wish he hadn't been here. In some ways it would have been easier. I wouldn't be able to picture him in New York. His beautiful face wouldn't be redrawn in my mind.

But it doesn't make me miss him more. That would be impossible.

"Mommy, I wish we could watch her again tomorrow night."

"That would be super fun," I reply. Maybe I would have been able to take it in a little more if I saw it again. All I could think about was Fisher. "But she's not performing tomorrow night. This is the only show she's playing in the

US this year. You're a very lucky girl to have gotten to see it."

"I'm a lucky girl," she says. "But not just because I got to see Vivian Cross tonight. Because you're my mommy."

She flings her arms around me and squeezes me tight, and I kiss her on the head. Being able to bring her here, to see Vivian Cross, to experience New York—it's been such a complete privilege.

The lights go up in the auditorium, and I deliberately don't look over to where Fisher was sitting. Seeing him again was bad enough. We don't need to draw it out.

"Follow them out of the seats, Riley," I say, nodding toward the people leaving our row. "I'm right behind you." I follow her out of the opposite end of the row to where we were talking to Fisher. I just want to get Riley into bed and have a few minutes to myself. I need to stop thinking about how unfair life is. Life is *good*. It gave me Riley. It gave me my ability to paint. It's beautiful. I'm being selfish for thinking anything else.

"Juniper!" Fisher calls from behind us. I pretend I don't hear. Prolonging this isn't going to help anyone. "Juniper!"

Fisher's behind us, and despite wanting to keep walking, I stop, like my brain isn't in charge anymore and my body is just doing what it's told by Fisher.

"Hey, Riley. Hang on a second," I say.

She turns, and her eyes light up as Fisher comes up behind us. I can feel his presence like you can feel when it's going to rain. The air shifts and there are connections your brain makes.

He came back.

I turn, and he's smiling at Riley.

"Did you guys enjoy the show?" he asks, scanning my face.

I shake my head slowly as Riley squeals and tells him all her favorite parts—which is all the parts. I can't lie to him. I didn't enjoy the show. All I was thinking about is how much I miss him and how I'll never be truly happy, now that he's gone.

Fisher's gaze flits between us. He's trying to listen to Riley, but I can see he's concerned. I've given up trying to hide that I'm okay without him. I've given up trying to pretend that a clean break is going to make everything okay. Because it won't. Nothing's going to stop this hurt inside. I'm just going to have to learn to live with it.

"Let's get you out of here," he says. "I have a car downstairs."

"We walked," Riley says. "Our hotel is only a couple of blocks from here."

"It's late. My car will get you back more quickly," he says.

I let Fisher guide me and Riley downstairs and along corridors until we go through another door, and suddenly we're on the street.

"Here's my car," he says. He opens the back door, and the three of us slide inside, Riley in the middle. I should say no, but I don't. He asks where we're staying, and Riley gives him the name of our hotel and then jabbers on about the concert.

We arrive outside the hotel minutes later.

"Thanks for the ride," I say, and I reach for the door handle.

I'm still getting out of the car when Fisher appears and offers me his hand to get out.

I smile weakly at him. "Thanks. You didn't need to."

"Yeah," he says. "I did."

I don't have the energy to argue with him. Not even

when he insists on seeing us into our room. "I'd like to talk. If not tonight, then tomorrow."

"We're on an early flight," I say. "We have to leave the hotel at seven. And I need to get Riley into bed."

"I'm so tired, Mommy," she says, rubbing her eyes.

The three of us step into the elevator.

"Tonight then," he says.

"Riley needs to sleep," I say.

"I know," he agrees.

We get to the door of our room and all I can focus on is Riley. She's about to fall asleep standing up. "Sit on the bed." I take off her shoes and socks and pull back the covers on the bed we're sharing. "You can sleep in your leggings and t-shirt."

"What about my teeth, Mommy?" she asks, as she crawls over to the pillow.

"They'll survive one day."

She falls onto the bed and closes her eyes. "I love you, Mommy."

I pull the covers over her and press a kiss to her forehead. "I love you more," I reply.

"Thank you for bringing me to New York."

"You're very welcome," I say. Despite having to endure the pain of seeing Fisher again, it was completely and utterly worth it.

I turn, and Fisher's watching us. The room isn't big, and he's only a step away from the bed. One step away from me.

Riley shifting on the bed catches my attention, and when I look around at her, she's on her side, fast asleep.

I turn back to Fisher. He's smiling.

"She was tired," I say.

"I've missed you," he says.

I sigh. Despite it feeling good to hear those words

coming from Fisher's lips, it's not what I need. Maybe if he announced he was getting engaged or something, that would be easier.

"I want us to talk," he goes on. "I want to see if we can find a way through this. Maybe we can split our time between New York and Colorado. Or maybe I can just come to live there—"

"Fisher," I say, shaking my head. "We've known each other five minutes. You can't be giving up your life here after five minutes. Who knows if we'd even like each other after a month."

He fixes me with a look that tells me I'm being ridiculous.

"I don't think even *you* believe that we couldn't like each other after a month, a year, a lifetime. I know you've got a list of reasons why it might not work between us, but I know it will. I'm sure enough for both of us."

"Your life is in New York," I say, but my voice is weak.

He shakes his head and takes a step toward me. "It feels like I'm giving up my life by not being with *you*, Juniper. You're my life. I know it hasn't been long, but I know that I'm never going to feel about anyone the way I feel about you. It's impossible. It feels like you're a part of me. Maybe it won't work out." He scoffs. "I actually don't think that's even a possibility. It *will* work out. We were meant to find each other. I was meant to find you in Star Falls, and you've been there your whole life waiting for me. I've never been surer of anything in my life."

He sounds so certain, like maybe his iron will could carry us both to the finish line, but it's not enough. "I have a child to think about." She's had a happy, stable life in Star Falls. "I can't have men coming in and out of her life. It's not fair."

"I'm here to stay," he says. "I adore Riley. I'd do anything for you both."

Tears gather in my throat. It feels so unfair that I'm not allowed to have this man in front of me. He's everything I ever dreamed about.

"I love you, Fisher, but even though I want to, I just can't see a way through." My voice breaks on the last word. He puts his arms around me, and I sink into him.

"I love you, Juniper. And there *is* a way through. I'll show you. We can take it slow if that's what you need. I can stay at the Colorado Club. We don't even need to move in together. And then if you're not happy—if you're not the happiest you've ever been in your life—I'll walk away and you'll never see me again."

Tears fall at the thought of never seeing Fisher again.

"I want to believe you and I could work somehow, but I'll hate myself every damn day if you're stuck in Star Falls. You have a business and a life here. I don't want you to give it all up for me."

"You're more than worth it. None of it means anything if I can't have you."

"Maybe... we could be in New York when school's out," I whisper against his chest.

"We can do that," he says, dipping his head to try to meet my gaze. "I don't want you to be sad," he says. "I want more than anything to make you happy."

"You do," I say. "I've never been happier than being with you and Riley and watching movies and eating pancakes."

"Well, why don't we do that forever?"

I gaze up into his blue eyes and wonder if this is really possible. Could I really have a life with this beautiful man who's holding me in his arms?

"You can split your time between Star Falls and New York during the semester—"

"Juniper, we can work out the logistics. But I need to know this is what you want."

I nod, scared to say the words. I don't know if I'm allowed to have a perfect life when I get my beautiful daughter, my dream career painting, and the man that makes everything make sense.

"Tell me, Juniper." He takes my face in his hands and searches my eyes.

I take a deep breath. "You're what I want, Fisher."

It feels like an end of something, but I don't feel sad, like I'm grieving anything. Maybe because it's an end to my life without Fisher.

Tonight's the beginning of something: our life together.

FORTY-TWO

Juniper

I haven't managed to sleep much. It's like I'm too eager to get on with my new life.

"Mommy, where are we?" Riley says, as she sits up in bed next to me. I've been scrolling through my phone, trying to resist Fisher, who's in the bedroom next door.

Fisher carried a sleeping Riley back downstairs after our conversation last night, and we all went back to his place. There's so much I need to know about his life here. I wish we didn't have to go back to Star Falls.

"We came back to Fisher's apartment last night," I reply, pulling my daughter in for a hug.

Riley squeals. "Does that mean we can have pancakes?"

I check the time on my phone. "It's six oh five. We have to leave in just over an hour to get to the airport."

There's a knock on the bedroom door. "Are people awake in here?"

Fisher pokes his head around the door. I can't stop myself from smiling.

He blows us both kisses. "Anyone for pancakes? I heard someone mention something."

"I don't think we have time before we leave," I say. "Our flight is at ten fifteen."

"Do you have plans today? If I can get us all on another flight later on, would that work?"

"But we've paid for the flights already. We can't change them."

The corners of his mouth twitches. "Riley, do you want to stay in New York for pancakes and get home a little later?"

"I want to stay in New York forever! You know I'm coming to college here," she says.

Fisher chuckles. "Well, that only gives us the next ten years to deal with."

"What does that mean?" she says.

I need to tell Riley what's going on. She deserves my honesty. "Sweet girl, Fisher's probably going to be spending more time in Star Falls. With the two of us."

"Cool!" she says, glancing down at her Vivian Cross t-shirt.

"And maybe we'll spend some of the school vacations in New York."

Her head snaps up, and she looks at me as if to check what she heard was correct. "Really? We get to come back to New York?"

"She's a fan," I tell Fisher.

"I'm glad. What about you? Do you like New York?"

"I do. Just as much as I thought I would before... before life got complicated."

He tries to suppress a smile. It's cute that he likes me liking his city. Just as much as I like the way he likes Star Falls.

"Are you and Fisher boyfriend and girlfriend now?" Riley asks, and my stomach dives to the floor.

"Um, I, well, I was—" I can't get my words out.

"Is that something that you'd like?" Fisher asks, proving to be a much better parent in this moment.

"Yeah. I told Mommy that ages ago." She shrugs like it's no big deal.

"No one's ever going to replace your dad, though," I reassure her.

"I don't really ever see my dad now anyway. So..."

"That sucks," Fisher says.

"Yeah," Riley replies. "But I have the best mommy, so that makes me lucky."

"I vote pancakes," I say.

"Maybe they'll make one in the shape of a love heart that you and Fisher can share."

"That's an awesome idea," Fisher replies. "I'm going to ask them if they'll do that."

Riley gets out of bed and slips her hand into Fisher's and leads him out the bedroom door. "I think you have to give me a tour. Especially if I'm going to be staying here a lot, what with you being my mom's boyfriend and everything."

I scurry to the bedroom door so I can overhear their conversation.

"Sounds fair," Fisher replies. "Maybe you could pick out one of the rooms as a bedroom, and I can get it redecorated for when you're next here."

"Really?" Riley asks. "I've always wanted a bunk bed."

"Bunk beds are cool," Fisher agrees.

I can do nothing but smile. If the man I love wants to spoil my daughter, who am I to stand in his way?

EPILOGUE

Three months later

Fisher

I've had a charmed life, but I've never felt so lucky as I do now. I get to spend my life with the woman I love and the girl who becomes more and more like my own daughter the longer I spend time with her. They are my family. They are my world. There's nothing I wouldn't do for either of them.

I also got to choose the movie this afternoon, so I'd say I was on a winning streak.

"I have something to show you," I blurt out, as the credits start to roll and before we can start debating who enjoyed the movie. "And I don't want you to freak out." I've been keeping this secret for a while now. And I'm not sure how it will land.

"What?" Juniper asks, sitting up a little straighter across from me. Riley is in between us.

"Well, I was thinking that I'd like to move some more of my things in here."

Juniper's eyes widen. I know it's not because she's afraid of me moving in. More that this place is so small, there's not a lot more that *would* fit.

"Yes!" Riley says. "Then you can stay for longer instead of flying back to New York so much."

We've agreed that while we're based in Star Falls, I'll spend four days in New York every other week. It's not ideal, but it's better than not being with my family at all. From September, the three of us will spend more time in New York during school vacations. But during this summer, Juniper needs to paint. There's no point wasting time trying to find studio space in New York and then her having to settle in. There will be time for that when she's built up some pieces for her show.

"What's your plan?" Juniper asks.

I stand and head out to the porch, where I've stashed the plans that I've had drawn up. Juniper and I have talked about getting a place together in Star Falls, but houses don't come on the market that much.

"Come see these drawings."

Juniper's eyes go wide in that oh-no-you-didn't way she has.

I shrug. "See what you think," I say. "I haven't committed us to anything."

Riley opens the tube, and I help her take out the papers and spread them on the dining table.

"So what's this?" Juniper asks, as she approaches the dining table.

"It's a house we could build," I reply.

"In Star Falls?"

"Yeah. And I thought we could all live together in it. The builder that's doing Rosey and Byron's could do it."

"Between the two of you, you've got to be keeping the Colorado construction industry afloat." She trails her fingers down my back in that absentminded way that sends me absolutely wild.

I don't know why either of us thought what we had couldn't work out. Everything's felt so easy since the night of Vivian's concert at Radio City. Everything's slotted into place. In a way, I have Vivian to thank for all of this. Maybe she'll play at our wedding.

"This place is huge," she says, as she takes in the plans. "And do we really need two kitchens?"

"And a pool, Mommy, look!"

She shoots me a look that says, *Stop spoiling her*.

"What?" I say. "I want a pool in our house."

"But we don't need all these guest rooms," she says. "Your friends will stay at the Club when they come to visit, won't they?"

"Yeah, but I thought..." I don't say exactly what I'm thinking. We've talked about having children together. Eventually. Obviously, we haven't said anything to Riley yet.

"But what about for my brothers and sisters?" Riley says.

Juniper and I burst into laughter.

"And I thought a guesthouse would be nice. Maybe for when your parents get older. And of course a studio so you don't have to leave home to paint."

She tilts her head and gives me the look that says she wants to jump my bones.

My eyes widen. "Thoughts of your parents make you think like that?" I ask.

"No." She shakes her head. "You being thoughtful and generous and an all-round perfect human makes me think like that."

"Well, save that thought," I say.

"Four bedrooms is plenty," she says. "Where were you thinking you were going to build this house, anyway? I don't even know how you'd get all the permissions for a new place—"

"Here, Mommy," Riley says, taking the words out of my mouth. "In Star Falls."

"I'll figure it out. We have what we need. The house is just frosting." I've already visited a couple of plots that already have some permissions already. It's not going to be as hard as she thinks it is.

She glances around at the tiny house "Riley and I have lived here since she was a baby. It's served us well. You took your first steps in this house," she says to Riley. "Said your first words."

"Right. And I'm growing up and we'll make new memories in the new house," she says. "On top of the old ones. They'll be the foundations to grow up on."

I smile. This kid is wiser than her years.

She looks at me. "Life is moving on."

I nod at her and slide my arm around her waist. "Life is getting better."

"Is Uncle Jack coming today?" Riley asks, at the same time there's a knock on the door.

"That must be him," I say. Before I can get to the door, he lets himself in.

"Hi, everyone," he says. He offers me his hand to shake, just like he always does, and I ignore it and give him a hug. Riley grabs on to his waist. His poor upper-class nervous system can barely take all the physical affection.

"Okay, okay. Enough of all that. Here, I brought Riley a present."

"What is it?" Riley asks.

He presents her with a Tiffany-blue box, and Riley squeals. I'm pretty sure she's never even heard of Tiffany.

She opens it, and she's completely delighted by the pretty bracelet inside and gives Jack another big hug.

"You really don't need to buy her gifts," Juniper tells him.

"I know, I want to. She's a cool kid. And I like being an uncle. Especially to Riley. Felicity is a different story. She's a walking sass machine."

The door rattles, and in comes Juniper's mom. She's sitting Riley tonight while the three of us go to Grizzly's. Life's very different to New York. I'm not out at a new bar every night. Movies and Grizzly's wings are where it's at.

"We've just been looking at some plans for a new house," I say.

"In Star Falls?" Jack asks. I nod and he sighs. "You're all moving out of the city. Who am I going to play with when you're all gone?"

"I'm going to NYU to college," Riley says. "Only ten years to wait."

"It's good to have a plan," Jack replies.

"And we'll be in New York plenty," I reassure him. "This is for when we're in Star Falls."

"Anyway, I'm going to find you a nice small-town girl, Jack, and then you'll be building a place right next door."

Jack laughs. "Wouldn't that freak Joan out," he says, referring to his mother. "Finding my bride and the mother of the future Alden generation in Star Falls, Colorado, rather than on Fifth Avenue."

"You can't rule anything out," I say. "There's magic here in the air in Star Falls."

Jack chuckles. "Maybe. But I'm confident when I say, I'm not moving to Star Falls because I fall in love with a small-town girl."

Juniper shrugs as if to say, *it could happen.*

Even I don't think Star Falls' magic is that powerful.

At least I don't think it is.

A month later

Juniper

As I hang up the phone, I'm pretty sure I'm about to explode. I pull up in front of the house Riley and I have lived her entire life and Fisher comes out onto the deck to meet me. My stomach still lifts every time I see him for the first time. I wonder how long that will last? A lifetime maybe.

He grins as I get out of my car. A car Fisher has tried to convince me to replace at least three times in the last week. As I keep telling him, there's nothing wrong with the car so long as it keeps going. He says he wants to ensure Riley and I are safe. I've never felt safer than with Fisher in my life.

"Hey," I call out as I get out of the car.

He jogs down the stairs to meet me. He's watching Riley as I wanted to have a long day in the studio.

"I have news," I say, beaming at him.

He cups my face and presses his lips to mine with a sigh, like all's well in Fisher's world now that I'm back home. I know that feeling. It's exactly the one I feel when he kisses me.

"That's a coincidence," he says. "Because I have news too. You go first."

Fisher's news is always more exciting than mine. He managed to secure a plot of land just on the outskirts of town to build our new home. He's already secured some of the permissions I never thought he would. Plus his news from New York usually involves someone I've seen on page six. My news is big to me, but will be small fry compared to whatever Fisher's going to tell me.

I shake my head. "You first."

He pulls in a breath. "I spoke to Gerry today. Turns out he's now a fully paid-up member of the Colorado Club."

My eyes go wide. "He is?" I don't want to pry, but I can't decide if that's weird or not. Gerry's been obsessed with Fisher over the years and now their relationship is in new territory. Does he think this is a good thing?

"Yeah. I just got an email from him. He said he thought it would be good to spend some time together when he's here next—which is the week after next."

"Wow," I say. "How do you feel about that?"

We wander back to the porch. "I feel good. I think. I know it's just biology, but we're half brothers. I think he wants that to mean something."

I don't say anything, but I'm still salty about the way Gerry's handled himself. Fisher didn't deserve any of the things Gerry's done to him over the years. Fisher's got broad shoulders, but I don't know how you can move forward with someone who's acted the way he has. I take a seat so we can have this conversation in private.

"And also, he told me that Re Records hasn't signed The Homecoming Kings."

"Oh," I say, taking in his expression. "Did you know that?"

"I'd heard that negotiations had been tricky."

"So you think Gerry didn't sign them because he stole them from you and he wants to have a better relationship with you or did he not sign them because they couldn't make a deal."

"He says it's the first reason. But either way, if he was still trying to stick it to me, he would have signed them whatever the deal."

"You going to try and get them back?"

He shakes his head. "I don't need them. They should go to a big label and see how that works out for them. Maybe it's what they need. But I'm not holding on to musicians who want to go elsewhere. Whatever the reason."

"So you and Gerry are going to grab dinner or something?" I ask.

"I guess. I can show him the land where we're building the house. Take him to Pizza Meet Ya. Get him to sample the wings at Grizzly's."

I laugh. "It always comes down to the wings."

"Every time," he agrees. "So tell me your news."

I can't hold back my grin. "I sold the blue painting."

Fisher jumps to his feet. "Really? Already? Is that even up in Grace's gallery?"

I shake my head. "No, she's saving it for the show. But she showed a collector and they loved it. Apparently they're interested in some of the darker stuff the Club didn't want as well."

"This is incredible."

Riley pokes her head out of the front door. "Do you guys want privacy to make out or something?"

"Your mom just sold a painting!" Fisher says like the Yankees just won the World Series.

"Which one?" Riley asks. "The blue one?"

This kid has a knack of knowing exactly what's going on at all times. It's mildly terrifying.

"Yup. The blue one."

She sighs. "I love that one. I knew it would sell super quick."

"We should celebrate. Shall we go up to the Club for dinner?"

I glance at Riley. She's always been at the center of all my celebrations since she was born. Everything to celebrate was celebrated with her. I don't want to leave her out of this. It feels like a big deal—a New York gallery selling something of mine—the girl who never went to art school who paints in an abandoned candy store in rural Colorado.

"All three of us," Fisher clarifies as if he's reading my thoughts. "We should celebrate as a family." His words make my heart melt. Of course he wasn't suggesting we leave Riley out. That's not who Fisher is.

"I have questions," Riley says.

"Let me have 'em," Fisher says.

"Questions about what?" I ask.

"Well, you said that when you sold a painting, you might give up work. Are you going to do that?" she asks. "What happens if you don't sell another one. Can you get your job back?"

The question catches me off guard. Riley's growing up every second. I don't want her to have to think about things like this. It's not for her to worry about. But it is for me to worry about. Riley and putting a roof over her head are my responsibility, even though I'm with Fisher. "I haven't thought about it yet, Riley. But I promise when I have, we can talk about it."

"Okay. Seems fair. And also, Fisher, you're in love with my mom. And you say you want to celebrate as a family. So, when are you going to marry her?"

I'm sure I turn beet red, but Fisher chuckles. "Any time I think she'll definitely say yes."

"Well, I found a ring with a huge sparkly stone that looks like a diamond in your coat pocket and I figured that you were going to propose, but you haven't and I want to know when it's going to happen."

If ever I've wanted the ground to swallow me whole, it's now. "Riley!" I say. "You can't—"

"She absolutely can," Fisher interrupts. "She's got skin in this game." He gives me a reassuring nod, but I'm a thousand percent more embarrassed than when she announced to Marge that she liked to fart.

She's the love of my life, but honestly, I could happily murder her right now.

"I have a dilemma," Fisher says to Riley. "I want to marry your mom. I've wanted to marry your mom for a long time now. But she's just about to become this art star. And I don't know if she's going to say yes when she's got all this other stuff going on. And she's smart and independent and I think she might want to go to her first show as a single woman rather than as a woman engaged to me."

My heart squeezes at his words. He's thought about this way too hard but I love him twice as much for it.

Our eyes meet and I see all his vulnerability. All the love he has for me. All his heart.

"There are no circumstances where I don't want to be engaged to you," I say in a whisper. And then I stop myself. "That's not true." Fisher clutches at his heart, dramatically and I grin. "I mean, I don't want to be engaged to you when we're married. But I'd never say no to you. I love you. For the rest of my life."

"I know," he says. "I'm not unsure of your love for me. But you got Grace's attention on your own. You signed with Rachel because you're talented. I don't want other people to think you got this because of me."

I slide my palm up his cheek. "I don't care what other people think. Fisher, will you marry me?"

A small smile curls around his lips and it turns into a chuckle. "Here? Now? Like this?" I know he will have been thinking up some elaborate way to ask me to marry him, but I don't need any of that.

I shrug. "Why not?"

"You're right," he says. "Star Falls works in mysterious ways. But the three of us are here in the place I fell in love with you. So, this is the perfect place for a proposal. Of course I'll marry you."

"I'm going to get the ring," Riley says. "You two can make out while I do."

We both laugh and Fisher pulls me toward him and into the best kiss of my life. Every single one of his kisses is better than the last. I just know that's how it's always going to be with us. Things just get better when I'm with Fisher. Life is better with him. That's how it is and how it always will be.

Are you curious about Vivian and Beau? You can read their book, **Dr. Fake Fiancé**!

Love Hard is the next book in the series, and it is Jack's book!

For Louise Bay news and releases, including bonus content, sign up to my newsletter at https://louisebay.com/newsletter/.

Find more books by Louise Bay in Kindle Unlimited, Paperback, Hardcover, and audiobook!

www.louisebay.com

You can also find your favorite tropes on my website under the reader guide!

Colorado Club Billionaires

Love Fast - Byron & Rosey

Love Deep - Fisher & Juniper

Love Hard (2026) - Jack & Eden

New York City Billionaires

The Boss + The Maid = Chemistry - Bennett & Efa

The Player + The Pact = I Do - Leo & Jules

The Hero + Vegas = No Regrets - Worth & Sophia

Doctors Series

Dr. Off Limits - Jacob & Sutton

Dr. Perfect - Zach & Ellie

Dr. CEO - Vincent & Kate

Dr. Fake Fiancé - Beau & Vivian

Dr. Single Dad - Dax & Eira

Related to the Doctors Series

Private Player - Nathan & Madison

Mister Series

Mr. Mayfair - Beck & Stella

Mr. Knightsbridge - Dexter & Hollie

Mr. Smithfield - Gabriel & Autumn

Mr. Park Lane - Joshua & Hartford

Mr. Bloomsbury - Andrew & Sophia

Mr. Notting Hill - Tristan & Parker

Royals Series

King of Wall Street - Max & Harper

Park Avenue Prince - Sam & Grace

Duke of Manhattan - Ryder & Scarlett

The British Knight - Alexander & Violet

The Earl of London - Logan & Darcy

ABOUT THE AUTHOR

Louise Bay is the USA Today and international bestselling author of contemporary romance novels that make you laugh. Louise was inspired by such bonkbuster authors of the eighties as Judith Krantz and Jackie Collins, but wants to be Emily Henry when she grows up. Writing is just a side hustle to her full-time career as a personal butler/driver/chef to her kid. IYKYK.

For more information, visit www.louisebay.com.

Instagram and Facebook: @authorlouisebay

TikTok: @authorlouisebayofficial

www.ingramcontent.com/pod-product-compliance
Lightning Source LLC
Chambersburg PA
CBHW030535190726
48283CB00006B/1933